LOVE, PRIDE AND MURDER

To Nancy —
Nice to know that
another "New England"
lover reads! Enjoy.

[signature]
7/16/23

DENNIS A. FEECE

ISBN 978-1-68526-923-4 (Paperback)
ISBN 978-1-68526-924-1 (Digital)

Covenant Books
11661 Hwy 707
Murrells Inlet, SC 29576
www.covenantbooks.com

1

I was enjoying a genuinely nice California Syrah, plucked from a case of twelve given me by a client who *had connections* in Napa Valley. It was about eleven thirty on a Tuesday night in July. During most years, July and August are the most congenial months in New Hampshire, and this year seemed especially nice. Holding my wine by the glass stem, carefully, I lifted it up to the light, noting both the deep-red color and the rainbow effect of light refracting along the wine's robe. Walking to, then opening, the french door screen, I stepped out onto my deck. I built it the previous summer, so it still seemed like a novelty, and I was proud of the accomplishment. I am not particularly handy with carpentry or anything like its ilk, but it was a nice addition to my little house in the woods. I had stained it, rubbed polyurethane over it, then added a couple of planters along the sides and a nice, rough-hewn table and padded chairs. The extra touches made it just what it should be.

The stars were clear and seemed almost accessible to outstretched arms; I reached up with my left hand and swept it across my field of vision, spreading all fingers and, in my pleasantly enhanced state, laughed for no good reason at the effect. Blackness was complete but for the stars; no moon could be seen.

I stretched, experiencing the marginally cooler air outside, and stepped up to the rail, leaned against it, and closed my eyes. Everything swirled softly, and I had an odd though distinct sensation akin to contentment. My thoughts drifted and came to rest on a small nicely constructed lady who had appeared in my office around twelve hours earlier.

***

My office is found near the center of Concord, so within shouting distance of most of our city and state offices. Concord is a small city, but then New Hampshire is a small state, so it is proportional. The office is on a street northwest of the immediate center but easy to find if you are looking for it and still, because of the semiresidential feel of the street, not public, an important consideration for most of my clients. The building is two stories, housing a barber shop, an antique shop, a small take-out place (specializing in a variety of sandwiches and some pretty-fair coffee), and on the upper level, next to a real estate office, my place: Stone Investigations. Yeah. I am one of those guys.

Clients were steady though far from plentiful, generating enough revenue to keep the agency going for almost seven years now. I investigate virtually anything, assuming what the client wants is legal. And yes, I have turned down a few potential cases that were decidedly shady, so my reputation tends toward honesty rather than whatever the opposite is these days.

I have a secretary, really an assistant, Julie (Jewels) Ellis, who files papers, sorts through email, and does some general telephone answering and/or surveying; she's efficient and discreet, and she guards the office like a Doberman, although to be fair, Jewels is always cordial and seemingly empathetic. She also has a knack for gathering useful information from clients. Despite my curmudgeonly ways, she seems to enjoy the work.

Jewels stuck her blond head in the door and announced a visitor. "TB, that woman who was here yesterday is back." She raised her eyebrows, indicating that I should probably see her.

"Okay," I said. "Show her in. Thanks, Jewels."

The lady walked in. And she knew how to walk, not that I'm in the habit of noticing such things. She was wearing designer jeans and a silk-sheened green top with sleeves that terminated at her elbows. Expensive-looking sunglasses were perched, or maybe nestled, in her wavy dark hair, just above a high forehead. She wore minimal makeup, just enough to accentuate full lips and high cheekbones. And her eyes—yeah, deep, dark, intelligent eyes that a man could explore interminably.

She sat down in one of the two chairs I had in front of my desk, the one on the right, which, probably not accidentally, let a streak of morning sunshine accentuate, well, everything. She crossed her legs. She smiled and said, "Good morning, Mr. Stone."

I smiled back and said, "Good morning, Ms.?"

She raised her eyebrows and said crisply, "Miss Nardone. Lucia Nardone." She smiled again and said, "Miss, because I'm a little bit old-fashioned. Please call me Lucy."

I grinned back at her and quipped, "Lucia? Lady of light?"

This time, the smile defined the name, and she replied, "Yes. My father is a very traditional Italian. I was named after my grandmother, who truly lived up to the name." With this she shifted in her chair and rearranged her face, saying, "Maybe we should discuss my reason for being here."

I leaned forward, hit the appropriate button on my phone, and said, "Jewels. Could you bring in two cups of coffee, please? Thanks." I looked at Lucy, raised my eyebrows, and she nodded. I said, "So what can I do for you?"

"Nine months ago, my fiancé was killed in an accident. His car ran off the road and over an embankment. He was alone at the time, at night, driving back roads up near 93 between Woodstock and Franconia Park. It was snowing, and apparently, he slid off the road. He was trapped in the car, injured, and wasn't found until morning. By the time a passing road crew spotted his car the following morning, he was…" At this point, she broke eye contact, looked down at her hands, and paused. I waited, watching her face and body; both were tense. She looked back up. She smiled softly, shook her head, and said, "I'm sorry. If only he had been found earlier, but the weather made visibility difficult, and it is pretty isolated up there."

"I'm very sorry, Miss Nardone." I opened a drawer in my desk and retrieved a box of tissues and pushed the box in front of her. She smiled again and said, "No, I'm sorry. It's been almost a year, and I should be past the crying stage by now." She quietly blew her nose, charmingly, I thought, but then internally kicked myself for being so vulnerable. Sometimes that happens.

"Anyway," she said, "it all came as a huge shock to, well, everyone—his family, all the employees in his business, friends, and just everyone. He was well-thought-of. It just seemed so sudden and unlikely."

"I can appreciate that. Was he a young man?"

"We were the same age, so I suppose he could qualify as young. He seemed in many ways even younger than his actual age. He was a competitive skier and looked like an athlete. His business was successful and growing. He was outgoing, friendly to everyone. He was even approached last year about possibly running for a state office." She looked out the window, over my shoulder, momentarily lost in remembering.

A soft knock on the door preceded Jewels delivering our coffee. She walked behind Lucy with the tray, looking at me with those perceptive eyes and eyebrows arched quizzically. Jewels is as subtle as a brick. *Maybe she's right*, I thought. *Maybe I should turn off my libido and concentrate on what was being said. Maybe. Still, I'm a seasoned veteran—I can do both. Yeah.*

Jewels put the tray down on the side of my desk, within easy reach. Before exiting, she poured two cups of very black coffee. She said, "Cream and sugar, Ms. Nardone?" Lucy shook her head, smiling pleasantly.

Jewels smiled in return and walked back out, heels clicking loudly on the hardwood. The door closed.

Lucy reached for her cup. I reached for mine and said, "You were telling me about your fiancé?"

"Yes. I'm not sure what else to say. What would you like to know?"

"Well, some basic information. Start with his name?" I sipped more coffee.

"Oh! Of course. Giorgio Abraham Adamo." She smiled somewhat in mock apology. "I know it's quite a mouthful. He was named after both of his grandfathers, hence the Italian Giorgio, his paternal grandfather, and Abraham, the maternal. His grandmother's maiden name was Chiellini, Maria. Her family emigrated here during the thirties." She took a long drink of her coffee and said, "Excellent coffee! Strong. I'm surprised."

"Why surprised?"

She smiled, eyes twinkling just enough, and replied, "Aren't you hard-boiled detectives notorious for bad coffee?"

I chuckled. "You can thank Jewels for that. She is rigid regarding two things—coffee is one of them."

"And the other?" The twinkle was not going away.

I looked at her for a moment and said, "Maybe we should get back to why you came here. We were working on basic information. Where does the Adamo family live? I guess the next thing is, what exactly do you want me to investigate?"

The twinkle was gone. She shifted in her chair, cleared her throat, and said, "I assumed you recognized the name, but the Adamo family live in the Hanover area, while corporate headquarters are located in Concord. Some manufacturing is in Manchester, but most of the holdings are, well, all over New England." She gave me a knowing look.

"Ah. That Adamo family. Sorry, it was obvious, but frankly, I'm unaccustomed to dealing with clients who are, well, you know." I shrugged and tried to look apologetic but probably failed.

She smiled and said, "You are wondering why I came to you rather than someone closer to Hanover?"

I grinned at her, nodded, and said, "Yeah, that will do."

"There are two reasons, actually—first, because you are unknown up there, and second, I checked around, and you have a reputation for honesty and persistence. I was told that you never give up when you believe in something and that you couldn't be bought off." She smiled.

I cleared my throat and said, "That's flattering. At some point, you'll have to tell me where you heard all of that and from whom. I might have to add somebody to my Christmas-card list or some such." I shuffled my notes. "Okay. And why the investigation?"

"Of course. Well, I'm not convinced that Abe, my fiancé, died by accident. I think there may have been more to it." She gave me a piercing look. "I think he may have been killed or, at the very least, left to die by someone." Now the look went from piercing to defiant.

"Okay," I said, giving her a neutral look, deliberately attempting to bring her from defiance and anger to a more reasonable place. "You will need to tell me why, and try to include as many objective aspects as possible. It's the best way for me to understand the situation. Okay?"

She blinked, looked down at her hands then back up, making eye contact again, and this time, her face was rearranged differently, calm but determined. I had a feeling that this sort of exchange was nothing new to her. Maybe regarding the death of her fiancé or maybe just because of the way she was as a person. Either way, it was a better starting place.

"Abe was an outdoorsman. He grew up in the mountains, skiing anything that could be skied and some that shouldn't have been. When he was a young teenager, he and a couple of friends would go into the wooded areas, far from most people, and camp for days at a time during the summer and on weekends in the winter months. In short, surviving in the cold and unpopulated areas was second nature to him. He was also, not coincidentally, an incredibly determined man. You might be interested that he was in the Marine Corps for six years and served in Iraq for a tour. He joined after college, counter to the usual way of doing things. Also, it's worth noting, I think, that Abe graduated with honors from an elite, decidedly liberal college in upstate New York. The general tone in classes was certainly not promilitary. I have always thought that part of his choosing to join up immediately after school was in reaction to the implicit propagandizing at the school." She stopped speaking, cleared her throat, sipped her coffee, and continued, "I'm telling you all of this to underline the clear fact that of all people—of all the people I know, anyway—Abe would be the least likely person to, first, slide off the road under any condition, and secondly, if he did slide off, he wouldn't have died of exposure, broken leg, broken arm, or whatever. It just would not have happened." With this, she tightened her lips, and the defiant, angry demeanor reappeared.

I held her gaze for a moment and said, "Earlier you indicated that your fiancé was trapped in the car. Couldn't that have prevented him from escaping and, presumably, finding help?"

"Perhaps, but I doubt it. I saw the car after they brought it in, and the damage was significant, especially around the driver's side, where it slammed into the trees, sliding down the embankment, but not severe enough to prevent Abe from wriggling free. I can't be convinced that he wouldn't have gotten free. He was just too stubborn to be trapped that way. If you could see the car, you would agree."

"Okay. Let's suppose the damage couldn't have prevented his escape—why was he found still in the car?"

"Well, that's part of what I hope you can find out, but I do have a theory…" She finished her coffee and put the empty cup on the tray, leaning back and straightening her hair.

I watched her closely to determine how certain she was about her claims; she seemed to believe what she was saying. "So what is your theory?"

"I think he was killed before he could escape. I don't know how or by whom, but he did not die from being trapped in the car. It was something else." Her hands were clenched and her voice elevated. Self-consciously she unclenched her hands, examined them, and rested them in her lap. Looking up at me, she said, "So what do you think? Can you help me?"

I stood, walked around my desk, and stopped halfway between her chair and the closed door. Looking at her, I said, "Well, possibly. I will, of course, need more information, and some of that will require more than you can provide. However, you and I need to work out exactly what you know and what you don't know. It may be that, at the end of this fact gathering, I will decide not to pursue it any further. If so, you need to understand—hopefully, you will understand—why. But even if you don't, you will have to accept it. Think you can do that if need be?"

She held my eyes for a long moment then replied, "I think so. And even if I can't, you will never know it. I'll just leave. Is that acceptable?"

I smiled at her. "Perfectly acceptable." I liked this lady.

She cleared her throat and, in a determined sort of tone, asked, "When can we get started? Today, I hope?"

"Not today. I have other business that needs some attention. But you can fill out some forms and make a deposit. Jewels will help you with the paperwork. Some of the information I need will be asked on the forms. Jewels is very discreet, and there is nothing you would tell me that I wouldn't share with her anyway. Okay?" She nodded her head and started to rise. "No, no. Just stay put. Jewels will come in here and take all the information. I have to step out for a bit now, so I won't see you again until we meet next for the more detailed information gathering. Jewels knows my schedule, so she can set up the meeting. Also, the rates for my service are standard, and Jewels will explain all of that, as well."

She stood up and extended her hand. I smiled and shook it, nodded, and opened the door. I stepped over to Jewels's desk, explained what was going on. Jewels smiled in her satisfied way and stood with the info packet already in her hand. I smiled at her and winked. She scowled and shook her head. I walked out the door, thinking about whistling, but decided against it.

2

What Lucy didn't know was that the "business" I had before officially starting the investigation included doing some preliminary research. Now, it could be said that I was misleading my new client, but that's not true. In fact, the investigation proper would start after I gathered some info from sources that Lucy need not know about, nor should she, because as much as anything, I was planning to double-check what she had already told me. Yes, she seemed credible, and yes, she also made a compelling argument, but that turnip truck I didn't fall off of had driven out of my life many years ago.

I walked out the side door and two steps down to the little inset from the street where I parked my car. It wasn't a Maserati, but I like it—a '75 Fiat 124 Spider, all original factory restored, dark green, with black leather interior. I inherited the car itself from my father, who bought it new. When he passed a few years ago, the car was part of my inheritance. I restored as much of it as I could myself, including the interior. The paint job was handled by an old college friend, Joe DeMoro, who loved classic cars and specialized in restoration. To be fair, he also advised me as I worked through it. I'm not much of a mechanic, but with his help, it turned out pretty well. Oh, and it was restored exactly as originally manufactured, but for one small detail: it has a 4.3-liter V6 with all the attendant underpinning. And no, I didn't do any of that either; Joe recommended another specialist from Manchester who, though painfully expensive, made everything work: engine, transmission, rear end, all of it. The engine is largely aluminum, so it's surprisingly light. It gets me where I want to go in style. It was completed two years ago, and every time I see the little green beauty, a smile comes unbidden.

Unlocking the door (with a key, thank you very much), I slid into the sweet smell of the leather seat, inserted the ignition key, pressed the accelerator once, and turned the switch. A muted roar reverberated from the buildings on either side. I smiled again.

This afternoon, my goal is to corner Mr. Benjamin Katz, an attorney who, among other things, works at some important level in the state government. Don't ask me exactly what he does for our idyllic little state, but whatever it is, it hasn't interfered with our friendship, even though I had repeatedly pestered him for information over the years. Ben and I met during our high school years. We became friends and remained so since then. We both entered the same law school though at different times, where Ben excelled and I did not. After two semesters, I realized that pursuing law just wasn't a good fit, at least not at that time. My father was ill, and my brother was busy chasing after a musical career somewhere on the West Coast; it was up to me to handle all the details involved with his dying. So considering my disillusion with the pursuit, leaving law school was an easy choice. Anyway, Ben had remained in my life and was now a good friend.

As I turned off Cote onto Broadway, I accelerated to merge, and well, another unbidden smile greeted the smooth pressure against the back of my seat. Midmorning traffic was light, so I drove a bit over the posted limit until reaching the I-93 interchange and then exit 13 onto Old Turnpike. After two more miles north, with a bit more congestion, I swung onto Hazen. Ben's office was a little bit south of 393. I found the side street and pulled into an empty parking space, next to Ben's gray Mercedes. I climbed out, walked up the steps to his office building, and entered through the double glass doors.

It was one of those multioffice buildings with the office and services leased for each business. Most of the businesses were government related, including attorneys, lobbyists, financial advisers, etc. A few steps from the entrance, a horseshoe shaped desk with a receptionist was located. I walked up to the desk where a cheerful young woman looked up at me, smiled and said, "May I help you?"

"Yes, please. I'm here to see Attorney Katz."

"Do you have an appointment?"

"No, but Mr. Katz will see me. Tell him Tom Stone is here." I used my most charming smile, such as it is.

"One moment, please." She pressed a button on her console, waited, and said into her headset mic, "Mr. Tom Stone is here for Mr. Katz? He doesn't have an appointment." She looked up at me, smiling and frowning at the same time (which must be an art form taught in receptionist school); listened; said "Thank you"; and hit another button. She said, "Go right in. Mr. Katz will see you. Office number 3, second on the left." She pointed off to her left down a hallway. She also smiled a happy-face smile and gently swiped a stray lock of auburn hair back in place.

"Thank you." I smiled back. Maybe my charming smile still had a measure of effectiveness, after all.

I walked down the hall, opened the door, and was greeted by Doreen Clark, Ben's legal secretary and all-purpose everything. "Hi, TB! How are you? It's been a while." She walked out from her desk and gave me a sincere hug.

"Doreen, it has been too long. It's really good to see you," I said, and I meant it. Doreen is a fifty-something sweetheart who could and would rip you to shreds with her tongue if she didn't like you, but if she likes you, she has a way of making you feel like the world revolves only around you. I put on a mock-serious face and asked, "Is Ben busy?"

"Nope. He's waiting for you. Just go in." She gave me another smile and asked, "Your usual or without?" She was referring to coffee, knowing that the coffee was definite but not necessarily with a bourbon additive.

"Ah. Doreen, if I weren't girl shy, I'd have married you years ago—the smile, the hug, and coffee? Today, I'll take it without. I just started a new case, and I need to keep my senses unfiltered. But thanks for asking." She nodded and gestured toward Ben's door.

I walked through Ben's door and closed it gently behind me. He was sitting in his comfy swivel desk chair, leaning back with his feet propped up on the antique cherry executive desk, with a big grin on his face. "Hey, man! Decided to slum it again, or do you truly feel guilty about abandoning your old comrade for so long?" He dropped his feet, stood up, and walked around the desk, hand extended.

I took his hand in both of mine and laughed. Then he laughed, giving my face a mock slap. Then we hugged briefly, slapping each other on the back. I said, "Good to see you, Benny. Looks like you are doing pretty well lately, what, with the new Mercedes out in your parking space. An upgrade from the Beemer, huh?"

"Well, you know, Tommy, it makes no sense to stand still especially in my line of work. Sit down, for God's sake! You look tired. Taking care of yourself or just moldering away up in the woods?" He grinned his patented grin.

I sat down in a nicely padded wing chair, one of two in front of the desk; Ben went back to his chair. "Yes, Mother. I eat regularly, and the woods have fresh air and something other than bureaucrats to look at. I'm probably healthier than you are. You still running, or have you given that up along with your conscience?" I made a face at him.

"Now, now, Tommy boy, all us lawyers aren't criminals and hypocrites—just most. And yeah, I still run. How else would I look so fit and trim, not to mention good-looking?" He put his feet back up on the desk, linking his hands together.

"Yeah, yeah. Fortunate son that you are, think you could let me pick your brain for a bit? Not that I'm in any way dismissing the pure pleasure of your company for its own sake…" I waited.

"Of course. Anything I might know is yours, you know that." The perpetual smile gradually faded, and his eyes turned serious.

A soft knock came at the door. It opened, and Doreen quietly came through, balancing a tray with coffee, cream in a silver pitcher, sugar, and what appeared to be little sandwiches. She smiled, put the tray down on Ben's desk, and turned to leave. She patted me softly on the shoulder in passing.

Ben dropped his feet, rolled his chair closer, and reached for the coffee. He poured a cup, placed it on a nice matching bone china saucer, and handed it to me. Then he poured a little cream in a second cup, added one teaspoon of sugar, and poured his coffee. He stirred it with the spoon, sipped it, and smiled. He said, "You know, if Doreen lacked her legal mind and could only make this coffee, she'd still deserve a raise." He smiled.

"Not to mention her capacity to set you straight when necessary."

"That too. So what kind of information do you need, Tommy?" He sipped more coffee, looking down at his cup.

"Well, a new client just brought an interesting case in this morning. She gave me her story, and on the surface of it, there may be something worth investigating. The problem is, I don't know her, but I do know, at least by reputation, the family that will be involved in the investigation." Ben raised his eyebrows inquiringly. "The

Adamo family, Tony Adamo himself, well, actually, his son."

Ben leaned forward, passed a hand over his face, and said, "You do know how to get yourself into deep shit, huh?"

"That's just it. I'm not fully committed just yet and won't be until I get some corroborating information. Stirring up Tony Adamo for no good reason would be something other than good business. So can you help me or not?"

Ben sighed and said, "That depends. I know people who know people, but like you, asking questions about the dealings of Tony Adamo, the guy who owns a large percentage of business in New Hampshire, has major interest in the Boston area, and hobnobs with most of the politicians in my little town, well, it could be a disaster." He sighed again, rubbed his chin, took off his glasses, and then said, "Tell me what you are looking for. Maybe it's nothing I need to worry over." He pulled a yellow legal pad over and grabbed a pen.

"My client is Lucia Nardone, who was Alex Adamo's fiancée prior to his car sliding off the road and, according to the official report, resulting in his death, presumably from a combination of injuries sustained and exposure to the elements. It happened at night, in winter, in an isolated stretch of road in the northern part of the state. Miss Nardone believes that Alex was too savvy to slide off the road in the first place and then die from exposure in the second. She's convinced the real truth is something else."

"Interesting. I'm guessing you want me to get some details. Maybe the official accident report?"

"Yes, and the coroner's report would help. If this is just a case of denial on my client's part and it was really an accident, then I can save myself a bunch of grief. She seems like a nice person. I don't want to take her money just because."

"Yeah, like you would do that. Give me a break. Okay, I can get all of that without ruffling any political and/or personal Adamo feathers. Some of it you could get yourself. Any reason why you haven't taken that avenue?"

I looked at him for a moment then said, "As I said, she seems like a nice person. I want to be absolutely objective about all of it. If you handle this piece for me, the preliminaries, and something in the information seems amiss, then I'll know it has nothing to do with bias on my part."

Ben smirked, placed his hands flat on the desk, and said, "It's like that, yeah? A *nice* person? Since when have you had trouble partitioning your objective investigative work from your personal interests? There has to be more to it. What aren't you telling me?"

I gazed past Ben through the window behind him, thinking about what he said, as well as what he was inferring, and said, "I really don't know how to answer any of that. There's something about this case, as new as it is, that makes me uneasy. Call it intuition based on experience, or call it jitters or whatever else, but the point is I don't want to dig into it in the usual way. There are certain things I will do myself, but until I get some reassurance that this is a straightforward case of questioning a death by accident—and this isn't my first—I won't rush into it headfirst. Does that make any sense?"

"I think so. Are you sure it's not just that the lady is, maybe, attractive and you have mixed feelings? I know you take care not to get tangled up with your clients, and I think that's good policy, but could these 'jitters' of yours be caused by her? To be frank?" He was not smirking this time.

"I can't be absolutely sure, but it seems unlikely. It's something else."

"Okay, pal. I'll get on this right away. Not to screech into another direction, but can you spare enough time for lunch?"

"I really can't. By the time I get back to the office, Jewels will have gotten all the paperwork gathered together, which should include the insurance company that covered the auto accident. That's where I can discreetly begin. But, hey, maybe when you get the other info, we can discuss it over lunch or maybe dinner. I'll spring, you pick the restaurant. Will that work?"

Ben scowled mockingly, stood up, and said, "It will have to do. This will probably take a couple of days, so I'll call when I have it." He walked around the desk, slapped me on the shoulder. "Great to see you, man. Let's not limit seeing each other to an annual event, okay? One of these days, you should go see Mama Katz, you know. She asks about you every time I see her. I still think she likes you more than me, her only son."

"You still haven't given up that tired old line. You walk in the light for that good woman, I am but a shadow that follows said light." I grinned at him.

With a pained look on his face, he said, "Yeah, I think she likes you because you are as inscrutable as a goy could possibly be. But whatever, you need to see her. Let me know when, and I'll come with. Maybe I can run interference for you and deflect some of the grief she will give you over 'never' visiting her. Okay? Can you do that for the poor old woman?" He bent over, with raised arms, hands extended pleadingly; then he wiped false tears from his eyes.

"How can I, in good conscience, turn my back on such a plea? Let me see what I can do today, figure out whether this is an investigation worth doing, and I'll call. Maybe you will also have some luck with your piece of it. Then, I promise, we can go see Mama."

3

D riving back to the office, I kept running it over in my mind—why am I so uneasy about this case? Yeah, the Adamos are an important, influential family, true. But their reputation is not a bad one. In fact, as powerful, politically connected entities go, they have a fairly benign reputation; that can't be what bothers me, or better, it's improbable. So what is it?

Rain clouds were starting to come down from the north, smearing yellowish color across the horizon, where the sun met clouds. I had my FM tuned to '60s tunes, and "St. Stephen" was playing with those odd lyrics and rolling guitar riffs. Somehow it all blended: rain threatening, my nagging intuition about the case, and the weird light. Occasionally, a convergence of seemingly unrelated events creates an intense awareness for me, an expectation of sorts, but of or for what? An image of rain in the north, in Hanover, suddenly entered my thoughts. I could picture the gray sheets of rain shifting and dancing on familiar streets. Hanover was a nice little college town, clean and obviously well-to-do. In the summer, when most of Dartmouth's students were gone, the locals were more active, especially in touristy parts of town, selling homemade goods and antiques. But the rain had them scattering, finding shelter where they could, their stalls and stands shuttered and draped with blue tarps. I caught myself, shifting attention back to the street in front of me. And what exactly, I wondered, did these images have to do with my uneasiness?

Letting out a long breath, I turned into the side street beside my office building and found my little parking niche. I got out, locked up, and headed over to the office.

Trying to force the quasi-vision from front to back, to let it simmer until something useful emerged, I walked slowly up the stairs. The floor was quiet, a little stuffy in the afternoon heat. I pushed open my business office door. Jewels was busy at her PC. I took two steps toward her desk, and the phone rang.

"Stone Investigations. May I help you?" She looked up at me and said into the receiver, "Mr. Katz's office?" I nodded and walked quickly into my office. My phone buzzed. Lifting the receiver and sitting at the same time, Jewels said, "Ben Katz for you, TB."

"Thanks, Jewels." I hit the button and said, "Hi, Doreen, what's up? Yeah, let me talk to him, thanks." I leaned back in my chair. Ben came on the line, greeted me officiously, and began telling me about his initial findings. "Whoa, Ben! Let me get a pad and pen. I literally just walked into the office. I can't believe you already have anything. Okay, shoot." And he did.

After hanging up, I sat considering what Ben had passed on. Apparently, according to Ben, two reliable sources, both having checked recorded documentation, found no reason to suspect anything other than the official story: Giorgio Abraham Adamo died as a result of injuries sustained in an automobile accident mitigated by subfreezing conditions and a collapsed auto frame. The exact medical judgment of the county coroner was death by blood loss and severe shock. Ben had copies of both the coroner's findings and investigating sheriff deputy's report. He was faxing it to me. He also told me that his contacts relayed that there was no hesitancy in releasing the information. In other words, no one who was questioned seemed suspicious of the inquiry. Clearly, if Abe Adamo did not die from the accident but from some other cause, whatever that might be, it was well and maybe professionally covered up. On the other hand, reason suggested strongly that Miss Lucia Nardone was mistaken, perhaps in denial, about her fiancé's death. But then, on the third hand, Lucy was so certain that Abe had not died from the accident, or at least not exclusively from the accident. And accidents certainly have been staged before and, yes, occasionally by professionals. So. Reason or the *little voice*?

I stood up, looked through my window down at the street. Not much traffic, the rain had started, and the sun, under low dark clouds, was shimmering through the new rain. Quite the spectacle. I stretched and thought that before deciding whether or not to pursue the case, I would see what Jewels had gotten from her paperwork questioning of Lucy.

Swinging my door open, I said, "Jewels. What did you get from Ms. Nardone?"

"Ms. Nardone, or *Lucy*, as she insisted I call her, answered all of the standard questions, but I did manage to get more than that, of course." She looked down at the ever-present yellow pad and continued, "I'm sure some of this you already gleaned from your time with her," and she read off everything on the pad.

"Well, there are some new bits, like Adamo's brother. I didn't know he had a brother. Did you get his name?"

"No, but she did mention that he and Abe shared a great deal of the family business between them, so it would be pretty easy to find out, as well as how to contact him."

"Yeah. Don't do anything about it just yet. I'm not entirely sure I'll be taking the case after all."

Jewels gave me one of her disdainful looks and said, "Really? She's convinced that you already have taken the case"—she waved her hands over the small stack of forms on the corner of her desk—"as witnessed by all of this and the deposit!" She lifted a check in the air as evidence.

"I know, I know. I was largely convinced by her argument and, well, her sincerity. But after hearing Ben's findings, I'm not so sure. The last thing I want to do is support what may be no more than an elaborate denial on her part. So don't pursue anything until I give you the go-ahead, okay, Jewels?"

"Yeah, yeah. I understand. Honestly, before I questioned her myself, I had my own misgivings, if you know what I mean?" Her eyebrows raised in emphasis. "But she convinced me. Something else that she mentioned that I noted as fairly significant was her conversation with the father, Tony Adamo, right after the funeral. He seemed to her angry, not mournful, and was impatient with her when she asked for some details on the accident. Doesn't that raise a suspicion or two?"

"Yeah, I caught that when you reviewed your notes. I'm not so sure. If considered objectively, it could easily mean that Tony was angry because of the accident itself—who wouldn't be? And being impatient with her? It was right after his son's funeral, and Lucy is asking detail questions about the accident. Hell yes, he was impatient. That was the last thing he wanted to discuss. I don't know, Jewels, it's starting to look like Miss Lucia Nardone may be going down the wrong path."

Jewels sniffed, pursed her lips in disapproval, and said, "It's certainly possible. Your arguments are reasonable, granted. How about this—go home, open a nice red, and mull it over before you make a final decision. Getting away from it for a little bit may allow that weird second sight of yours to suggest something new. That's also possible, right?"

"Probably a good idea. In your sage capacity as my most trustworthy adviser, what's a good wine to conjure up this transformative experience?" I grinned.

She looked up at me, not entirely sure if I was kidding or serious, and said, "Either you are being an ass or expecting a lot from a secretary." She looked back at her screen then back up at me with no discernible clue as to her decision regarding my intention. She was like that. She was also practiced at being able to switch a conversation from receiving a verbal spike to returning it with finesse.

"Okay, Jewels. You are right. Thinking about it is good advice. You know me well. And you are my trusted adviser. Seriously." I wanted to be clear, and she accepted it: a tight little smile and a nod of her head proved it.

I gave her a mock salute and walked to the outside door, opened it, and before I closed it while leaving, I heard, "A young Italian red. Miss Nardone would approve." Closing the door, I laughed and said quietly to myself, *Smartass.*

***

It had stopped raining but looked like it could start up again at any moment. Walking across the wet alleyway, dodging puddles, I crossed into the parking space. Opening my Fiat, careful not to accidentally splash water inside, I climbed in. The scent of rain-soaked air blending with the leather interior was sweet, and I sat for a moment, enjoying the sensation. The engine turned over with a satisfying rumble. I switched on the wipers and backed out.

On the way to my place, it began raining again, making the usual staccato white noise on my ragtop, not an unpleasant sound. I turned off the streaming music and listened to the rain. It was late afternoon, so traffic had picked up, and my attempts to avoid truck backwash were futile. On the positive side, washing, polishing, and generally doting on my little Fiat was like a gift, and I'd have a legitimate excuse this time.

Pulling into my drive I stopped the car, jumped out, and quickly pulled a handful of mail out of the box. The rain persisted. Driving slowly up the gravel drive, dodging puddles, I hit the remote, and the garage door opened. Entering, centering, and noting how the engine noise seemingly increased in volume, reverberating off the two-by-four skeleton structure and the metal roof of Fiat's shelter. Switching off, I hit the remote, and the door closed creakily. I got out, stretched, and walked up a low step and then into my house proper. Doc, my cat, trotted up to me, obviously glad I was home. Kneeling, I scratched his head with both hands and said, "Doc! How you doing, my friend?" He purred. I stood up, reached above my head, and retrieved Doc's dry food from a cabinet. Doc made his usual noises in expectation, and I poured a generous amount in his bowl. He immediately squatted down and began eating. I checked his water, and it was okay. The autodispenser held half a gallon, and gravity dispensed it as needed.

I flipped a switch, and lights came on in the kitchen area. Opening the fridge, I retrieved a glass container of beef-stew leftovers, put the cover in the sink, pulled a double sheet of paper towel from the roll, and covering the container with the towel, slipped it into my ancient microwave. After setting the timer for four minutes, I quickly moved to the wine rack, grabbed a bottle of Italian Bardolino, and stepped quickly to the counter. Reaching above, I selected a stemless wineglass. Glancing over at the microwave, which had counted down to 2:50, I extracted my favorite corkscrew from a strategically placed basket and began circling the bottle band with the attached small knife blade. Sliding the tip of the blade under the cut band, I popped it off. Inserting the screw in the cork, centering it carefully, then screwing down to its base, I pulled the cork. The microwave read 1:20. I sniffed the cork. It was fine, and I chucked it in the basket. Pouring a small amount in my glass, I put my nose a little beyond the rim and inhaled deeply—fruity, hints of chocolate. Then the taste. Perfect! And the microwave beeped. Exact timing and efficiency in the bargain! A small victory, granted, but nevertheless.

So with stew and a young Italian red in hand, I went out on the deck. The rain was more of a drizzle now, and thanks to my retractable overhead canopy, most of the deck was still dry. I put stew and wine down on a small table. I sat, I ate, I drank.

***

Having finished my meal, relaxing with it, I sat comfortably in my chair with over half a bottle of the Bardolino by my side. The rain had stopped, and the sun was beginning to shine through the remaining clouds. It was time to make a decision regarding taking the case. It seemed logical to pass on it, considering Ben's findings, but it felt like I should take it, based on Jewels's generally reliable intuition, as well as some of her arguments. Really, it was a fifty-fifty split. If only my own moment of inscrutable confluence would congeal into understanding, the balance would be favored one way or the other, but so far, it remained unclear. Okay. Ben's findings were factual. If Ben had sensed anything out of synch, he would have passed it on. So his facts, based upon prior experience with his help in the past, were credible. On the other hand, Jewels's intuitive recommendations had almost always been reliable, if at times somewhat myopic. So her sense of Lucy's argument was also credible, if personalized. My own interview with Lucy was mixed, I suppose, but immediately following it, I was strongly leaning toward pursuing the case. It was only later, after reason kicked in, that I questioned my initial reaction.

And then there were other factors. I could use the income; that much was always true. The business was solvent, but only just. Who knows when another case would present itself? It was also true that I'd never been involved with such a potentially high-profile case. The Adamo family interests were far-ranging. If Tony Adamo was satisfied with the official police investigation, and he had virtual access to any level of follow-up investigation, who was I to argue? Still, Lucy wasn't shy, and my guess is that if Tony wanted her to let the whole thing drop, she would never have shown up on my doorstep.

I swallowed the remains in my glass, reached for the bottle, and poured another half glass. Young Italian red, indeed. Yes, Lucy was a very compelling, attractive young woman, and I couldn't deny that she struck a chord in me and that might be clouding both reason and intuitive assessment. But knowing how I am, however sweet the distractive elements, I am capable of focusing on a decision free of such compulsion. It takes gritting my teeth and sweating, but still. Sitting here, I wondered if I was not overcompensating for the *distraction*. No, that was not it. What prevented me from making this decision, one way or other, was my prerain quasi-vision earlier today. There was something else going on, and whatever that something was, it was not surfacing. Generally, even historically, these odd imaginings coalesced quickly, and that was not happening, which alone was suggestive. And that, in all its peculiar glory, was the impediment. I took another drink.

Staring off into the trees, up the hill, and on up the mountain, I let my thoughts relax into the pine trees. A dark late afternoon blue rose above the tree line, above the granite, and into a brighter shade of sky. Closing my eyes, a kind of calm gently washed over my body, ascending into, behind, and then beyond my vision. So many shades of blue filled me, lifting, carrying, supporting the place where thought emerged unbidden and unburdened and whole.

My eyes opened. I smiled, laughing quietly as the blue mists receded. Got it!

4

The following morning, driving back to the office, I mentally planned my approach. First, brief Jewels. Second, get Lucy back in the office, and go over everything in detail and, if possible, free up more useful information. Based on that, draw up a list of people to question, places to visit, and people/places for Jewels to call.

The front door was open, so Jewels was already hard at it.

"Jewels. Good morning." I stood in front of her desk. She looked up and gave me her guarded, professional smile.

"Good morning, TB." She leaned back, pointed to my closed office door, and said, "Miss Nardone is in there waiting for you." Then in a hushed tone, she continued, "She has been here since eight thirty and, I'm guessing, longer than that in the parking lot. I thought you would want to see her, one way or the other." She nodded her head then shook her head in quick succession, raising her eyebrows for an answer.

I gave her a thumbs-up as answer, keeping a straight face, and said softly, "Is there coffee in there?" She made a face, indicating sarcastically that I was an idiot for even asking. Then I smiled, walked to my office door, and entered.

"Good morning, Lucy. This is a bit of a surprise. You must be a morning person, yes?" I walked around my desk and sat down.

She smiled pleasantly and said, "Not really." Then looked at me expectantly. Today she was wearing a casual sort of summer business suit, made of lightweight tan fabric with a muted light-blue pattern. Her shoes were flat, comfortable, and light brown. The effect was "I'm serious but relaxed with it." I liked the look. It matched her hair, the highlights.

"I see. Okay. Let me bring you up to speed." And I did, after pouring myself a cup of coffee and taking a sip. I gave it to her without icing, without artifice, all but the reason for my decision. I didn't know her well enough for that.

She gave me a blank stare, shifted in her chair, slowly took a drink of her coffee, and said, "Are you now satisfied that I'm not just another hysterical, grief-denying female grasping at possibilities?" She carefully, delicately, placed her empty cup in its saucer. "Should I have another cup, my third, or should I be on my neurotic way?"

I held her softly defiant, unblinking stare for a moment. I reached for the coffee and poured another cup for her then me. "I think, Miss Nardone, that you and I will be working together on this investigation. It will be important that I learn everything about the accident, your late fiancé, and the circumstances surrounding the incident. I'll be frank, the questions all seem to be answered, so at this juncture, there is no logical place to start. So we need to find a place to start—the proverbial rock to turn over."

"Could I tell you something, Mr. Stone?" She emphasized the *mister* part.

"Of course, Miss Nardone." I emphasized the *miss* without a sarcastic tinge, and that was hard.

"You have a decidedly unconventional way of screening your clients." Her eyes lit up like a cop's flashlight in a dark alley.

I rocked back in my chair and said, "Yes, ma'am! That's a pretty fair assessment!" And I laughed softly. A tap at the door sounded. "Yeah, Jewels."

The door opened. "More coffee?"

***

We sat in the little sandwich shop on the lower floor of my office building. The coffee fresh and every bit as good as Jewels's but industrially served in round-topped white mugs with handles that were suited for three fingers. Sandwiches were ordered. I said, "Just what I need—more coffee." I blew steam away from the surface then sipped carefully.

Lucy smiled and said, "So where exactly do we start? I thought that between you and Julie, you had gathered everything from me. What more is there?"

"Well, details, primarily. I'll need a list of all of the people that were close to your fiancé: relatives, employees and workmates, friends, and potential enemies. After that, what had Abe been doing the last few weeks prior to the incident—jobs, projects (both working and personal), recreational activities, and anything that doesn't fit into those categories, like political activities for example? And then, uncomfortable as it may be, was there anyone who had been upset with him? And this doesn't have to be an enemy. It could be a work associate or relative or even someone you didn't know but knew about in some way?" I sipped more coffee.

The sandwiches arrived. We made the usual appreciative comments as we arranged plates and applied condiments. Lucy said, after taking a healthy bite of her tuna melt, "Very nice!" She held her hand over her mouth, chewed a few times, then said, "Oh. Do you want me to continue calling you Mr. Stone or what?"

"Ah. No, you can call me TB. Everyone does."

"Okay, TB. Your initials?"

I chewed then replied, "Thomas Bradley. My father's brother's name. He and my father were close."

"Is he still alive? Your uncle?"

"No, he was killed in Vietnam. Went down in a chopper he was piloting. He took a round in his leg, hitting an artery, but he landed it prior to losing consciousness and saved the troops onboard. It was a hot zone, and he died before anyone could get to him."

"Oh, I'm sorry." She actually seemed concerned. Fascinating.

"He was always a sort of legend when I was growing up. My father never got over it completely. In fact, we used to go to DC once a year, on my uncle's birthday, and visit the Memorial Wall. My father was a strong man, but every year, every time, he would stand in front of that shiny black wall and silently cry. When I was a teenager, it was uncomfortable seeing that kind of emotion from my father. It left me with a certain amount of bitterness for that war. You know, the ongoing consequences of questionable political decisions? As brave as those guys were, others had to suffer. But then I was a naive teen."

She didn't say anything.

"I didn't know my uncle, but my father was never bitter about the war. He generally didn't judge people, and now, I guess I'm old enough to understand why." I cleared my throat. "But that's much more than you want to know. Sorry."

She said nothing but smiled in what I took as a sympathetic way.

We exchanged a look, then I said, "Let's talk about the case. That way I can write this lunch off as a business expense, okay?"

She nodded noncommittally and replied, "What first?"

"Tell me about Abe's family first."

"Tony, the father and patriarch, runs the various businesses through his sons and, to a lesser extent, his daughter. Tony, as I'm sure you know, owns real estate all over New England: commercial buildings, apartment complexes, that sort of thing. He also holds mortgages on many of the buildings and many individual homes through his banking interests. Six years ago, Tony named Abe president over all the real estate businesses. Obviously, Tony was still involved, but the actual daily operations were Abe's. Now that Abe has passed, Tony has reassumed all of that. He is in his early seventies, so it's unlikely that he will continue with it for any length of time. Tony is one of those persons who can charm you into agreeing with him on virtually anything. Over the years, he has been approached numerous times to run for political office, but it never interested him. I asked him about it one time, out of curiosity, and he told me that he loved the country too much to go into politics. I don't know if that's true, but I do know that he really does love this country. Do you know that he met Frank Capra years ago? They became friends of a sort. Frank was an immigrant, and of course, Tony was also. They were many years apart in age, but they had a common perspective on the opportunities this country provided to people with ambition. Tony quotes Frank as saying to him once, 'Love God, your family, and this beautiful country, but never forget your roots.' And Tony took that to heart. He is easily the most honest, loyal, and just fundamentally decent person I have ever met. Of course, Abe was very much like him." She stopped, shifted her eyes to the side, and took a slow breath. She looked at me. She smiled.

"The eldest brother, Marco, has always been responsible for *expansion* businesses, the start-ups. Five years ago, as an example, he opened up Adfam Tech Inc. in Boston. It is, today, the most prosperous business of its kind in the area. Software, hardware, social media, artificial intelligence, robotics, and his latest interest, holography. *Wall Street* has dubbed him the East Coast version of a Silicon Valley czar. On a personal level, Marc is extremely bright, holds an MBA from Harvard, and was a Rhodes Scholar. He is stoic, all business, and can be charming if somewhat single-minded. It is difficult to get to know him. I like Marc, but he and I do clash occasionally. I'm not sure how relevant it is, but we actually had a relationship at one time. It only lasted a few months, and it was an amicable parting. Then, over a year later, I bumped into Abe and we started dating." She paused, then she asked, "Is this what you are looking for?"

"You are doing fine. Just keep going."

"Okay. Marco is now married to a beautiful local girl, Cynthia. They are expecting their second child in a few months. The whole family is excited about it. I don't know her at all. When Abe passed away, everything changed for me, and my ties to the family have gradually faded." She reached for the coffee carafe, poured, sipped, and smiled half-heartedly.

"The daughter, Maria, is fairly young, so her responsibilities are limited at this point. She finished college two years ago and is now orienting herself to the family business in Concord, spending time with all of the various corporate heads. It is likely that she will assume some administrative position in a year or two. Eventually, she will take on more responsibility in the financial end. Both her education and interests have always pointed her in that direction. She's bright, insightful, and seems mature for her age. Unlike the two sons, Maria is an introvert, so her personal interests tend to be bookish. She has a close relationship with her mother. That has evolved over the years into friendship. She adores her father, but the friendship component is secondary to her respect for him. Tony is noticeably protective of her, like most fathers, I suppose. My opinion is that Maria, as she grows older and acquires experience, will become a significant force in the family business and perhaps beyond."

"Okay. All good information. How about the mother?"

"Ah. I've intentionally saved her for last because of everyone else in the family, Gianna is the most, well, inscrutable. I can tell you what I know about her, but it isn't much. And in case you are wondering, I'm not alone in this. Everyone outside of the family has an opinion about her, but no one really has anything other than that—opinions. It is said that Tony, after making his first million, went back to Italy to find a wife. He was unsuccessful, but as luck would have it, he met Gianna, who was visiting relatives in Italy, Milan, in fact. Her family, after leaving Milan in the early 1900s, had settled in the Philly area. Beyond that, who knows? When Abe and I announced our engagement, she sat down with me, and we spoke for over two hours, discussing Abe, the family, marriage, in general, all sorts of things. She was cordial, warm, even inviting, but at the end of the conversation, I knew no more about her than I did before. And I was paying attention!"

"Now that's interesting. Is it a learned sense of privacy, do you think? From her birth family?"

"Maybe in part, but there's more to it. I asked Abe about it, and he just shrugged and said that it was just *Mama's way*. When I pressed, he smiled and suggested that over time I would get to know her better. Of course, that wasn't good enough for me. She would be my mother-in-law, so I wanted to know more, but I never had the chance. Again, things changed."

"Okay. Anyone else in the family I should know about?"

She frowned and said, "Well, Tony's brother, Sal. But he rarely comes to the States. Tony has an import/export business, and Sal heads up the Italian side. It's a small business, and Tony handles the American side himself. I'm not sure what all is involved, but wine and olive oil are imported. I don't know what is exported. Computer components, maybe? I don't know."

"And that's it for the family?"

"Yes. I believe so. At least the ones I know."

"Okay. I may have more questions as we dig deeper into all of this, but starting with investigating the family is generally the most fruitful. Patterns usually emerge that may not lead directly to the answers but usually suggest a direction for pursuit." She nodded. She seemed tired, her face showing it. I said, "Are you ready to go? We have a lot to do today."

"Yes, I'm ready. What exactly will we do next?" She stood up slowly, stretching her shoulders, and moved away from the table.

I stood, walked out and raised my arm to get the attention of our waitress, and pointed to the table, where I left payment. She nodded and waved.

"Lucy, are you feeling all right? You seem tired, no?"

"Talking about the family like that is taxing. They were so close, and now..." She shrugged and forced a smile. "But I am ready to get started on all of this. Whatever you want me to do." She straightened herself and walked to the door. I followed, smiling to myself, and reached in front of her, opening the door so she could pass through. She did.

Later that day as Lucy and I were up on 93, headed to the accident site, my phone rang—well, actually, it intoned the sound of a large bell, paused, then rang again. I reached for the cell and said, "TB here." I listened. "Okay, thanks, Ben. Yeah, I will. See ya."

Lucy looked at me and asked, "Everything okay?"

"I'm not sure. That was a lawyer friend of mine. Yesterday I had him run down some reports for me concerning the accident. He got back to me later in the day and reported the information and, more importantly, that he had no difficulties getting the information."

"Why *more importantly*?"

"All of the records are public and, aside from the usual bureaucratic red tape, should be easily accessible."

"So what's the problem? I don't get it."

I paused before answering, considering, then said, "It may be a problem because he received a call this morning from a clerk at the coroner's office, one of Ben's friends, and the guy told him that the office received two calls re the inquiry. The first was cordial, the second not so much. Apparently, just questioning the accident stirred up some concern. That's a red flag."

"Who made the calls?"

"Ben didn't know because his friend didn't get the names. The coroner's secretary took the calls, and when Ben's friend asked her about it, she clammed up. She wouldn't say anything and wasn't particularly nice about it. Ben said he would see if he could find out for me, but under the circumstances, he needed to be somewhat discreet about it, so it might take a little time."

"What do you think it could be? And who?"

"Good question. Another question is how much information did the coroner pass on to the callers about us? And about my friend Ben, who officially asked for the information? Whoever called is obviously concerned that questions are being asked about, not only the accident, but also Alex's death."

Lucy was quiet. I was thinking. Someone out there had more going on with all this than the official story of the accident suggested. That small voice was chittering away in the back of my head. I felt my hands tighten around the steering wheel. I consciously loosened them, breathing out slowly. I smiled. This might be an interesting case, after all.

"Lucy. You know that rock we were waiting to find?"

"The one that might be turned over to our advantage. That one?"

"That's the one. Well, it might not be turned over just yet, but someone is circling around and guarding it. And if we find whoever that is…" I turned my head and caught her eyes.

"Then we will find the rock." She sat back, then she said, "Is there any doubt now?"

I stared at the road ahead and, after a few minutes, replied, "Something is amiss, that much is certain. I'm hoping we will find more at the accident site." I wasn't sure, so I asked, "Did you check it out yourself? The site?"

"Yes. I didn't see much that meant anything. I went up by myself a few days after the accident, so everything was still visible: tracks through the snow, the broken saplings and brush where the car ran over the embankment"—she paused—"and the tree where the car hit and was stopped. To be honest, I was too emotional to notice anything other than the obvious."

"This is a long time after the accident, so it's unlikely we will find anything new. What I'm looking for is just an idea of how and where the car lost traction and then, judging by the terrain, how fast it might have been traveling. Really, I want to recreate all of it in my imagination and then possibly consider other alternative causes. It may be that, after assessing the area, the official reported version will be the most reasonable cause."

She looked out the side window and, judging by her silence, wasn't enthusiastic about any conclusion that eliminated foul play. Stubborn lady.

"How far yet to the side road?" The traffic had thinned out to all but nothing. I checked the dash clock, three thirty.

"Not far. Another fifteen, twenty miles. It's so beautiful up here. It never gets old. Do you get up here very often?"

"Not really. Last time I was this far north was last year. I took a couple of days to unwind from a difficult case."

"Did it help?" She had turned, shifting her shoulders to partially face me.

"Actually, it did help. The case dragged out for almost four months—a lot of time spent on research— and then, about a month and a half into it, I got the crap beat out of me by a couple of pros. A week in the hospital later, I was convinced the trail was heating up!"

She covered her mouth and turned back around, facing her side window. She was stifling a laugh.

"What's so funny? They did a number on me. Two broken ribs, bruised kidney, and I couldn't see out of my right eye for three days! I wasn't amused."

"I'm sorry. It's just that I had this image of you bandaged, lying in the hospital saying to yourself, 'Well, guess I'm making progress,' and it just seemed funny. Sorry!" She patted my shoulder and giggled again.

"Well, you can see why I needed to unwind." This time she laughed out loud and kept on laughing.

5

The traffic was picking up again. New York, Massachusetts, Vermont plates on the cars. Some New Hampshire. "Lucy, where do I turn?" She looked at the road signs and said, "Turn on 49. It curves around a bit, heading into the State Forest area. Right up here." She pointed.

I slowed and turned. Some state signs indicating tourist attractions ahead. "Now where?"

"Another two or three miles. You will see a dirt road on your right."

The traffic was intermittent, more headed west than east. It was approaching four o'clock.

"Okay. Slow down, it's not far now. See those trees up there? Just past. Yeah, right there!"

I saw the road and slowed. The road made a sharp turn, immediately crossing a one-way wooden bridge. I slowed to a crawl and thumped across. The stream below was still, and summer greenery reached out over the water, very scenic and placid. Reaching the other side, I pulled over to the right and stopped, letting the engine idle. Lucy looked at me questioningly.

"How far from here? I want to approach it slowly so I can see everything."

"Not far at all. Actually." She leaned forward, studying, and said, "I'm pretty sure it's just around that bend up there, on the left. There's an embankment." Her eyes were large and obviously alert, and I couldn't help noticing the greenish flecks that accentuated the brown. But that was another matter.

I reached up and disengaged the convertible top then leaned over in front of Lucy and released the right-hand lock. Returning my arm to my side, I realized that I was extremely close to Lucy. I paused; she gave me a look that was something other than uncomfortable. With the closeness, that is. We held the look between us. She said, "What now?"

"We take the top off."

"What?"

"The convertible top. I want to have an unobstructed view of the accident site."

"Oh. Yes, of course. That makes sense."

"Okay. Let's get out and pull the top back. It's not automatic." We broke eye contact and exited.

After pulling the top back and fastening it, we reentered the car and drove slowly forward. Removing the top had enlarged everything. We were in a small valley area, pine trees everywhere with some huge deciduous growth, as well. And then the mountains, surrounding us, rising up green then gray and brown then white clouds mixed with blue sky. Quite spectacular. And it almost captured me, but for the business at hand.

We approached the bend, began the turn, gravel scrabbling below the tires, and then a fairly steep decline. I could see the embankment on the left and the mountain skirt of pine on the right. I stopped the Spider, shifted out of gear holding the brake. Looking down the road as it curved out of sight below, I noticed a wide spot directly opposite the embankment, obviously a pullover. Above this, well above, was a jutting large chunk of granite almost covering the pullover, which, this time of day, shadowed the wide spot below. It could have been widened to provide a tourist sight for the overlook—it was a beautiful spot. Or more likely it was widened for safety; I could imagine using the wider road to navigate more carefully on a snowy day. Serendipitously, it would make a perfect meeting spot for someone who wanted privacy. Interesting thought.

"What do you see, Lucy? Anything occur to you?"

"Well, when I came out here before, a few days after the accident, as I mentioned, I went directly to the embankment. There were tire ruts in the shoulder, running down to the trees. You know, where the trees were skinned up from his…" She stopped and looked at me forlornly, cleared her throat, and said, "Sorry."

"So am I, Lucy. Maybe it's too soon to come back here."

Her chin tightened. She said, "No. This needs to be done. Don't worry about me. Just do your detective thing, and tell me what you see, because all I see is what I saw before, and that doesn't help. Okay?"

She meant it, even though I knew she was hurting. Stubborn and strong. Good combination. Lucy, two more points—world, zero. "Okay, Luce. Well, I noticed a couple of things. Access to the embankment from our direction, downhill, would require slowing down considerably even in good weather, but on a snowy, icy night, it would be treacherous to make the turn at a speed of even twenty miles per hour. Coming up the hill would be easier, but if the road were icy, especially at night, driving more than thirty to thirty-five mph would be equally dangerous. Also, see that wide spot up there on the right? Below the overhang? Might be ideal for a meeting, especially if you didn't want anyone to stumble across said meeting. It could be nothing, but still, it's worth noting for future reference." We slid back into the Fiat. I put the car in gear and started creeping forward.

"So just so I understand, you are imagining how someone might slide off the road, from either direction?"

"Yes. Traveling too fast, not realizing the risk."

"Forget that. Abe knew these roads around here like you know Concord. And his favorite time of year was wintertime. He couldn't get enough. But he was cautious and always respected the potential dangers that came with winter. I rode along with him over many of these backroads and trails all over this area, and I can assure you that he never would have accidentally slid over that embankment. Period."

"Okay, but what if he was being chased by another vehicle? Or what if someone had been waiting for him, car hidden in that pullover? Or what if someone, coming from the opposite direction, swerved into him and he slid over the embankment?"

"Oh." She thought about it. "Do you think that happened?"

"I have no idea. I'm just speculating at this point. If it's impossible that he could have accidentally gone over that embankment, then we need to consider all other possibilities and then eliminate them one at a time. Make sense?"

She nodded. I engaged the clutch and pulled over beneath the overhang.

"Let's get out, check the area a little closer. Okay?" I watched her reaction. She wore the now-familiar determined face. She pulled at the door latch, opened the door, and stepped out. I waited until she closed the door, then turned the ignition key off, pulling the park brake. I got out.

Stretching, I waited for Lucy to join me on my side. We walked to the middle of the road. I looked back up the hill then down the hill; this really was an isolated spot. At this point for maybe fifty yards or so, the road was flat. It would be virtually impossible for a car to approach from either direction without being heard well before it came into view, and at night, headlights would be visible against the trees. The big hunk of granite now reaching out over the Fiat seemed somehow ominous. A truck could get under it, like a small snowplow, but anything bigger would be tricky. Probably not relevant, but interesting for some reason. The embankment on the other side was also preceded by a wider shoulder but not enough for a car to comfortably park. It was fine for observing the downhill view.

We walked over to the embankment side. The shoulder sloped up just a bit and had a kind of rocky lip all along its edge, almost like a poorly formed step. It wouldn't be enough to prevent a car moving at speed to go over, but it would surely slow it down. I walked slowly, carefully along the edge, trying to find any indication that a car had gone over. It was probably a fruitless effort, but whatever. I did find a break in the lip, the step, that in the last few months had been covered over somewhat by rain and mud and road grading. I squatted, roughed the area with my hand. Yes, it was loose. I brushed it, and the gravel and sediment easily came away. Lucy knelt beside me and started helping. After ten minutes or so, we had cleared away three shallow breaks in the lip/step, two close together and one distant from the other two by several feet. I stood up, reached into my pocket, and extracted my cell. I snapped half a dozen pics from various angles, close and a few feet back.

"I don't think you ever told me what kind of car Abe was driving, Lucy."

"A Range Rover."

"Huh. Certainly not a vehicle that would be out of place up here. Well, if it slid over the side, at an angle, it would have gone over right here." I pointed to the spot. "At an angle, let's suppose, the two front wheels would have gone here"—I pointed to the spot where the two indentations were close—"and the rear wheel would have gone here." I pointed to the separate, distant indentation.

"Why wouldn't there be two marks back here?"

"Probably by the time outside rear wheel would have reached the lip, the car would be tipping up as the front began going down. It is a fairly steep and immediate descent."

She looked thoughtful and said, "So if all of this is true, he would have been driving up the hill, not coming here in the same direction as us?"

"Yes. Or he could have been pushed over from the road, after having stopped. But in either case, his car would have been pointed in this direction, opposite the way we entered. Does that matter?"

"Well, I'm just curious why he was coming from that direction"—she pointed downhill—"rather than that direction." She pointed uphill. "The only thing back there is heavy forest. It wouldn't make any sense, especially if he were here to meet someone. And if he came out of the forest, really almost wilderness, who would be chasing him?"

"Good questions. Tuck those questions away for future reference." She nodded.

"Okay, Luce, I need to go down the embankment and examine the area. See if there's anything that was missed by the cops. You can stay up here, if you like."

"Not gonna happen. I'm coming with. Besides, I can show you the tree that stopped his car, as well as describe the angle and final position. All that."

"Okay, but for safety's sake, follow me down. If I stumble, you will be forewarned." She agreed though, I suspect, reluctantly.

The steep path down was difficult with loose gravel, sharp rocks jutting out in spots, and slippery algae growing on some of the exposed granite. Even months later, there was a wide area that reflected the path taken by the vehicle: bark scraped from trees, places where the car sheared off humps of gravel and dirt, creating shallow, trench-like spots. By moving carefully from tree to tree, we reached a flat area that with three tall old pine trees. One of the pines was badly damaged, a large piece gouged out and smaller places that looked like random axe indentations running down from the larger wound. Obviously, this was what stopped the vehicle. Lucy was now standing beside me, face sober, panting from the exertion.

"Luce, anything you recall from your first visit?"

"Not really. I didn't come down here then. Of course, the downward path the Rover made was fresh, so smaller trees were bent, some broken, and there were spots dug up along the way. This tree looked even worse. It looks better now than I would have expected."

I took several pics of the crash site, walking around the tree, and then a couple of shots looking back up at the road. As I circled the tree for the second time, I noticed something in the weeds. I leaned down, pulled the growth back.

"Luce! Look here." I pointed to a sharp piece of rock jutting out from the ground a foot or so from the tree. There was a smear of gray-green paint on the rock. She knelt.

"Oh! That's from the Rover. I always liked that color. I picked it out when Abe bought the car." She sat down, put her hands over her eyes, and quietly sobbed, shoulders shaking.

I reached over, put my arms around her. She nestled up and let it go.

After Lucy was ready, we walked back up to the road then across to my car, tucked beneath the overhang. Before getting in the car, I examined the bottom of the granite more out of curiosity than anything else. I noticed an irregularity in the rough surface, but it was too dark to make out. I hit the flash icon on my phone and ran it over the granite above. Sure enough, the irregularity looked like something had scratched the surface and left a small smear of blue in its path. I took a couple of pics from different angles.

Lucy asked what I was doing. I told her, explaining that a snowplow had probably scratched the underside accidentally, but then again, maybe it was something else. Might as well get as much physical evidence as possible while we were here. She nodded half-heartedly.

6

On our way back to 93, a little before six o'clock in the evening, the light compressing like melting butter across the road in front of us suffused everything inside and out in soft gold. Before leaving, we had retopped the Spider, but the windows were still partially open, allowing warm air to shush speech and eliminate any need to talk or listen or worry about either. Lucy looked straight ahead; I scanned for oncoming traffic or hikers or straying wildlife. My thoughts were softly engaged but nonverbal and remote, subconscious and conscious mixed with melancholy, though a muted and tame sort of melancholy. Probably communing with the light. Maybe replaying Lucy's tears.

When we reached the on-ramp to 93, Lucy squeezed my arm and said, "Pull over up here before getting on the highway." I looked at her, but she was looking ahead. I pulled over on the side of the road and shut down.

It was suddenly very quiet. Lucy said, "TB, I'm not really looking forward to the drive back to Concord. Maybe we could go up to Woodstock and stay the night. I know we weren't planning this, but I could really use the time to regroup. What do you think?"

"Well, I haven't been up there for years, but assuming we can find someplace to stay, it might be better than spending the next couple hours in the car. It's, what, twenty, thirty minutes up?"

"About that. And I know we can find a place because my aunt Connie has a cottage just west of town. She retired up here." She smiled brightly, nicely.

I cocked my head, squinted my eyes, and replied, "Aren't you full of surprises. You can just walk in on her, without warning, not to mention having me in tow, and she will be happy with it?"

"Oh yeah. Aunt Connie is always after me to come visit, and she is the sweetest person I know. Also, Italian that she is, the food will be exceptional and plentiful. Maybe we can stop off in town and pick up some overnight things and a bottle or two of wine?"

Without speaking, I started my car and pulled out.

We stopped at a little shop (Ye Olde Wine Shoppe) and bought two reds and one white. Surprisingly, despite the cornball name for the place, they had a fairly broad selection, organized by region and/or country then by varietal. It made shopping convenient and as speedy as you might want it to be. Leaving there, we walked down a block and entered another small store that carried all sorts of odds and ends, including toiletries, some clothing, and even snack foods. We purchased what we needed.

We walked back to the car, slowly enjoying the final setting of the sun. I looked down at Lucy, her face bathed in red gold, and thought about her name: Lucia. It certainly fit. The dimming light seemed to accentuate everything I was beginning to appreciate about her—intensity, sensitivity, pride, intelligence, and a certain mystery, intriguing but welcoming. Suddenly I could hear Ben Katz saying to me out of my subconscious, *Careful, Tommy, careful.* I told him to shut up.

We only drove a few blocks north then made a turn on a side street, drove a short distance, through strung-out gas stations and specialty stores, and then almost immediately into the twilit countryside. After a mile or so, Lucy said, "Right up here on the right. See the sign?" I saw it, a smallish, tasteful sign, Cottages for Rent, lit by an overhead spotlight. I pulled onto a gravel drive, crunched up to an office/cottage building, and stopped the car. "You didn't tell me about your aunt's business."

She smiled and said, "Should I have?"

"I suppose it doesn't matter. Is your aunt in the office?"

"Yes and no. The front room is the office, and behind that is where she lives. You'll see. Come on." She climbed out, carrying our bags. I picked up the wine and asked, "Should I leave the car here? Seems like it might be in the way."

"Just leave it. We'll figure out the accommodations, and you can move it then. She only has six cottages, so we may be staying with her. I'm not sure." She walked up to the door and pressed a lighted button. I locked the car and joined her. Two large windows framed the office door, which was also heavy gauge glass. Lucy looked at me and smiled. "I think you and Aunt Connie will get along famously."

"If you say so. I'm not accustomed to having 'famous' relationships."

She laughed and replied, "That's why!"

"What?"

A door opened at the back of the office, and a small, thin woman in her late fifties, with short gray hair, walked to the door. When she recognized Lucy, her face went from expressing seriousness, bordering on severity, to what could only be described as absolute joy. "Oh my god! Lucia!" They hugged, they teared up, they babbled. I stood at the side, taking it all in.

Aunt Connie said, "Come in, come in! And who is this?" Lucy turned to me, reached for my hand, and said, "This is my new friend, Thomas Stone."

She seemed to radiate approval, which caught me a little off guard. "Hi. Very nice to meet you, ma'am." I reached out to shake her hand.

"Call me Connie, Mr. Stone. Please, you two, come in." We walked into the office. Connie locked the door behind us and said, "Come on. My home, a sanctuary of sorts, is back here." We followed her through the back door. I was not sure what I was expecting, but not what I encountered. The door led into an open large room that was much larger than the little office suggested. A dark hardwood floor extended conservatively thirty feet back to a wall that was almost entirely glass but for a low wall, perhaps two feet high, and a section a few inches from the ceiling. The walls were plaster, subtly and min- imally stylized and painted off-white. The ceiling had open dark beams approximately three feet apart that seemed to be sunk in the same whitish plaster so that the effect wasn't "rugged" so much as it was quietly substantial. There were thick, patterned rugs that were all dark burgundies and blues, patterned but not intrusively so, strategically placed in what might be high-traffic spots. Chairs, couches, and other necessary accoutrements were dark wood and comfortably functional looking. Upholstery leaned to medium shades of blue, burgundy, and the occasional brown; patterns were nicely random. Lamps were Tiffany and burnished dark metal, a couple of floor lamps, the rest on tables. If I had to guess at a style for the whole room, it would be unselfconsciously Victorian. But then, what did I know? What I did know was that it looked like the kind of place where you could relax in style. Oh! And best of all, both side walls had tall old dark stressed wood bookcases, the kind that might have come out of a late-nineteenth-century library. And books? They went on forever. I liked this room.

I suddenly realized that it was very quiet. Both Lucy and her aunt were looking at me with big smiles. "Hey, I'm sorry. Guess I got lost in this room of yours."

"I'm pleased that you appreciate it," said Connie. "Some do, some don't. Feel free to explore the books." She reached out and patted my shoulder. "Come on, Lucy. Let's go open some of that wine."

Lucy laughed at me and said, "Enjoy." And they walked to the end of the room and exited through an arched doorway. I turned back to the rows of books. On each side, one of those rolling ladders that let you get to the uppermost shelves hung. Damn! So many books, so many topics. It was incredible.

***

After half an hour or so of exploration, I picked a Kierkegaard collection of essays. I sat in one of the wing chairs, table lamp on the left, and started to read. Not five minutes later, the two ladies came in with a bottle of red, some sandwiches and pasta salad on a platter, and smug little smiles on their faces. I stood up, hanging Søren over the chair arm. Connie put the platter on a longish table central between two chairs (one of them mine) and a sofa. Lucy, bottle in one hand and three glasses, stems interspaced between her fingers, placed the open bottle on the side of the same table that was nearest me. She said, "Would you please do the honors?"

"Of course. Let's see, what do we have?" I checked the label: Italia, Sangiovese, Toscana, 2014. The vineyard, Fattoria La Loggia. "Holy shit! Do you know this vineyard was started by the Medicis? You gotta be kidding me!"

Connie laughed. "Lucia told me that you enjoyed wine. I thought you might like this one. I picked up a case three years ago at the estate. I tasted it when I was there, enjoyed it, so here it is."

"Ah. I have never been to Italy, but a guy can dream. And wine like this is one way to kick off some sweet dreams. Thank you!" I poured a small amount in one of the glasses and offered it to Connie.

She shook her head, smiling, and said, "No, no. Please."

I gave her a little bow and held the glass up to the light, swirling the wine, slowly letting it breathe, then held it still and watched the legs run down the interior sides. I passed the glass under my nose, having released the bouquet, and the scents swirled softly upward: fruity, tart. Then I swirled it again and stuck my nose past the rim and inhaled. A combination of scents, complex and promising, exploded from nose to the back of my palate. I took a nice amount into my mouth, let it ride on my tongue until the cherry, raspberry flavors emerged clearly, then sloshed it until the tannins stung pleasantly. As I was swallowing, the soil, musky and acid and almost like mushrooms, presented. And despite the full range of flavors, both subtle and bold, the finish as I swallowed was gentle.

I looked up. The ladies were staring, Connie with a satisfied look and Lucy with a look I didn't recognize at first but later did. I said, "I have always enjoyed Italian wines, Chianti one of them, but Sangiovese has never been like this, blended or otherwise. It's like discovering new depths in conversation with a friend and then realizing that you never knew that friend. Does that sound crazy?"

Connie said, "Sounds plausible to me. I'm just pleased you appreciate it. Wine is to be enjoyed!" She motioned toward the platter. "Mangia."

I poured the other two glasses, handed them to each, and then returning to my chair, poured my own. We all dove into the platter. Connie ladled pasta into bowls for all of us while Lucy placed sandwiches on saucers and handed them around. She then distributed the pasta. We dug in.

***

After the meal, we were sitting comfortably, sipping one of the reds that we had brought, a seven-year-old California Cab. It was nothing like the revelation that was the Sangiovese, but it was nice, nevertheless. We were talking about all sorts of things, learning about each other. While I was speaking midsentence, my phone intoned, once, twice. I found it, swiped, and answered.

"Tommy! Glad I got you, man." It was Ben, agitated and loud.

"Ben, what's going on? What's wrong?"

"Aw, someone broke into my office, and Doreen was here for some reason. The ambulance is here now for her."

"Doreen? How bad, Ben?"

"Well, whoever it was hit her on the back of the head. She has a pretty bad gash and a concussion. They are taking her to the hospital to be safe, you know, in case of internal bleeding, I suppose. Aw, man. It happened about an hour ago. Doreen managed to call me though she was unconscious for a while before. I rushed over, and she was sitting up, blood all over. I called an ambulance then the cops. They are doing their thing. The cops, that is. Doreen is being carried out to the ambulance right now. I have to go. I'll call you back after we get her checked in. Bye." He was gone.

"TB! What's going on?" Lucy was standing by my chair.

"That was Ben. His office was broken into, and Doreen, his secretary, was hurt."

"Oh no! Is she okay?" She was genuinely concerned.

"Well, as a precaution, she's being taken to the hospital, but it appears to be a blow to the back of her head, apparently cutting the scalp. They are sure she has a concussion. Ben will be calling me back with more information." Lucy reached out for me and gave me a hug.

"Do you need to get back tonight?"

"I'm not sure. I'll wait for Ben to call back before deciding." I thought about it for a moment then said, "I'll also find out then why it was so important for him to call me, literally as they were carrying Doreen to the ambulance. We are friends, yes, but Ben's not a guy who would call without a reason, especially so soon."

Lucy sat next to me on the chair arm, and although I appreciated it, it also triggered my curiosity, which, in turn, distracted me from Ben's situation somewhat. Curiosity because we had only known each other a few days and her response seemed somehow overstated. Then again, whenever stress kicks in, I tend to close up. Maybe I'm the one who's out of synch.

Connie was still sipping her wine, watching the two of us, her expression inscrutable. She finished her glass and stood, looked at us, and said, "Anyone for coffee?"

Luce and I both nodded. "Please," we said simultaneously. Then, again simultaneously, we looked away from each other. Connie smiled, gathered up the dishes, and walked out of the room. In the still that followed, we could hear her rattling utensils. We made eye contact again. Lucy said, "So what do you think?"

"About Ben, you mean?" I said it, unintentionally, in a flat voice.

She held my eyes before answering, "Yes. I'm wondering if maybe the break-in had something to do with me, with the case. Is that possible?" She shifted on the chair arm then stood, walked to the couch, and sat, tucking her legs up.

"Good question. That would certainly explain why Ben called me rather than, well, anyone else." I cleared my throat, imagining Doreen on a stretcher.

"It's crazy. Why Ben's office and why hurt his secretary? Why not come after me? I'm the one who started all of this." She shook her head, face blank, eyes wide. "Maybe it has nothing to do with the case."

"I don't know. Whoever it was probably wouldn't have known why Ben was making inquiries. Maybe that's what he was looking for, more information. We will know more when Ben calls." I checked my watch. "It's been about twenty minutes. He should call soon."

Connie walked back in, placed the same tray on the same table, and asked, "How do you take it, Tom?"

"Black, please. And friends call me TB." She smiled, handing me a cup, a spoon, and a saucer. Then she put sugar in a cup, poured coffee, and handed it to Lucy, saying, "One spoon, right?"

Lucy nodded. "Thanks, Auntie."

I sipped. It was strong, more like espresso than straight coffee, but it was excellent. Then my phone sounded. "Yes. Ben. How's she doing. Okay. That's good.

Tomorrow? I'll bet she argued about it, huh?" I listened. Ben then gave me all details of the break-in. "Okay. Well, sounds like there's not much I can do tonight, but I'll be back first thing tomorrow. I'm up in Woodstock. Yeah. I'll be there at your office, around nine. Okay, Ben. Take care, pal." I took another sip.

Lucy, with Connie next to her, said, "And?"

"Doreen will be fine, but they are keeping her over night as a precaution, so that's a relief. Apparently, after she left the office, she went back half an hour or so to retrieve her sunglasses. The door was unlocked, so she thought that Ben must have come in to do some work, which is not unusual, so she thought nothing of it. When she went in, she saw the light in Ben's office on. She turned on the main office lights and walked into Ben's office, and that's all she remembers. Next thing, she wakes up, her head is pounding, and all of the lights are off. She manages to get to a light switch then slides down to the floor again. She waits for a bit then crawls to Ben's desk and calls him. When he gets there, he calls the ambulance."

"Thank heaven she's all right."

"Yeah, she's a tough lady. She didn't want to stay in the hospital, but Ben told her he'd fire her if she left." I chuckled. "She called him something colorfully derisive but agreed to stay."

They both laughed. Lucy asked, "Any idea who broke in and why?"

"Yes. It seems that the Adamo file was missing, the record of his research. A bunch of other files were missing, but that particular file was the only current one. There may be more missing, but he won't know until he cleans things up. Apparently, they trashed the office, overturned filing cabinets, threw stuff all over, pulled out desk drawers, and spilled the contents. They also dumped a trash can on Doreen's desk, made quite a mess. Most of the destruction must have been done after she was knocked out, or she would have seen it when coming in."

"So what do you think is going on, Tom?" I noticed again that Luce was calling me Tom. No one called me Tom except Ben. Interesting.

"My guess is that someone found out that Ben was checking up on the accident and wanted to know more about why. Of course, since more than that file was taken, there's an outside chance that it had nothing to do with our case. Until we sift through the office tomorrow, we won't know for certain."

Lucy thought about it, sipped her coffee, and said, "But you think it has to do with our case, right?"

I nodded. Connie was sitting quietly, listening to us. "Connie. You are very quiet." I raised my eyebrows questioningly.

She gave me a piercing look, reached over to Luce, and squeezed her hand. She said, "Well, as you might guess, Lucia and I have discussed 'the accident' at great length many times over the last few months. I'm a little puzzled by all of this because I thought it was over, that Lucia had accepted the death. Now I don't know what to think." Luce leaned over and put her head on Connie's shoulder.

"I can't say that I haven't had doubts myself," I said, "but there were enough oddities, especially at the accident scene, to shift me over to suspicion. What I do know for certain is that I won't be satisfied of any part of this case without further investigation."

"Investigation? How long have you known, Lucia?"

I looked at Lucy and said, "She doesn't know?"

"No. I'm sorry, Auntie. I was planning on telling you tonight, but I was waiting for the right time." Her voice had a pleading tone. Connie gave her a look, a mix of sympathetic mouth and stern eyes.

"Please tell me now, Lucia."

Lucy glanced quickly at me. I gave her a quick nod, and she said, "Tom is a private investigator. I hired him to check into the accident. I'm sorry, Auntie, but I just can't dismiss it. I know how you feel about all of this, and of course I respect your views, but I needed confirmation. From an objective source, that is, before I could find peace. Is that such a bad thing?"

Connie sighed, kissed Luce on the forehead, and stood. She walked slowly over to a nearby bookcase, adjusted the position of a stylized ivory statue of the Buddha, and turned around to face both of us. She said, "Give me the whole story, from beginning to end. Everything."

I looked at Luce, who shrugged and gave me a tired smile, nodding. I motioned for Connie to sit, saying, "This will take some time, so please be comfortable, Connie." She sat but in the chair opposite me rather than the couch, presumably in order to see both of us, maybe to distance herself from Lucy, or both. Whatever her intent, the choice implied a serious discussion.

I disclosed all the details from my perspective, and Luce filled in her view when pertinent. An hour or so later, I stood, stretched, and said, "That's it. You are now fully informed or at least as much as we are." I asked where I could find a bathroom, and receiving said information, I excused myself.

Upon returning, I found the two of them in a somewhat heated though civil exchange. Lucy's face was red, and Connie's face was stoic. When they saw me, they both stopped talking and gesticulating. Into the silence I bravely strode, chest out, jaw jutting. I said, "Please. Don't let me interrupt." I smiled winningly, even charmingly. They both stared at me. "Or I could go outside and watch the stars. You know, seek out portents and such." They stopped staring and, looking away, simply dismissed me. I tried yet again. "Seriously, if you two want me to go, I could always head back to Concord. No big deal."

"No, no," Connie said, "we were simply in disagreement about something. It's a conversation that can wait." She stood, walked over to the corner archway, and exited.

"Tom. Don't worry, it's just the same old business about me not letting the accident remain an accident rather than, to quote, 'entertain this conspiracy theory.' I'm used to it by now." She folded her arms and struck a pose that belied her words.

I sat in my chair, leaning forward, putting arms on knees, and said, "It's not too late to back out of this business. At the risk of sounding callous, whatever we find at the end of this investigation, it won't bring Abe back. It just won't, Luce." I watched her face. There it was again: that stubborn face and resolute eyes.

"I am perfectly aware of that. As I have explained, this is about finding the truth, not resurrecting anyone, not even myself." She stood up, walked to the same archway, and exited. I wondered at that moment what the Italian phrase was for déjà vu. But then that's just me.

The phone call and subsequent flurry of words and emotion had predictably brought me to a state of calm distance. Odd as it may sound, I have always reacted on some visceral level in the same way. Not sure why, but everything draws down to a kind of rational, objective, alert state. It's almost as if a part of me, a part that waits in reserve, takes over and brings a situationally appropriate mode into being. It is not infrequently misunderstood by those caught up in the "flurry" as withdrawal from the moment but is exactly the opposite. Ben, not surprisingly, is the only person who has gotten it. He compares it to a happy-go-lucky hunter traipsing through the woods who, when suddenly confronted with a pack of wild wolves, immediately grows still and wary and focused. Now, granted, the comparison on the surface might seem a bit lurid, but under the surface, Ben's assessment is exactly right. It is a kind of survival response that seems to be hardwired. It has always been there. Anyway, I sat there waiting for the moment to unwind, ready to respond as needed.

The silence continued for fifteen, twenty minutes or so. Then, softly, both Lucy and Connie walked through the archway side by side, smiling. Lucy spoke, "Sorry to leave you in here alone, but we needed to patch some things up." She looked at her aunt.

"Yes, but please know that we frequently go through these charged disagreements, and just as often, we reach agreement. It's all a process developed between us over many years." They sat down together on the couch.

Again, keep in mind that I was still in my focused mode, and seeing the two of them together—same posture, same expression, same casual smile—it was obvious that part of their rapprochement had to do with me. I smiled and said, "So now what? If you are of one mind, is sharing with me possible?" A little sarcastic but just enough.

Lucy leaned forward. "Of course. That was part of our agreement"—she looked at her aunt—"and considering this latest news, about the break-in, it's apparent that you are invested. Right?"

I watched Connie closely, and she watched me every bit as closely. I replied, "Of course. I did take the case. And though my chosen vocation isn't replete with honorable practitioners, I can assure both of you that I'm not here to collect a fat paycheck. My business is solvent and likely to remain so without this case. Having said that, I'll bail whenever you wish."

Lucy started to respond, but her aunt stopped her with a double pat on the knee. "Mr. Stone, TB, it may seem as if I have objected to your being involved in all of this, but that's simply not true. It is true, however, that I have been skeptical of any foul play regarding the accident. Lucia was justifiably distraught when Abe passed away, and it was my opinion, at the time, that she was in denial and that she would come to her senses after the grieving process ran its course. She knows this and accepts my reasoning. Now, after hearing the arguments, as well as recognizing the probability that your initial inquiries prompted the break-in at your friend's office, it becomes clear that Lucia's suspicions are likely justified. So even though I'm not directly involved in any of this, my concern for Lucia's well-being remains, and because of that, I am pleased that you are working with her." She looked over at her niece then continued, "I know nothing of detectives and such, but you strike me as a responsible, capable young man. So at the risk of putting words in Lucia's mouth, as if anyone could"—she made a surprisingly funny face for Lucy's benefit—"we are both hoping that you will not bail on her." She sniffed.

Now, I have to say that the sniffing caught me off guard, but the rest of it worked. It appeared that client, client's auntie, and yours truly were all on the same page of the same odd book. Now I could start putting a few pieces of the puzzle together and maybe even figure out what the hell kind of puzzle it was. Oh, and my focus mode evaporated, probably with the sniff.

We drank more coffee, chatted about the case, and ever so slowly eased into personal matters. Well, more Connie and TB matters because we both knew Luce, although my familiarity was limited. Anyway, among other things, I learned that Connie was a retired teacher and her husband, prior to his passing, had been a successful real estate broker; he had left her financially comfortable.

"Connie, what did you teach?"

She looked at Lucy. Luce made a face at her and said, "She taught philosophy at Dartmouth. Auntie was a tenured full professor but likes to play that part down."

"Lucia makes more out of it than there is. Strip away the title, and it still comes down to teaching. And quite honestly, that's the only part of the job I ever enjoyed. All the other nonsense was more interference than anything."

"Why did you leave the university? Sounds like an ideal situation." I was genuinely curious.

She sighed, looked at Lucy, smiled sadly, and replied, "When my husband passed away, I took a breather and just never returned. Somehow, the joy of teaching got lost. Odd how associations, linkage between parts of one's life, are never acknowledged or even recognized until some critical catalyst brings it all out into the open. I was teaching when I met Louis, so my interests were set deeply prior to knowing him. Meeting him and then getting married, well, my life's vocation should have had nothing to do with any of that. However, when he passed, something just changed. It's almost as if my life shifted, irrevocably setting me upon a different path." She looked past me, into a space very personal and private.

I said nothing, waiting.

She made eye contact, smiled, and said, "Oh, I still write and stay in touch with former colleagues. And my studies continue. Actually, now I have shifted from philosophy to theology, strange as that may sound. The two are like cousins anyway, one borrowing from the other. I grew up Catholic, of course, so making the intellectual transition wasn't uncomfortable. Well, not for me." She smiled to herself. "Certain of my colleagues find the switch discomforting, but I suppose that is to be expected." She softly laughed.

"Theology? I had eight years of parochial school growing up and then attended Villanova on scholarship. Of course, the Augustinian fathers insisted that we take a certain number of religion courses prior to graduation. I liked the courses enough to get a minor. Granted, that certainly can't compare to your level of study, but believe it or not, I continued reading on my own. I've never lost interest. In fact"—I reached down to the side of my chair—"this is the book I was reading before you served the wine." I held up Kierkegaard.

Connie laughed. "Well, that's certainly an interesting choice. He was a multi-interest scholar, philosophy and theology primarily, but also psychology, poetry, all kinds of other things. What exactly is your interest in him?"

Now I was in trouble. What was that saying about fools rushing in? Tentatively, I replied, "Understand that I am not a theologian, just an interested fellow traveler, okay? But I think his notion of the individual's relationship to Christ, the subjective reality of it, is fascinating. Does that make any sense?"

"Oh, sure. But keep in mind that with Kierkegaard, you have to consider the breadth of his approach, as well as the specifics. He believes essentially that there is no solely objective truth unless that truth is true to the subject and, in this instance, meaning that to believe in Jesus Christ is to be changed and directed by that belief. For him it is impossible to say, in effect, that one believes in the truth of Jesus Christ as an objective reality, but not as something that has any bearing on the subject. It all comes from Kierkegaard's questioning Hegel's commandeering of Christian thought, that is, of objectifying the Gospels and making that the basis for a rational understanding and effectively distancing the subject."

"Does that mean that the subject then creates truth?"

"No. Although to some extent, the subject is necessary for the truth, that is, to recognize it. In other words, he is saying that *truth* cannot be solely objective, sort of perched up on some metaphoric mountaintop of rational thought, particularly with regard to Christianity. Of course, Kierkegaard was challenged in his day and still is by some. Does that help?"

I thought about it but decided discretion was, in this case, the better part of agreement. "I think so. I'll have to chew on it awhile. Is there something else I could read that might help bridge the gaps?"

She laughed and said, "Well, you might read Hegel's *The Phenomenology of Mind*. That should help you get a handle of some of it." She stood up, walked over to one of her bookshelves, and located a volume, bringing it over to me. "If you are going to be around for a bit"—she looked over at Luce—"let me know if you want to discuss it further. We could take an afternoon and dig into it."

"Thank you! I can see why you enjoy teaching." I examined the book, grateful for her help but wondering if an intellectual lifeguard might be more help.

Luce looked over at me. "I'm not sure about you, but I'm getting really tired."

I nodded, yawned with honesty and purpose. "Same here."

Connie said, "Well, I have an extra bedroom upstairs for Lucia, and this couch"—she patted the couch—"is very comfortable. I'll make it up for you, TB." She walked out of the room.

I looked over at Luce, who had an odd expression. Responding to said expression, I said, "Well, that eliminates an awkward moment, huh?" She grinned sheepishly.

"When Aunt Connie and I were out in the kitchen, I told her that we really didn't know each other very well, so I'm guessing that she assumed separating us would be appropriate, of course."

"No doubt she is wiser than I. In many respects," I said, lifting Hegel as example.

She chuckled. "Trust me, Auntie suffers no fools. If she didn't want you to read it, you wouldn't be holding it." She stood and walked over to me. She reached for the book, thumbed through it, and handed it back, taking the opportunity to squeeze my hand. She cocked her head and gave me a lesson in how a woman can control a man with her eyes. Hegel I'm not too sure about, but those eyes? Lesson learned, memory encoded.

7

W e rose early, grabbed a quick muffin and some of Connie's strong coffee, and drove south. Luce was quiet. I was quiet. My thoughts were circling from the accident to the break-in and back again. By tying the two together, assuming Ben's office was breached to find out how much information he had gathered re the accident, it seemed clear that someone didn't want an investigation. No matter how I shuffled the facts, let alone the assumptions, it was impossible to draw any other conclusion. And by assaulting Doreen, whoever broke in wanted the information bad enough to attack a defenseless woman to get it, and from there, it ratcheted up. Contrary to popular fictional TV, it's not easy to intentionally hurt someone under any circumstance. An angry dispute can lead to physical action, sure, but to hit a fifty-year-old woman in the back of her head is quite another thing, a cold-blooded thing.

I glanced over at Luce and asked, "So why so quiet?"

She looked over, smiled, and said, "Thinking about Aunt Connie. She spends so much time alone these days, I hope everything is all right with her. When Uncle Lou was alive, she was always around people: friends, relatives, colleagues. After he passed, she gradually withdrew from all of that, and when she retired, it seemed as if her withdrawal was complete. I have always been close to her, growing up, but in the last few years, my own life led in a different direction. I just worry about her."

"Can I ask a question?" She looked at me and nodded. "What was your uncle like?"

"Well, this will sound odd, but I'm not sure. He laughed a lot, joked around. Was very busy with his real estate business. He was one of those people that everyone likes, and I certainly liked him myself, but I don't believe I ever had a conversation with him for longer than a few minutes. Isn't that terrible?"

"He sounds like an outgoing person, yes? Always organizing things when the family got together? Talking people into doing things, going places?"

"Yes! I remember one time, when I was around eleven or twelve, we were all at their old house for a summer barbecue, and Uncle Lou talked everyone into piling into cars and driving down to Lake Sunapee for a dinner cruise out on the lake. Looking back on it, how he ever did that is beyond me. All of my relatives, many stubborn Yankees, agreeing on a road trip especially after spending most of the day eating and drinking, with children yelling. And how did he arrange for a cruise on such short notice? But yes, that's what I remember most about Uncle Lou." She smiled, wide and enthusiastically.

"That's it then."

"That's what?"

"Your uncle complimented your aunt's natural personality, drawing her out, encouraging her to do things she probably never would have done without him. She adjusted to his cheerleading, his bigger-than-life persona. Now, after that lifestyle is no longer part of her world, she has reverted to her natural way of dealing with the world. A quiet life, books, her thoughts, and only people who are either necessary or relatives and the occasional close friend. She hasn't really withdrawn at all. That's just how she prefers it." I checked how she was taking it. She frowned, considering.

She said, "I guess that makes sense. So you don't think she's lonely or depressed or anything?"

"Look at the facts. She has been a bookish person all of her life, that incredible personal library proves it. And what did she do after coming into a bit of money? She buys a business that requires minimal attention but still keeps her connected to the world, and she only has to deal with strangers who come and go. She is within an easy drive of Dartmouth, where her colleagues are accessible on her terms. It all fits. She is independent, self-reliant, satisfied with her own company, and in her own way, a charming person. I don't know about you, but I should be so content!"

Luce looked at me with those piercing eyes (yes, piercing, yet another manifestation of those eyes), and smiled just a bit, then she said, "You think she's charming?"

"Hunh."

***

When we reached the outskirts of Concord, I asked Luce if she wanted an early lunch. She declined saying that she needed to get back home, make sure her cat was okay, and check her voice mail. We agreed to stay in touch by phone. I gave her a quick call from my cell number so we were connected.

I parked my car. We got out and met at the back of the car. Luce looked up at me and said, "Quite an adventure, Tom." She reached up and kissed my cheek, turned, and walked across the street toward the front of the building, where her car was parked. I touched my cheek.

When I entered the office, Jewels rose from her chair in greeting, smiling, then she frowned and said in her inimitable disapproving tone, "So a telephone call would be too much? To let me know what's going on?" She had her fists firmly planted on her hips.

"I'm sorry, Jewels. It all happened so fast that I didn't have time. Sorry!" I gave her my best hound-dog look.

"Maybe you were preoccupied? Maybe Miss Nardone's car still parked in the same spot as yesterday has something to do with it? Look, Stone, what you do with your own time is your own business, but how am I supposed to do my job if don't have any freaking idea of where you are? I get a phone call from Doreen, in the hospital, for God's sake, telling me that you are in the White Mountains while she is getting her head caved in! What was I to think? And on your way back down here, presumably this morning, you couldn't call?"

She was genuinely upset. Calling me Stone was a dead giveaway. "You are right, Jewels. Okay? I'm sorry."

She made a dismissive noise and sat down.

"When did Doreen call?"

"This morning, while I was on my way here. On my cell—you know, my mobile phone? I believe you have the number?"

I sighed, and trust me, I rarely sighed; I gave it up, along with the vapors, years ago. But I sighed. "She's still in the hospital? Ben told me last night that she was being released this morning, no?"

Jewels shuffled some papers on her desk and said, "Before leaving the hospital, she called. She was going home for the day. Then Jewels sighed, and for her that wasn't just unlikely but unthinkable. Anyway, she said, "You know how Doreen is, she downplayed the whole event. What really happened, TB?"

She called me TB! I'm forgiven, thank the Lord. I sat on the edge of her desk and gave her the whole story as I knew it. We talked about it for a few minutes, and then I told her that I was going over to Ben's office to see what I could find that might be helpful.

"Ben's expecting you?"

"Yes, and I need to get going. While serving nature, could you put a healthy dose of your most medicinal coffee in my carry mug? Please?" I blinked my eyes at her.

She screwed up her face, stood, and headed for the coffee area.

Before leaving, I grabbed my coffee, gave Jewels a quick kiss on the top of her head, and jumped away before she could hit me.

"TB, I called Ben and let him know that you were running late. Let me know if you need anything." She extended her thumb and her little finger, putting the hand to her ear, mimicking a phone.

***

As I edged into traffic, as much traffic as ever on a summer morning in Concord, with tourists getting an early start and commuters getting to government jobs, my driving was set to autopilot because all thinking bunched up on what might be waiting in Ben's office. At nine, the sun was intermittently blinding as it flashed between buildings, trees, and high-profile trucks. And with every flash, my thoughts cleared just a bit, almost rhythmically. I stopped at a light. As the cars passing in front went by, they picked up the rhythm of the sunlight, and my thoughts distilled further, becoming crisp and pointed. When the stoplight turned green, I knew what I wanted to check out in Ben's office. I'm sorry, but that's how my head works sometimes. When I was younger and sharing was acceptable between friends, I talked about this unique way of thinking and soon learned two things: first, other folks thought I was weird; and second, certain things should remain solely in my head. Stubborn Irish that I am, I didn't think it was weird, and I continued to let it play out. As time passed, I realized that in some ways it gave me an edge. I didn't have to rely on intuition or even rational synthesis to provide "aha" moments. I just kept my subconscious unbridled and let it mingle with my conscious experience, and voilà, an inspired conclusion sprung, fully formed. Weird, huh?

I drove the final couple of blocks, humming a long-ago tune, and pulled into Ben's parking lot. His Mercedes was in its spot. Before getting out of my car, I looked at the parking lot, office building, walkway, and the overhead lights. Stepping out of my car, I stood, taking it all in. The intruder last night no doubt studied the area in a similar fashion, and it could very well be that he was here earlier to make certain there would be a favorable entryway and, perhaps more important, an exit way. I noted that there were no CCT cameras mounted on the face of the building or anywhere else, for that matter. It was also worth noting that some nice trees and bushes blocked much of the building face; it would be easy enough to approach the front door surreptitiously, particularly after dark. The only time he might be seen was when he actually breached the door. I walked to the front door, stood for a moment, checking out the exterior lights that would have been on, as well as the lobby lights that were always on. Going in through the front door, without a key, would have been problematic. The lock itself was standard: engage a push bar on the inside. I opened the door and knelt down. The lock insert wasn't damaged; however, I did find a small bit of heavy plastic on the floor of the entrance. I put it in my shirt pocket. I stood up. The receptionist was watching me, and so was Ben, with that patented sardonic grin on his face.

"The cops checked all of that out, you know."

I nodded, reached into my pocket, and extracted the piece of plastic. Walking over to Ben, I held it between my thumb and my index finger, directly below his nose. "They missed this."

He looked at it, shrugging, and asked, "What's that?"

"Maybe nothing, but I suspect it was used to prevent the lock from engaging fully. It would have been inserted in the lockhole so the lock tab couldn't fully engage."

Ben shook his head. "But what if he came in after Doreen was already here? She says she didn't lock the front door because she was only going to be here for a few minutes. The guy comes in, assaults her, and then finds and takes the files."

"Well, that may be, but if he planned to be here, he wouldn't have known that she would be here. And with the lobby lights on, he probably was as surprised as Doreen when he made his way to your office area. But none of that matters. If the lock was disabled, it was disabled during office hours, which means…" I cocked my head, raised both arms, and waited for it to sink in.

Ben stared at me for a second, grinned, and said, "Then he was here sometime yesterday."

"Exactly. So let's check the sign in sheet, yeah?"

The receptionist had already turned the sign-in book to the previous day's records. She said, "I don't know very many of your clients, Mr. Katz, let alone any of the other offices, but I do have a pretty fair memory. If you see a name that doesn't seem right, I may be able to give you a description." She handed the book to Ben.

"Thank you, miss?"

"Archer. Melissa Archer, sir."

"Tommy and I will be going over this in my office. Since Doreen isn't here today, please hold all calls until I let you know otherwise. Okay, Ms. Archer?"

"Yes, sir. Can I ask how Doreen is doing? I know she was hurt last night."

"She's okay, though she is resting at home today. Thanks for asking."

We walked into Ben's office. I pulled a chair up to his desk, and Ben opened the book. Three pages were full and part of another. The building housed a dozen or so businesses, so there were many names, almost all likely unfamiliar to me, but Ben should have better luck. While Ben was perusing the list, I was looking around the office. It was largely cleaned up since the cops had finished their due diligence. The filing cabinets would be in the outer office, where Doreen had ease of access, and I would inspect that area next, but Ben's office did have a credenza behind his desk that served for personal files, and his desk drawers, of course, contained still more.

"Ben, real quick. Where did the intruder find the Adamo file? In here?"

"Yes. In this top drawer"—he pointed to the right—"I wanted it to be handy in case you needed information."

"Thanks." It probably meant that the thief, if he had even a vague idea about what he was seeking, would have checked the desk first. I would have. And if that were true, then all the disarray, the vandal's touch, was intended as pure distraction. "One more thing. Sorry, but you said last night that more than the Adamo file was taken. Do you know what?"

"Yeah. Everything in that top drawer, five different client files, and my day planner. Is that important?"

"Maybe. But we'll get into that after." I pointed to the sign-in book. "The day planner—names, numbers, appointments tucked in there. We may find a lead for the intruder and, maybe, whoever hired him, because ultimately we want to know who initiated the inquiry into the Adamo accident." I made a mental note to ask Ben about details later.

"Well, there was no one who signed in to see me that would be a suspect. There are nine other offices in the building: three attorneys, two accounting firms, and four government-related offices, two of which were closed yesterday. So we are down to seven offices. I have run down the list, and I know maybe a half dozen of the names out of a total sixty-two, leaving fifty-six possible. What now?" He asked.

"What I will do is go from office to office and question receptionists first, then secretaries, and so on. If all goes well, that list will boil down to four or five good candidates. A long, tedious process, but it's what I do. The cops may have done some of this already, but their priorities depend on the importance of the case. Assault and robbery may not be at the top of today's list. Unless they think the case warrants a detective, my questioning will be more thorough. Anyway, I'll need a copy of that book, segregated by the names for each office."

Ben nodded. "Okay, let me make the copies, and you can finish up looking over my office." He headed for the outer office.

I inspected the desk, floor, credenza, phone, and so on. Any fingerprints or any other obvious thing would have been taken by the cops last night, so it didn't take too long. Half an hour later, Ben came back in.

"Here's the info. One sheet per office, and I crossed out the names I know. Is this good?" He handed the sheets to me. I sorted through them.

"Looks good. The names you crossed out—are you sure they are unlikely suspects?"

"Yes. Three of them call on me and have for years, and the others are sales types I can vouch for. A couple of the names I know but not well, so I left them."

"Sounds right. Okay. Before I start, let's sit and drink some more coffee and talk." Ben looked at me, nodded, and went through the door. He came back in a couple of minutes with the coffee. We sat.

"How are you doing? Must have been a trying experience, yeah?"

Ben rolled his eyes, shook his head, and said, "Well, Doreen is okay, so that was the most upsetting part of it, of course. Last night, I just wanted to take care of her, so I didn't really have a chance to think about it, you know. But the whole thing was a shocker, and this morning, I have been trying to figure out what might have triggered such a reaction. I mean, breaking in and assaulting a fifty-year-old woman just to get information that could be so easily obtained elsewhere. There was nothing in that file that was damning or even sensitive. I just can't figure it."

"My guess is they were more interested in *who wanted* the information than the information itself. They knew that you were looking for it, somehow, but between the file and your day planner, could they piece together more? Like me or Lucia?"

"I don't think so. I'm pretty sure your name wasn't written down, and certainly not Lucia's. Since my services were pro bono, as always"—he made a face—"for you that is, I didn't write your name down. No reason to."

"Okay. Well, if you are willing, while I'm questioning the folks in the building, I'd like for you to call your contacts again, the ones who helped you gather the info, and tell them about the break-in and the assault. Again, only those contacted the first time. Play up the assault. See how they react. What you want is to find out who they might have told, either intentionally or unintentionally."

Ben had a blank look, thinking about it, and said, "Isn't that potentially dangerous? I mean, won't the culprit find out?"

"Yes. That's what we want. We want a reaction. And if we don't get a reaction, then that will tell us something different. Either way works to our benefit. Look, Ben, when you tell your story, let them know that the cops were here and that they are investigating it. As far as your contact knows, you don't suspect him or her, and your intention is to find out who might have *cared* about the inquiry. Yes?"

"Yeah, I get it. Should I let them know that there is anyone other than the cops investigating? Not necessarily your name."

"No. Here's what I think. The person who actually broke in is not the same person who initiated the break-in. We want both. And don't forget, it's pretty clear by now that the Adamo accident was more than the official story tells. Who knows how far this search may lead? I'm also guessing that the person who broke in, once we start pushing on all of this, will be in big trouble. And that can only help us. Anyway, the less they know about another person investigating, other than the cops, the better. This will give us an advantage. Understand?"

"I think so. You can operate without them knowing about it. They won't be expecting it."

"Yes. Depending on how this plays out over the next few days, they may not see me coming at all. Not until I'm in front of whoever it is."

"And assuming you remain unexpected, what then? I mean when you find whoever it is?"

"Well, if I find the guy who assaulted Doreen first, and I expect to do so, I will express my displeasure with the break-in." I smiled softly.

***

I found the stairs and walked up to the second floor then to the rear right office. I started upstairs because information, rumors, really, generally start on the first floor of a building and gradually move up. This was true of all office buildings, or so the sociologists said. And in my experience, it tended to be true. The name on the door read, "Harris and Andrews, Attorneys at Law." I opened the door and walked in. The secretary was seated at an inward-curving dark wood reception station with two large potted plants flanking it. As I walked toward the secretary, her name plate attached to the center of the station indicating Ms. Stacy Evans, she reached for what must have been her appointment book. I smiled, putting both hands on the chest-high counter, and said, "You won't find my name in your appointment book, Ms. Evans, because I don't have an appointment."

She gave me a defensive look and said, "May I help you?" Her tone sounded like the one I always use when a telemarketer managed to fool me into answering my cell.

"Yes. Actually, I probably won't need to see anyone other than you." I smiled sincerely and winningly but not quite as sincerely or winningly as a salesman would. She smiled back, a touch less defensively, and leaned forward in her swivel-backed highboy stool expectantly.

I changed my sincere smile into my concerned-yet-ever-so-pained frown and said, "Well, I'm sure you have heard about the break-in last night? Ben Katz's secretary was knocked out and hospitalized."

She immediately became serious, attentive, and nodded. "Yes. It was terrible! Doreen is such a sweet person, I can't imagine who would want to hurt her!"

"And that's why I'm here. We believe that the assailant was actually in the building earlier in the day, you know, to check out the place?" She nodded knowingly. "I have a copy of Ms. Archer's master sign-in sheet, and I'm hoping that you can look over those who visited you yesterday. Maybe one of the names will jump out as questionable?" I smiled tiredly but patiently and handed her the sheet.

"Of course! Anything to help." She looked down the list carefully and shook her head. "No. I know all of these names. They have been clients for years. All check out. I'm really sorry, Detective…"

"Stone." I shook my head wearily and said, "Well, thank you, Ms. Evans."

She handed the list back and said, "You are welcome. Good luck. I hope you find whoever did it."

"Thank you. We will." Putting a steely look on my face, I walked out. After closing the door, I smiled to myself. She called me "Detective," thinking, no doubt, that I was a cop. And she would call or email a few of her friends in the building, informing them of my visit. Excellent! They would all assume that I'm a cop, and that would serve two purposes. First, it would insulate me from the bad guys, and second, it would expedite the balance of the questioning. I walked over to a men's room, used the facility, washed, ran a hand through my hair, stared out the window, and wasted about fifteen minutes. Now everyone in the building would know that the police were here. Whistling softly, I exited and walked down the hall to the next office: James Harrington, CPA, general accounting.

I walked out of the last office at 11:30 a.m. Not a bad round of info gathering. I had three possible subjects, two new and unknown subjects, and one highly likely nonshow candidate, William Warren. The nonshow guy signed in at the reception desk but failed to make an appearance in the Environmental Action Group office, a PAC. The folks in the office had never heard of him, which for them is not surprising, considering their general clientele. So my next stop would be Melissa

Archer. Maybe she would recall Mr. William Warren and be able to give me a description.

Melissa did remember him. Her description was this: "Medium height, midthirties, fit looking, white, no distinguishing characteristics other than an odd tattoo on the back of his left hand. It was Oriental looking, just one character. He was polite, all business, quiet, and walked toward the appropriate office. He came back through only forty-five minutes or so later, but since it was late afternoon, I didn't think much of it." I asked her if there was anything else, anything at all. Nothing.

Melissa's description didn't help much, but it did eliminate tall, short, old, young, nonwhite, blond, heavy, skinny, female, talkative, and tattooless folks. That was something, I suppose. The sign-in sheet had his supposed phone number and address. I called the number but doubted I would reach anyone. The area code was for the Concord area. It rang three times, then a recorded voice politely indicated that the number was out of service. So it seemed we found the guy, at least in theory.

***

I made my way back to Ben's office. He was on the phone. I waited.

"Thanks, Bill. If you hear anything, please let me know. Thanks." Ben put the phone down; leaned back, putting folded hands over his middle; and shook his head. He handed me his notes. "Take a look. Maybe you will see something there, but I doubt it."

I glanced at the notes. "Ben. It would be unlikely that you would find anything. Remember, all we wanted was to let everyone know that you were trying to figure out the reason for the break-in and, of course, the assault. As long as you sold that part of it, all is good. Now we just wait to see if anything else happens. You did let them all know that the police were involved, yes?"

"Sure did. And no one knows that you are on the case, well, at least not from the phone calls."

"Good. Change of subject—I finished questioning the receptionists and ended up with two possible and one probable. This guy." I handed him the names of the three candidates, with one circled. "The problem is that it seemingly ends there. Melissa is the only one who saw him, and aside from an 'odd Oriental tattoo on his left hand,' her description is very general."

"Yeah, I see that. Too bad she didn't recognize the symbol. So what now?"

"Of the calls you made, is there any way to prioritize the likelihood that they would have given up the information? That is, who's the most talkative, from 1 to 3? Who is the least reliable to you? Who might be able to gain something by passing the info on the someone else? And maybe who is in an office where a phone call might be overheard? Rank the three."

"Ah. Well, let me see." He pulled out a pencil, wrote down the names, and asked me to repeat my criteria. I did. Then I went to the outer office and refilled our cups with coffee, dawdled for a few minutes, and returned. I put Ben's cup on his desk and watched him.

Ben sat up, stretched, and handed me the sheet of paper. He had gridded the four criteria at the top and the three names on the side. He ranked the names 1 to 3 for each criterion and ended with a tally on the right side and another tally at the bottom. It looked like one candidate was least likely, but two were tied for most likely.

"Interesting. So John is least likely, and Bill and Al are most likely?"

"That's how it comes out. And that tells us what exactly?"

"Not much, but it does give me somewhere to start. I'll begin surveilling either Bill or Al first. Which would you suggest?" I looked at him and smiled beatifically.

"Oh, brother. I have no idea which one. This surveillance. What does it entail?"

I leaned forward, did a quick check to make sure no one was listening (very detective-like), and whispered, "Better that you don't know."

"Yeah, yeah. Seriously."

I sat back and said, "I'll sit in my car somewhere inconspicuous and watch his place of employment and maybe his home. I might get lucky and see something, someone that looks suspicious. If I do, then I'll plant a bug in his car or office. If not, then I'll go to the next one on the list."

"What if nothing suspicious happens with any one of these three guys?"

"Then the time I spend in the car will have been wasted. Or maybe not, because I'll have plenty of time to think of the next step or two. And in the meantime, something else could break for us. In the larger case, I mean."

"Huh. And I thought my job was boring."

"Your job is boring, Benjamin, which is why I quit law school all those years ago. Now I live on the edge."

At that point, before the effluent became too deep, Ben's phone buzzed. He answered, "Ben Katz." He listened. "Excellent. I'll pass it on. Thanks, Melissa." He gently replaced the receiver in its cradle and smiled. "Melissa, clever soul that she is, thought maybe you'd be interested in knowing that our building parking lot might be covered by an adjacent building's CTV security camera. Interested?"

"Holy shit! How is that possible? I checked that out, I thought."

"Well, she's not sure, but the building across the street, a three-story building housing state offices, has cameras that scan their entire property. It may pick up our parking lot during the scan. If we are lucky, maybe our suspect was getting out of his car, a car with a license plate, during the scan."

"It's certainly worth checking out." I stood and headed toward Melissa's station.

She saw me coming, big grin, a young kid happy with what she had done. I smiled back. "Melissa! You just might be my hero today. You know that, yeah?"

The grin got wider. "I just hope you can learn something useful from the cameras."

"Sounds like a real possibility. What are the details?" I leaned against the counter.

"Okay. It's that building over there." She pointed out the front window at a tall building across the street but maybe a hundred yards or so from the entrance. "It's a state building with lots of offices and fairly sophisticated security which includes a 24-hour CCT surveillance system. You can't see the cameras from here in part because they are intentionally disguised. Ernie tells me that there are two cameras that, during their scans, pick up part of our parking lot. With luck, maybe something will show."

"How do I get access to the tapes? If the security is tight, it's unlikely that they will let me view anything."

She positively beamed. I chuckled to myself. She said, "That's where Ernie comes in, my boyfriend. He is the IT manager and has already cleared it with his boss. Just go to the front desk and ask for Ernesto Delgado. You are expected."

"Melissa, thank you. I owe you." And I meant it.

Her face turned serious. "Just find the person who hurt Doreen. Okay?"

"We shall see what happens, but that's the plan."

8

Walking up to the entranceway to the New Hampshire State Memorial Office Building, I looked for the cameras and couldn't see anything. Whatever they did to camouflage the surveillance was successful. It was a newer building, very sleek, with shiny stone and glass surfaces, unlike most of the official state office buildings. From this vantage point, it appeared to be more than three stories, but that could be an illusion. I walked up the wide steps to one of the two different sets of doors. I opened the door and walked in. Very modern interior but for a bronze statue of Nathan Hale that served as a reminder of our heritage. I liked it.

A pleasant-faced woman in very proper business attire, with glasses hanging from a chain around her neck, smiled primly as I approached. I said, "Good day. Thomas Stone to see Mr. Ernesto Delgado."

She lifted her glasses, placed them in the proper place with both hands, looked down at a register of some sort, and said, "Please sign the book, Mr. Stone." She pushed a button, lifted a receiver, waited, and then said, "Mr. Thomas Stone for Mr. Delgado." She listened. "Thank you. Please have a seat, sir. Mr. Delgado will be down directly."

"Thank you." I walked over to a corner divan with a view of the entire lobby and sat. The interior was tastefully decorated with an assortment of plants, plaques, and unobtrusive paintings of New Hampshire landmarks. It was very quiet, with no sounds from outside or inside the building. Almost strangely quiet, as if everyone in this multistory large building were on vacation or sleeping. Then I heard footsteps, and a young man, tall, fit, walked out the hallway entrance and toward me. I stood.

He extended his hand, smiled, and said, "Mr. Stone. Ernie Delgado. Very nice to meet you."

I took his hand, a firm but not aggressively so grip. I said, "Please call me TB, Ernie."

"Please come with me, TB." He turned back to the hallway entrance. I walked by his side, our footsteps in synch and echoing softly. The hallway was long; the floor was some sort of polished tile. Like the reception area, the colors were understated browns and grays. Every twelve feet or so was a door, all were closed and without windows, nameplates, or anything other than a numeral for identification. I counted fifteen doors on each side before we came to another, wider, heavier door at the end of the hall in a recessed area on the right. This particular door had an electronic lock. Ernie ran an ID card through a slot, and the mechanism buzzed softly then clicked. He turned the latch, and we walked through. The door closed automatically and made another satisfied click.

I said, "Quite a bit of security. I'm surprised."

"True. Let's get to my office, and I'll brief you on what we do here." He continued down another corridor, though this one was narrower and the doors on either side all had electronic locks. They were spaced farther apart, all closed. Halfway down the corridor, Ernie stopped in front of one of the nondescript doors, slid his card through the lock, and opened it. We went in.

His office actually looked as if it were being used with a desk, chairs, a table along one wall, and above the table, a colorful large picture of a cobblestone street in some tropical locale, ocean in the background. Ernie gestured to one of the two utilitarian chairs placed at an angle before his desk. I sat.

Ernie reached to the credenza behind and, curving around the left side of his desk, popped a coffee pod in his coffee maker and a mug under it. He asked, "Coffee?"

"Please. Black."

He engaged the device then turned around and smiled. He opened a folder on his desk and read, "Thomas Bradley Stone, CID. Served for *officially* four years, stationed at Fort Bragg. Security clearance, top secret. The reason for your clearance is classified." He looked up at me.

"What is this? I am no longer in the army and haven't been for almost a decade. I thought we were going to be looking at some CCTV footage, and you are referencing this?" I was curious as much as surprised. "What's the connection?"

He sighed, never taking his eyes off me. "As you may have guessed, this building is not primarily a New Hampshire State office building. On the other side, we do have some general state bureaucrats using offices, but that's more for cover than function. In actual fact, this is a federal facility."

"What sort of facility?"

"Intelligence, primarily, though we do have some research going on upstairs. Let me give you some history. After 9/11, the most glaring lapse in our intel/surveillance was a lack of coordination between the various agencies. FBI, CIA, NSA only the more obvious, but also military intel and even various state agencies. It is now a well-known fact that the attack was predictable and would have been predicted had the bits known by each agency been put together, coordinated. Now, as you may know, the various agency heads all have a dotted line reporting responsibility to one person, whose role it is to sort through, in a coordinated fashion, all of the intel and make sense from the whole. And that looks good, at least on paper."

"Not to interrupt, but I have to ask, does it work?"

"Yes and no. Yes, the intel is consolidated, and yes, it has yielded fruit. We haven't had a major terrorist incident since 9/11."

"But…"

"But the bunker mentality still continues. No two agencies trust each other completely. Let's face it, intelligence work requires suspicion and distrust, and even under the best of circumstances, interagency rivalries will never disappear."

"I assume you are about to drop the other shoe, yes?"

He gave me a calculating look, shuffled some of the papers in my file, and said, "And so our group was formed."

"Your group. What exactly is your group?"

"Labels are meaningless, but suffice it to say that our intended purpose is to cut through all of the red tape and directly address potential threats, both external and internal. And we have, so far, been successful."

This was fascinating, but why in hell was I sitting here listening to all this? At the very least, combining internal and external intel ops is legally questionable. Granted, the Patriot Act blurred some of the lines, but as example, the CIA can't surveil US citizens within US borders, let alone directly deal with the bad guys. Yet here I was, listening to this stuff. I said, "My head is swelling with curiosity, but I have to know why you are telling me about all of this. I'm a civilian."

"Yes, you are a civilian, but you still have a top-secret security clearance. It was never rescinded. Technically, with regard to national-security issues, you cannot divulge any part of this conversation without severe consequences. To yourself."

"I understand that. I'm not questioning that. What I am questioning is why. Why tell me any of this?"

Instead of answering, he pulled out one sheet of paper from the folder, looked at me for a moment, tapped the paper with his index finger, and said, "Ostensibly, you were a CID agent, working on criminal cases involving soldiers who were breaking laws, both military and civilian. There is a record of that. But digging a little deeper, which is very much what we do here, it is also true that in addition to receiving police-investigation techniques, you also went through Special Forces training. It took some research, but we found out that you were trained primarily in interrogation methodology but also hand-to-hand combat and small-arms use. Now that is interesting." He looked at me, smiled softly, and continued, "Now since you were never enrolled in SF training officially and, of course, you didn't graduate, it seems pretty obvious that something else was going on. So we dug even deeper and found that you also went through a training regimen that has even less to do with military-police investigation work. You went to Camp Peary and learned all sorts of things about clandestine operations suitable only for espionage and/or paramilitary work. We also discovered that although you were officially a CID investigator, your workload was minimal, allowing you to travel to some pretty exotic locations, including, let's see—ah yes, the Middle East, Prague, Islamabad, and Guantánamo Bay, to name only a few."

"Okay. You get an A for your research. Congratulations. But the question still remains: why are you telling me all of this?" I had to admit that there was an edge to my voice, and it was only partially intentional.

"Tell you what. Let's go into the next room and look at those CCT records. I'll answer your question after. Okay?"

I nodded. We went into the next room. It was a large room, maybe sixteen by twenty-four, dimly lit, and one entire wall was covered with monitors, by count, ten large, fifty-inch screens. Obviously for security surveillance, they showed different views of the building's exterior. To the right of the first was another wall of smaller monitors, approximately two dozen, a few blank, but most showing various scenes: some long-distance city views of streets, some city buildings, and some within buildings. As I took this in, I noticed that a couple of the views changed completely. Below each of these monitors was a digital readout with time and initials, presumably indicating location. A third wall was covered by what appeared to be a conglomeration of digital equipment, some tables, some cables, and an assortment of sleek-looking cabinets. In the center of the room, angled with a view of both monitor walls, was a functional large computer desk with two keyboards below a large screen, a twelve-by-eighteen-inch slanted switchboard, an expensive-looking swivel chair, a small side table with piles of folders, and a coffee maker.

"This is my work office. Okay, let's see. Grab that chair, TB, and have a seat." He motioned to a rolling desk chair half buried within the confusion of equipment behind him. He sat at the desk and immediately began keying. An image popped up on his desk screen. "Okay, this is a piece of what one of our cameras caught yesterday."

I sat, leaned in to better see the screen. The image was moving slowly, showing a view of the street between his and Ben's respective buildings. As the camera panned, a late-model car appeared, turning into Ben's entrance. As the rear of the car came into view fully, the image froze and enlarged simultaneously. The plate was clear: Massachusetts, with numerals/characters easily visible.

Just below the image, a time stamp indicated 16.45.09. "That's great! But how do you know it's my guy?"

"Wait for it." The image disappeared, and a second appeared. It showed the same car exiting. The time stamp read "17.10.12." I looked at my new pal, Ernie, who nodded and pointed to the screen. A third image appeared, not as clear, but it showed the same car entering, 20.31.05 time stamped. Ernie looked at me with a goofy grin, the same grin that Melissa showed me only a little bit ago. I relaxed.

"That's great. I can trace the plate and, hopefully, track him down." Ernie shook his head. "Keep watching." The image changed yet again, but this view was from a longer distance, showing a part of Ben's parking lot. The same car came into the frame, pulled into a space, and a man stepped out. The frame froze and telescoped in, and now, happily, I had a visual. It was the guy, pretty much like Melissa had described him.

"Holy shit, man! It doesn't get any better. Can you get me a print of this?" Ernie reached over, opened a folder, and handed me four eight-by-tens of the guy and his car. Incredible. "Very nice indeed. Thanks!"

"You are welcome."

"Now that's out of the way. Why the investigation? And don't tell me it's for these pics, because assuming you ran a standard security check, just to make certain I was legit, all you needed to see was my ongoing security clearance. Why the deep dig?" I watched for his reaction. No reaction. No micros, no redirect, nothing.

He smiled, holding eye contact, and said, "I have a favor to ask of you. Tit for tat."

"Go on."

"Melissa told me about your investigation when she asked about the camera captures. And no, she didn't say anything that wasn't confidential regarding Ben's business interests. That would be unethical, and she is very much not that." He paused, leaning in while raising his eyebrows for emphasis.

"Got it. Melissa is one of the good guys. Continue."

"After I started dating Melissa, very casual at that point, I did a low-level sweep of the building businesses next door just to make sure. We do that sort of thing periodically, which I'm sure you can understand." He looked for verification.

I nodded.

"Of course, Attorney Katz was one of the businesses in the sweep. As with all of the other businesses in the building, our *tools* developed a list of his clients, and as luck would have it, your name showed up on that list. Automatically, a public search, all part of the software analysis, was made on every one of the names from all of the businesses. A few names popped up that were, well, interesting. But of all dozen or so names, your name was the only one that was red-flagged."

"The TSC?"

"Yes. The number of people outside of the intelligence community and quasi-intel folks like certain politicians, as example, who hold a top-secret clearance is small. So your name stuck. Of course, at that juncture, it simply went on a trigger list."

I interrupted. "Trigger list?"

"Nothing ominous, just a list of names that will be 'triggered,' cross-referenced, if any unusual associations are made, like an unexpected request for information from this department. And when Melissa made her request, your name popped up as *interesting*. And the rest you know."

"You still haven't told me about the favor you want."

"Of course. You know a little about what we do here. A few months ago, we received intel from another agency that Adfam, the Adamo tech company, was negotiating with a Chinese tech company for rights to a certain piece of technology that, when used inappropriately, could directly access US military satellite feeds. The tech itself has been used in the States to bridge communications between various computer platforms and, as a result, speed up information transfer. It operates as a very ubiquitous link between old tech and new and everything in between. The Chinese want it for other purposes, we fear. We want to know how far the negotiations have gone and who knows what within Adfam."

"Why haven't the Chinese just pirated it? It's not as if they have ever had any compunctions about stealing our technology."

"A couple of reasons. First, we have been much more vigilant in recent years in protecting our newly developed tech, and second, there is an encrypted software lock that launches an extremely hostile counter whenever the tech is threatened. Very hostile!"

"Okay. So where do I come in?" He looked at me, assessing whether or not I'd been suitably tenderized for the request. I didn't really know myself. Maybe, but it depended on what he wanted me to do—or not do. When I officially worked as an operative for, well, my country, I did all sorts of things for the greater good. Most of my activities were straightforward and ethically tenable, but occasionally I was tasked with some operational "details" that I didn't want to do at all. That was why I left the game.

"We would like for you to find out exactly who is behind these negotiations and why. Up until now, Adfam has been very careful about intentionally, and unintentionally for that matter, sharing both research and fully developed tech. If they weren't concerned about securing this particular piece of technology, why would they have developed such a robust protective lock? Some of the companies are not so careful, and we know who they are, but not Adfam. What has changed? With your military background, and considering your current investigation"—he pointed to the CCTV pics—"you are ideally suited for finding this out." His face was blank, waiting.

I tapped on the counter, considering. I looked at him. "I need to give this some thought. I do have some questions. If I decide to do this 'favor' for you, will I have all of your support? Or will I be effectively operating alone? And secondarily, how much can I share with, well, anyone?"

"You will have our full support, to the extent that we can. Before you embark on this 'favor,' if you elect to do so, you will be fully briefed, and your operational parameters will be fully explained. No surprises. In all probability, I will be your contact."

"And the second question?"

"I'm afraid that you will need to maintain complete silence. No one outside of this building can know what we are doing here. You might not be surprised to learn that a large percentage of the folks who work here, in this building, operate on a need-to-know basis. Only a handful know exactly who and what we are. You now know more than most." He smiled benignly.

I scowled and replied, "Thanks for sharing, asshole."

"You are welcome, *cabrón*," he said with humor in his eyes.

Smiling, in the conventional way, I said, "I assume that includes Melissa? She knows nothing about what you do?" I said this last bit with a hint of mixed apology and concern.

He blinked, showing just a small crack in his professional face, and said, "No. Not even Melissa."

I nodded, understanding. It was possible I could like this guy, but I did not trust him any more than I trusted my handlers before I left the military life. If I decided to cooperate with his request, I would have to trust him to some degree. Not an easy thing for far too many reasons. I said, "You know, of course, that I will need to meet your boss, at least, and preferably your whole team. Can you arrange that?"

He squinted then reached for his desk phone, lifted the receiver, paused for a second, then said, "Could you gather everyone together for a brief meeting with Mr. Stone?" He listened then said, "Good. We'll be there in a few minutes." He hung up.

"Wow! That was fast."

"This is important. National security and all that, you know?"

"If I had a nickel for every time, I've heard that…" I said it with less cynicism in my voice than I felt.

He chuckled softly, cocked his head, and said, "My father, who came to this country on a raft with nothing but the clothes on his back and determination in his heart, loved this country. He instilled in his children many things, but nothing so important to him as duty. He always believed that it was important to give back to this country even more than this country gave to him. I am first-generation American, and I do what I do out of duty. Doubt me, personally, for any reason, but never doubt that. Come on. Let's go meet the team."

***

We exited Ernie's work area through a second door, located on the fourth wall. This door, unlike all the others so far, had no lock. We walked down a narrow corridor illuminated by recessed lights located on the walls about two-thirds of the way up. It was, like everything else in the building, preternaturally quiet. Our footsteps were silent, and I could only "hear" my breathing inside my head, as it kept rhythm with my heartbeat. It struck me that this was overkill, but then just as quickly, I realized that aside from what Ernie had told me about the operations, I really didn't know what was going on here. And that was when my weird psychic antenna reached out and my senses became, well, whatever they became when truly odd and/or dangerous circumstances emerged.

We came to another door, this one sporting the usual electronic lock. Ernie keyed it, and the door popped softly. We walked into what appeared to be a standard conference room. In the center was a long hardwood table, with a dozen or so comfy-looking chairs neatly arrayed around it. Curiously, there were no monitors, phones, or anything else of a tech-centric nature. Five people were seated around the table, three women and two men. In front of each was a yellow legal pad. In one corner of the room, on a brass stand, was a furled American flag. The floor was covered with tight-knit, industrial-style carpet that allowed easy rolling of chairs. In the back, opposite our entrance door, was a second door with a table next to it, upon which were a coffee maker and the usual assortment of mugs, spoons, and additives. No one in the room had coffee, however.

Ernie gestured toward an empty chair for me and then sat opposite me. He said, "This is T. B. Stone. He has requested meeting our team before agreeing to assist us, which seems reasonable." All five looked at me with various facial expressions, running from welcoming to bored. "To start, let's introduce ourselves." He tapped his hand on the table close to the woman on his right.

"Mr. Stone, my name is Sue, I'm a computer tech. I assess incoming material and pass it on to the various departments." She turned to the woman on her right, who cleared her throat and said, "I'm Anne. On this team, I'm operating as a field agent. Tom." She passed the baton, as it were, to the man facing her across the table. "Hi, TB. I am Tom, and I also will be serving as a field agent for this little project." He glanced to his right, and the third woman smiled and said, "TB, I am Veronica, or Ronnie, as most call me. Generally, I serve as handler for the agents. Depending on the nature of the op, I provide support and resources. You probably know how that works." She smiled again and nodded to the last man on her right. "Henry, Hank. Like Sue, I gather and process digital streams of information, usually encrypted. Fun stuff."

Ernie said, "Thanks, folks. You know me already, TB, and as I have mentioned, I'll be your handler for this operation, assuming you elect to join us. I am also team leader this time around. Okay, that's out of the way, the floor is yours." He leaned back in his chair.

I thanked him, rolling my eyes. Veronica laughed; the others waited. I said, "I asked to meet with you folks for a couple of reasons, and I won't insult you by sugarcoating any of it. First, I left this kind of work many years ago, and I have absolutely no regrets, so dipping my toes back in isn't especially appealing. Second, and I mean no disrespect, but I'm not entirely sure I trust this whole enterprise. Hence, even assuming this is all legit, I ask myself, why would I want to do it?" I paused, gathered their facial and bodily reactions, tucked those away, and proceeded. "So the question for all of you is, why me? You can't believe that I have just been hanging around, hoping for this sort of recall into the game!" I stopped, leaned back in my chair, and waited for a response.

They all were looking at me, not at Ernie, not at each other. I continued waiting. After a couple of awkward minutes, Veronica, the presumptive people person, smiled warmly and said, "TB, I think all of us were surprised that someone with your credentials would just knock on the door, especially considering that we were trying to develop a plan for this op. Actually, *op* is probably the wrong word—more like *investigation*—but more to the point, you were already investigating a matter having to do with the Adamo family." She looked around the table, and almost on cue, all but one nodded. She said, "So maybe it's selfish on our part, but the question should maybe be, why wouldn't we want you to do it? Put yourself in our position." She shrugged her shoulders, questioning.

"Forgive me for being blunt, but again, why should I trust you folks? My experience with intel organizations isn't encouraging."

"Let me field that one, Ronnie," Ernie said, putting his hands flat on the table then spreading his fingers. "You and I discussed this just a little bit ago, right? Well, nothing has changed. Every one of us is on the same, exact page, at least with regard to our purpose here. Our psych profiles, despite some personality differences, are damned close to identical. I trust everyone at this table, and every one of us feels exactly the same way. Ronnie answered the only question you asked that was pertinent, namely, why you. The trust issue just isn't an issue. I have an idea. How about if all of us ask you a question? Each one asks one question, and then you respond. From that, you may learn something useful about our collective trustworthiness. Okay?"

"A bit unconventional, but sure." This would be entertaining, if nothing else. Actually, it was frankly such a naive notion that it already eased some of my suspicion. Hmmm. Maybe not so dumb.

Ernie said, "Let's start with Sue again and go around the table. Again, ask your question, TB will respond, then go to the next person. I'll ask the final question. Sue?"

Sue, slender, late twenties, well dressed but no jewelry at all, said, "A simple question: why did you retire?"

"Not so simple but easily answered, I was burned out. It was a decision based on an accumulation of unpleasant requirements. I can't give details because almost all of it is still classified." Sue nodded and turned to Anne.

"TB, my question is a practical one. If you accept our request, how will you go about gathering the info that we need?" Anne was average height, average weight, early thirties, wearing a watch and one ring on her right hand. She had a pleasant, attractive face.

"If I take this 'investigation' on, I'll use whatever resources I discover along the way. My primary focus will be on my original investigation, and this thing will be secondary, so I guess it depends. Again, if I take this investigation of yours, my original client comes first. That is not negotiable." Anne cocked her head, smiled, and looked at Tom.

"I don't know you, TB, obviously, so my question is pretty important—for all of us. Why should we trust you?" He looked at Anne then Ernie. Anne was looking at me, and Ernie showed a hint of irritation.

"Now that's a good question. My first reaction is that you probably shouldn't trust me. My second, more-thoughtful answer is that I don't have to prove my trust to you or any of you, for that matter. You came to me, not the other way around, so I truly don't give a rat's ass whether you trust me or not." I held Tom's eyes until he broke the connection. He turned his smirking face to Veronica. Tom was a good-looking guy, fit, well-dressed, and I suspected that his motive for asking the question had nothing to do with the op. Of course, his surface intention was to get under my skin, and he thought he did, but he did not succeed.

Veronica looked at me with a bit of a twinkle in her eyes. I suspected that she knew my game. "Okay then, TB. My question is perhaps a bit different from the others, but I think it matters. What kind of a person are you?"

I chuckled and said, "Just a regular kind of guy!"

She made a face at me. It made me smile. She was an attractive woman, though not my kind. A stray thought crossed my mind: I wonder if she *could* be my type if Lucy weren't around. Ah! Focus!

"Seriously then? Okay. Subjectively, which is really the only way anyone could honestly answer that question, I suppose that I'm inquisitive, usually happy, generous. I live alone, well, aside from my cat, in the country. I like people sometimes, and I don't like some people always. I'm sure you have read through my military folder, so you know a little about my personal history. Beyond that, who I am is my business, not yours. Respectfully." I smiled at her.

She smiled back and said, "I have one more question. What's your phone number?"

She caught me off guard, surprisingly. I laughed. Then everyone laughed.

Ernie said, "That's classified, Veronica." Everyone laughed again. "Hank, you go next."

Henry was maybe thirty, pudgy, and disheveled. He asked, "What can we do to help you in the field? Anything in particular?"

"Assuming I accept all of this, I would want immediacy of information. I wouldn't want to wait on some bureaucrat's approval for answers to questions that might be time-critical."

Hank nodded and grinned.

Ernie said, "All right. Unless TB has anything else to ask or say, we are finished here." Everyone stood, replaced their chairs, and left. Ernie and I were alone. He asked, "What do you think?"

"You know, of course, that I really don't want to do this, yes?"

He nodded and said, "I know that. And you have to know that I wouldn't be going through all of these hoops if I didn't think you were the guy we need for this. Just that simple." He sat calmly, waiting.

"Reluctantly, I will help you out. But after completing this undertaking, I never want to hear from you or any of your secret buddies again. Understood?"

He gave me a somewhat-inscrutable look and reached out to shake my hand. "Understood."

"What was that look? You know, the look that said 'I know something you don't.' That look."

Ernie chuckled and said, "Only that I was pretty confident that you would agree to help us and that you would want some sort of assurance that we wouldn't intrude in your life again."

Yeah, I was right earlier—I did like this guy. "Are you really as honest as it seems? Unusual for a spy, you know."

Ernie laughed. "Yeah, well, we all have our conditions for employment in this racket, TB." He laughed some more.

"Good luck hanging on to your principles, pal. You will need it."

He shoved a cell phone across the table to me and said, "This will be our conduit. Hit number 5, and it will automatically call this cell." He held up a duplicate. "I'm sure you know the drill. Use it only for calling me, always keep it on you. It's loaded with protection, so it can't be accessed or cloned, but as someone who knows about tech, it may be safe today, but tomorrow? When I call you, if you can't talk, either let it ring out, or answer it and say you have to call me back, whichever works better at the time." He shoved an envelope across. "Here is your expense money. It should be adequate, and if not, let me know. As for the op, just keep me updated. Questions?"

"I'm sure I will have questions, but not right now." I stood.

He opened the door and escorted me through multiple hallways, to the front door.

9

I walked back over and into Ben's building. Melissa grinned and asked, "How'd it go?"

"It went well." I held up the pic folder and said, "I have the information we needed to move forward. Thanks again!"

She beamed. "So Ernie helped? What did you think about him? A nice guy, huh?"

"Seems to be. But I probably never would have met him but for you. Thanks again, Melissa!" One of the many reasons I got out of the intel business was exactly this, the duplicity, the secrets even from people you trust, and constant worries about how much to say and not to say. Yeah, yeah, I understood the reasons for all of it, but I also knew how it ate away at your insides, both head and heart. And your stomach. In fact, looking at Melissa, with her obvious infatuation for Ernie, the "nice guy," made my stomach hurt.

I walked back to Ben's suite. I knocked on his open inner office door. "Hey, man. We hit pay dirt." I spread the photos across his desk. "This one is the guy's car coming in. The next one shows his license plate, and this one shows the guy."

Ben looked carefully and then said, "Holy shit, man! That's not pay dirt. It's freaking gold!" He shuffled through the other shots. "So that's what the bastard looks like, huh. He really is Joe Average. I don't know him, for certain." He pushed the photos back to me and leaned back in his chair. "What next? Turn this over to the cops?"

"No. I'll follow up with his license plate, though my guess is the car is a rental. However, it gives me a good place to start. I have a cop friend in Boston who can run the picture and the plates for me. We might get lucky. And assuming the car was rented, I'll chase down the rental agency and see what turns up."

"No cops? You sure?" He had a skeptical expression on his face.

"I'm sure. Remember the break-in is only a small part of my investigation, and I don't want the cops trampling over the rest of it. Patience, my friend." I used my most reassuring tone. The last thing I wanted was for the cops to wander over to visit my friends across the street and stir them up. This whole business was getting way too complicated already.

"Okay. You're the boss. But promise me that guy here"—he pointed to the picture of the intruder—"won't skate on the assault. Can you make sure of that at least?"

I gave him a long couple of seconds of cold seriousness and said, "Without any question."

***

On the way home, my head was filled with bits and pieces of the last two days, way too much disconnected crap. I put on some opera, *Turandot*, and let the melancholy sweetness flow through me, easing some of the cognitive stress. Odd that this opera, more than any other, should calm my thoughts, since the story was so irrationally disturbing on so many levels, but there you have it. I let out a breath.

Someone associated with the Adamo family, or possibly some family member, had something to do with Abe Adamo's accident. That much would seem to be true. The only other possibility was far too improbable. It was also likely that whoever broke into Ben's office, assaulted Doreen, and took, among other documents, the very thin file on the accident that Ben compiled by asking a few innocuous questions from some fairly trusted sources was sent by the same source. Why such an improbable reaction? Arguably, the death of Abe Adamo, made to look like an accident, was tangled up with something serious. It could have been personal; that is, some enemy of Abe, for an obscure reason all his (or her) own, staged the accident solely to eliminate him for purposes of revenge or money or even love. But my recruitment by Ernie and his merry band of spooks, presumably at the behest of Uncle Sam, stretches the *personal* motive beyond anything credible. I guess the two could be unconnected, but coincidence just didn't feel right. Why try to put that awkward square peg of coincidence into that perfectly round hole of synchronicity? Okay.

I reached down and forwarded the disk to act 3 so I could listen to "Nessun dorma." Seemed like I deserved a treat. Why was I thinking about Luce? Lucy? Lucia? Why did I get excited thinking about her? If it weren't for her, none of this unreasonable shit would be cascading through my comfortable life. The aria was starting. I listened and wondered about the threat from *Turandot* buried so sweetly in the melody.

I pulled into my drive and parked in front of the house. Walking to the front door, I realized that my small yard needed some attention—the grass was high, and weeds extending from the woods were starting to encroach on the lawn. Also, a dead branch was stretched across a flower bed that was planted by God only knows who but had become mine through too many hours of weeding. Maybe I need a gardener. Sure.

When the door was half-open, Doc started winding around my ankles, purring loud enough to score Richter points. I reached down. "Hey, pal! How are you doing?" Kneeling, I scratched him around the neck and under his chin. He closed his eyes and sat, expecting a major amount of attention. I split the difference with him for a few minutes then stood up and walked across the living room, into the kitchen, and opened the fridge. Not much there. Closing it, I reached across an adjoining counter and grabbed a can of food for Doc, popped the tab, and scooped a generous amount into his dish. He ate, still purring. I covered the open can and put it in the fridge, which now wasn't empty, unlike my stomach. I checked the freezer above: some unrecognizable packets of frost-covered whatever, ice cubes, and a half-used bag of peas. I thought about nuking the peas, but then thought better about it when I found a brand-new bag of chips in the cupboard! I grabbed the bag, opened it, and stuck a couple in my mouth. Not so new, but edible.

I walked back into the living room area over to the rough antique table that served as my desk. I sat. This would be a good time to call my buddy at the DMV. Maybe he could give me some quick info on the license plate of *the guy* (break-in guy). I picked up my cell, stared at it, and called Lucy. I should bring her up to speed on all that had happened. Yeah.

"Lucy? TB here. How goes it?" Why was I so freaking nervous? Probably lack of food.

"Hello, Tom. How are you?" She sounded fine, composed.

"I'm okay, thanks. Long couple of days, you know."

"That's for sure. When I got home this morning, I took care of some phone messages, drank some orange juice, and collapsed on the couch. I am not a nap person, but I was unconscious for almost three hours. I guess I needed it."

"Sounds like it. Listen, I have some news. Good news, I think."

"Great! What is it?" She was excited.

"Well, I was thinking that maybe we could get together and discuss it over a light dinner. There's quite a bit to discuss." I waited, feeling like the way I felt in the seventh grade on the phone with Suzie or Mary or whatever the hell her name was.

"Good idea. When and where?"

Excellent, I said to myself. To her I said, "How about my place, maybe seven o'clock, seven thirty?"

"I have another suggestion to consider. How about my place, and I can cook something for us here? Same time, seven or so. Would that work?"

"Of course, that would be fine. How do I get there?" She told me. I wrote it down. "See you in a couple of hours, Luce."

"See you, Tom."

It was five o'clock, so I had plenty of time to clean up and pick out a bottle of wine. Shit! I didn't know what she was cooking. Red or white? Screw it, I'd take both.

***

She lived close to Lake Sunapee, so it should take no more than forty-five minutes to get there. It was a beautiful, warm summer evening, maybe eighty degrees, with a soft breeze. I had the top down, and the air blowing over the windshield was sweet. I headed toward 89, winding my way over a couple of back roads. All the folks along the way seemed to be outside, barbecuing or sitting in deck chairs, a couple even tending flower beds. In New Hampshire, no one wasted the short summer months inside. The general attitude was that if God wanted to give us this incredible gift, then we were going to enjoy it, especially since it was free! Of course, no true Yankee would ever say it out loud, but everyone thought it. And then they smiled at one another in mutual acknowledgment and talked about the comparative merits of different styles of snowblowers.

I reached the lake with ten minutes to spare; now I needed to find her house or cottage or whatever. The directions suggested following 103A, toward Blodgett Landing, then the first side road running east. I found the Point then the road running perpendicular to 103. I drove a half mile or so, looking for a small Cape Cod-style house, blue siding, back from the road on the right. And there it was. Tidy, in a small green yard cut out of the woods surrounding it. I pulled into the gravel drive and crunched up to the house. I was five minutes early. I grabbed the wine, exited my car, and walked up the irregularly inlaid stone walkway and up to the porch. I reached for the bell, but as I did, the door opened. There she was. I grinned like a moron.

"Hi, Tom. Come in." She was wearing loose khaki shorts, sandals, and a burnt-orange designer T-shirt. Her hair was tied behind and up. Curiously, she had more makeup on with this casual outfit than she did when she last came into my office. But it looked good, so curiosity succumbed to appreciation. She turned and said, "Two bottles? One for each of us or what?"

"It could be, but honestly, I just didn't know what you were cooking, so…" I shrugged. Then smelling something other than her perfume, I realized that some sort of beef-dish aroma was wafting through. "Oh, unless my olfactory sense is cross-circuited, that's beef? No?"

"Very good. If you like Italian food, then my grandmother's lasagna should work for you. Follow me." And off she walked through a small but comfortable-looking living room, into a kitchen-dining area, which was obviously the center of her home. The smell was incredible. "Have a seat." She motioned to a padded bench that ran along one side for ten feet or so. Typically, benches are not all that comfortable, but this one had an inclined back, also padded, that came up to a window running the length of the dining area. Not only was it comfortable, but it also offered a perfect view of the entire room, as well as the backyard, through the window. The bench was built for the room, yes, but clearly its central purpose was for people to use it. In front of the bench were three small but sturdy, portable tables. The table closest to me had a couple of magazines and a half-filled, stemless glass of red wine.

"Looks like you got a jump on me, huh?" I pointed to the glass of wine.

"Yeah, I enjoy a glass when I'm cooking. The bottle is up there." She pointed to a bottle on a nearby counter. "Glasses are in the cupboard. Please help yourself."

I stood, took a couple of steps to the cupboard, and opened it. It held dozens of wineglasses, stemless and stemmed, all shapes and functions, some for daily use and some clearly expensive. I retrieved a glass that paired with Lucy's. I picked up the wine and inspected the label. Northern Italy, Barbera, a varietal from Puglia. I poured half a glass and tasted it. "Very nice. You want your glass topped?"

"Yes, please." She was busy at her stove. And stove it was! An old-style black country cookstove, or so it seemed. Six burners, two ovens, and twice as wide as a conventional range. On closer inspection, it was fueled by propane, and it had a grill. It was a replica but a good one. I added wine to Lucy's glass and took it to her.

"Here you go." I held the wine out to her.

She took it, smiled, and said, "Thanks." She faced me, sipped. "We have another ten minutes or so for the lasagna and then a few minutes for it to cool. Salad is ready to go—in the fridge when we are ready. Let's sit." She moved past me, brushing against my arm. We sat.

Quiet. Both of us, not looking at each other, and quiet. We sipped our wine, and after an awkward amount of time, she broke first and spoke. "Been a busy couple of days."

"Sure has. Nice to relax. The wine is nice."

"It works with lasagna or any other tomato-based sauce. Kind of a common wine, you know."

"Lucy. It's good to see you again. I mean, well, it hasn't been all that long, but wine, food, being here with you in your home all feels right. Does that make any sense?"

She continued examining her very common wine, without looking up. Then she lifted her head and caught my eyes with her eyes, and well, she won that exchange. I shifted over on the bench closer to her. I put my glass on one of the tables and slowly extended my hand and gently brushed her cheek with the backs of my fingertips. She leaned in, and in an exploratory way, we kissed. I cradled her face in my hands, letting my thumbs softly caress the skin under her cheekbones. She put her arms up on my shoulders, hands behind my head. She put her head next to mine and whispered, "I guess that's out of the way." I laughed, then I kissed her again.

She gently pushed away and said, "I need to take our lasagna out." And getting up, she did just that.

***

The lasagna was excellent. Different, but then every good lasagna is because it reflects the person who prepares it. I asked Luce what made it so tasty, and she credited her grandmother for it. I asked her if her grandmother taught her, and she said that her mother taught her. But her mama learned it from Noni. I asked if her mother changed the recipe, personalized it, and she gave me a look and said, "No! I don't think so anyway. Well, except for nonessential things, some spices and the kinds of cheese. Mama always taught us that Noni was the real cook." I pushed and asked if her mother was a good cook, as well, and she said, with feeling, "Of course. She learned from the best." I then pushed my luck one more time and asked if she, Lucia, had altered her mother's recipe. "Why are you asking all of these questions? Don't you like the lasagna?" At that point, I decided to let it drop, in the interest of preventing a complete meltdown.

After we ate, I excused myself, went outside to put the top up on my Spider and to retrieve the pictures Ernie's people had captured. When I reentered, Luce was sitting on the bench with two of the little tables joined together in front and coffee waiting and a small plate of biscotti. I sat down beside her and spread the photos out in front of us.

She said, "Well, that's helpful. Where did these come from? I thought that there were no cameras on the building."

Fortunately, when she asked the question, I was in the middle of taking a drink of coffee. I cleared my throat, paused for a second, and answered, "A bit of a story. The receptionist in Ben's building was a friend of Doreen, and she was upset about the assault. She has a boyfriend who works IT in that big building across the street. She called him to see if maybe one of their unobtrusive cameras might have caught some shots during the sweep of their property. He checked, and sure enough, this is what they captured. Of course, these are doctored, you know, enlarged and enhanced. I met her boyfriend, and he was kind enough to provide all of this."

"Nice break. Lucky for us Doreen has friends, huh?" Shuffling the photos, glancing at me between shuffles, she continued, "Do you know who this guy is yet?"

"No. Actually, I thought maybe it might be someone you would recognize. Not so?"

"Not a clue. Nondescript sort of fellow. How about the car? A Mass plate. Can you track him from that?"

"Maybe. I know some people down there that should be able to help. My guess though is that the car is a rental. But I'll track it as far as it goes. Having a photo of the guy will help, of course."

She leaned back. "If this is the guy who broke into your friend's office and took the file he had on the accident, do you think finding him will help us find out who killed Abe?" This she said with an edge.

I looked at her, shrugged, reached for a cookie, took a bite, and said, "Perhaps. But we are a long way from that. We need to be smart about it. The guy who broke into Ben's office may or may not know anything about the 'accident,' and we won't know until we find him. Even then, he will have to confide what he knows. Assuming he talks, we will have to verify it." I watched her face to see if any of what I was saying registered. She wanted what she wanted, but she nodded in understanding.

"Tom, it's hard for me to be patient. You get that, right?"

"Of course. All I can suggest is that the process will take some time. We can't move any faster than the evidence presented, and even then, we have to proceed with caution. This guy"—I shoved the photo of the guy in front of her—"put a fifty-year-old woman in the hospital. We need to be careful. Yes?"

"I suppose." She didn't like it.

"Luce, we have a great deal more information this evening than we had this morning. That's not a bad thing. Please trust me. It will all go forward, and we will find out what happened to Abe, but again, we must be careful. Okay?"

She smiled, reached over, and squeezed my hand. "Okay. But promise me one thing. You will keep me informed and, if possible, include me in the investigation."

"Yes to both. Now you have to promise me something."

"What?" Innocent eyes, skeptical tone to her voice.

"You won't do anything regarding this investigation without letting me know ahead of time. Nothing.

No inquiries, no searches on the web, and definitely no involving anyone else at any time. Can you do that?"

"I can do that. Eat your biscotti, drink your coffee, and let's talk about something else."

I ate the cookie. She ate her cookie. We quietly shared in the awkwardness of it all. She said, "More coffee?"

I said, "No, thanks. I'm good."

"Look, Tom, we don't know each other at all. Well, aside from our business together." She paused, uncomfortable.

"You mean aside from the investigation?"

"Yes. That. But in just this short time, I do feel like I know you, somehow, and better than our time together should have allowed. Why do you think that is? Or is it just me?" She looked down at her coffee cup.

"Lucy, I do know what you mean. It seems the same to me."

"Since Abe passed, I have had zero interest in any sort of relationship. It has almost been like that part of me passed away with him. So to have any interest at all is…" She shook her head disapprovingly.

"I can't say I fully understand how you feel. Mixed feelings, no doubt. I can tell you that I like this Lucia Nardone person. That's all I know for sure."

She smiled sweetly, openly, and said, "I just don't want to do anything or say anything that might mislead you. Or anything that I might regret."

She was being honest with me. Maybe that was why I liked her. One of the reasons, anyway.

"Lucy, can I tell you a story? From my teen years?"

She nodded.

"Like most adolescents, boys, anyway, I was restless and argumentative but also hostile and angry. Really, looking back on those days, I was a pain in everyone's ass. My only outlet was baseball. I played constantly. But even then, a lot of the guys didn't want to play with me because I was so damned aggressive, verbally and physically. I was better than average at the plate, both hitting for average and power. And I could play anywhere in the infield, but shortstop was my position of choice. I was quick, good arm, and generally anticipated well. I'm telling you all of this not to brag, but because it was the only thing that helped me channel my anger. Get the picture?"

She nodded. Attentive.

"Well, one day, we were playing a game with a rival team, and we were behind. For me, the worst possible thing was losing. Nothing was worse than that. I had hit a blooper between right field and first base. The right fielder ran for the ball, picked it off the ground, and threw it to second, where I was stretching for the base at full speed. The second baseman, while trying to catch the ball, swung his mitt down for both catch and tag, just as I was sliding in. Without thinking, I raised by leg and slammed into his outstretched arm with a little extra kick. I could feel the bones crack in his arm. He yelled, the ball dropped in front of his mitt, rolling into the infield. I jumped up and ran to third. I made it to third and was as happy as I ever was back then. I remember laughing because of the play." I stopped, remembering the moment.

"Are you okay, Tom?" She reached for my hand.

I took a breath, realizing that I was sharing something I really didn't want to share. I looked at her face, so open and so caught up in my story. Maybe it was time to get some of this crap out of my head.

"Yeah. So as I was congratulating myself, the other team's players were all rushing to second base, where the kid I had hurt was being tended. All I could see was the backs of the other kids. I couldn't see the kid himself. The third-base coach, our guy, jogged over to second to see how the kid was. I just stood on third, waiting. He walked back and told me that the kid's arm was broken, that both of the bones were sticking out and he was bleeding pretty bad. As it turned out, the kid went to the hospital, and after some surgery, they set his arm. It was never the same again, and he sure as hell never played ball again."

She waited, knowing, I suppose, that I wasn't finished.

"I had an uncle, on my father's side, that I was pretty close to during my teen years. I could talk to him, and he always had time for me. I told him what happened, and he listened carefully. When I finished, he put his arm around my shoulders and asked me what I had learned from the incident. I thought he was crazy. What had I learned? I ruined the kid's arm, probably for life, just because I wanted to win a game. A game! And what had I learned? It made no sense to me."

"So what did he mean? Why ask that particular question?"

"Well, he guided me over to a couple of lawn chairs that he had in the backyard and sat me down. Then he asked me how I felt about the accident. I told him I felt guilty, responsible for breaking the kid's arm—for my own selfish reasons. He reassured me that feeling the way I did was natural and showed that I wasn't the heartless bastard that I thought I was right then. When he said that, it put the incident into some perspective, I suppose. I needed to hear that. After I settled down a little, he asked me what I wanted to do about it. I had no idea. He suggested that I might want to visit the kid and maybe apologize for being such an asshole. I agreed.

"But my uncle wanted me to understand something more important than the way I felt right then. He told me to go talk with the kid then consider what could be learned from what happened. Then come back and tell him what it was."

"Tom! Come on, tell me, what happened? What did you learn?"

I chuckled a little bit and said, "Well, I went to see the kid, at his home. At first, he was hostile, as he probably should have been. But we talked about it. I apologized and even cried a little when he accepted my apology. I spent the rest of the afternoon with him, talking about all sorts of things, including how we both hated the Yankees but loved some of their players, especially Derek Jeter and Tony Fernandez. We established that since he was a Red Sox fan and I was a Phillies fan, we could coexist, at least until those rare series when we played each other. When I left later, his mom gave me a hug and told me that I should come back anytime."

"Whatever happened to the kid?"

I smiled. "He's my best friend, Ben. And every time the weather changes, his arm aches, and he blames me for it." I laughed.

"Ben? The same Ben? Oh my god, how cool is that?" She laughed and squeezed my hand.

"What did you say to your uncle? What did you learn?"

"You have to know what the man was like. He was older than my dad, retired. He spent most of his time reading. He read everything—fiction, history, philosophy, theology—and then he would talk about it in such a way that even a dumb kid like me felt included in the wonders, the treasures that he found. He once told me, when I was whining about being stuck in our little town, that 'if you can't be happy on the patch of ground you are standing on, you won't find it anywhere else.' He was a man, in the purest sense. Strong, always ready to help anyone who needed it, honest in every possible way, loyal to his friends, and a formidable foe to his enemies, the few he had. He was a persistent guy, never someone who would give up. He was a decorated soldier, wounded in combat, and fiercely patriotic. He always flew the flag in his front yard proudly but not ostentatiously. He had the most incredible garden every year, every vegetable you can imagine. And he had some beautiful flower beds, as well. He could quote Thoreau and, in the next breath, tell you Joe DiMaggio's lifetime batting average. And he truly believed that most people were good-hearted and that all problems in life could, and would, be worked out in time with persistence and the right attitude."

"Sounds like he influenced you in many ways."

"You flatter me. No, he was one in a million. I miss him. Uncle John."

"How long has it been?"

"He passed twenty years ago next month. On July 4, oddly enough."

"Come on, Tom. What did you tell him you had learned from your experience on the ball field?"

"I told him that I learned something about myself. That there were some things I shouldn't do just to win. Uncle smiled at me. Then he told me something I didn't really understand until years later." I paused, sipped coffee slowly, and continued, "Do you want to know what that was?"

She clamped her teeth and glared.

"Okay, I'll assume that means yes. Well, Uncle John was not a simple man, and I suspect he planted ideas in my head that would emerge over time when I needed them. He was always thinking ahead, especially when people he cared about were concerned. He said, 'Tommy, life has a way of circling around and returning you to where you were before. If you recognize those times, you can make important choices. The key is to recognize where you are.' I know now that he was right."

Lucy thought about it and said, "Karma. Sounds like it anyway."

"Yeah, I believe so. It also reminds of a line from Eliot, the one line I know: 'We shall not cease from exploration, and the end of all our exploring will be to arrive where we started and know the place for the first time.'"

"That fits. You read poetry?"

"Sometimes. More of a backward reader of poetry."

"What does that mean?"

"Backward reader of poetry? I read that line, the Eliot line, in a book and then looked up the source and read it. Backward from how it's usually done, I'm guessing. Anyway, Uncle John was quite the guy."

"I wish I could have met him. You know what? From your description, he reminds me of my aunt Connie. Does that sound silly?"

"I don't know her very well, but she strikes me as a person who lives more inside herself than outside, and Uncle John was the same way. Both well-read and both natural mentors. Not silly at all. They weren't from the same generation, so social influences would have been different. Also, my uncle was self-taught, and your aunt was obviously formally educated, but the end product sounds to be similar. Interesting, huh?"

"It is. I wonder what would have happened if they had met. Obviously impossible, the age thing, but what if? The conversations they might have had…"

"Hah! Yeah, that would have been fun to experience, even as an observer. Some popcorn, a good seat."

"Are you ridiculing my idea?" She wasn't smiling.

"No, no! Not even a little bit. In fact, I'm notorious for putting seemingly impossible scenarios together in order to synthesize something new. You know, during an investigation or sometimes just for fun. Ben tells me I'm crazy, but then he invariably joins in once I start combining oddities, unrelated images, and memories, even. No, I like that you readily do the same sort of thing! Having and using an imagination is an advantage in life, not to mention that it generally adds some joy."

She considered what I said and grinned. "Why do you think some people have imaginations and some don't? Why are some people unable to just, I don't know, speculate about the world around them?"

"I can only guess, but I think everyone has the capacity to imagine what might be. When you were a kid, it seemed as natural as breathing to imagine all sorts of interesting, exciting things. It made growing up easier because you could imagine, pretend things you hadn't done but probably would at some point. Imagination was the doorway into new spaces. Then as you got older, life presented obstacles to *pretending*. And as with any set of skills, your capacity to imagine diminished without use. So my guess is that some folks have just forgotten how to use their imaginations."

"That sounds true, but also, some people see vivid imagining as childish. That a more rational approach is required to navigate in the *real world* and that using your imagination is foolish."

I looked at her. "So you think active use of one's imagination, in the pursuit of learning something new, is childish?" I chose not to smile, just to see.

"God, no! I agree with you about thinking of a functioning imagination as an advantage and, especially, as a way to enjoy life more fully. Where would the world of aesthetics be without imagination? Human beings would still be living in caves without imagination, creativity, daring to speculate. All I meant was that not everyone agrees on the value of *active imagining*."

I thought about what she said and her intensity as she said it. Interesting. "Well. And how do you reflexively use your imagination? Or is it reflexive at all?"

She considered for a moment, stood up, and walked over to the table where we left the half-full wine bottle. She found her glass, poured the wine, and asked, "More for you?"

"Sure. Why not."

She poured the balance into my glass then brought both back, handing my glass to me. She sat, settled herself. "Honestly, I think I do both. I daydream frequently, reflexively. And sometimes I wake up in the morning, with a dream still in my head, and I just let it continue. But there are times when I intentionally imagine something in order to explore possibilities or maybe solve a problem." She stopped, sipped her wine. "Is that what you mean?"

"Yes. Do you think dreams are a function of imagination or something else?"

"Both. Imagining something is a broad way of describing a way of thinking or feeling. Dreaming could be described in the same way, but subconsciously. Does that sound right?"

I nodded. "Yeah, I have a theory that people who have vivid imaginations are drawing upon their subconscious, even merging conscious and subconscious processes. My language, the terms, may not be entirely accurate, but you get the idea. Getting older, it seems like accessing my subconscious is easier. Intentional imagining then becomes more useful and more trustworthy."

"Isn't that the same thing as just getting to know yourself? Recognizing your own patterns, preferences, and such. No?"

"Maybe. But try discussing all of this with someone else, and see what happens. You know?"

"I wouldn't do that. Maybe in a psych class or something, but not in casual conversation." She smiled.

"Why not, Luce?" I watched her closely.

"Because most people just don't talk about this sort of thing. Not easily anyway. It's somehow too…intimate, too personal." She blinked and seemed uncomfortable.

I didn't verbalize what was obvious, but the unspoken truth of this intimacy was suddenly embarrassing for both of us. We didn't really know each other, so why indeed were we digging into each other's heads like this? I didn't know.

10

The next morning, Lucy and I left Sunapee around eight o'clock. We were up at six thirty, showered, and had a light breakfast. Lucy filled two carry cups with coffee for the trip. And just to be clear, no, we didn't share the same bed the previous night. I slept on a very comfortable bed in a spare room.

As I pulled onto 89S, it occurred to me that Luce and I hadn't discussed whether or not she would accompany me back to Concord. In fact, even though unspoken, our agreement had been implicit all along. It just seemed right. As we settled into a comfortable speed, I glanced over at Luce. She was watching me. I turned my eyes back to the road ahead.

"Tom, what exactly is on the agenda today? This sort of thing is all new to me."

I considered her question, but having not really thought about her involvement in anything other than a general sort of way, I hadn't prepared an answer. "Well, first thing is to make some phone calls. Follow up on the license plate. Call Ben, and see if the cops have anything new. Then, assuming the car was a rental, visit the agency and try to get more information there. Of course, finding this guy presupposes that he will lead us to whoever initiated the break-in. I also want to do some research on the Adamo family, both the business end and the family itself. We don't have anything like a motive for, well, Abe's murder. Maybe you could do some of that."

She thought about it, or maybe she was just reacting to the notion of labeling it *murder* rather than *accidental*. After a few moments, she said, "I can do that. Anything in particular to start?"

"Yeah. You need to consider who might benefit from Abe's death. Business associates, customers, enemies, whoever. Then, even though it will be uncomfortable, consider who in the family might be responsible, even from a distance. Don't exclude anyone from consideration. I know there will be a few that you will immediately discount, but don't. Murder almost always happens for one of three reasons: money, power, or love. And love is likely to be tangled up somehow with the first two. Jealousy, revenge, spite, general craziness, even."

"I get that. Can I make some phone calls, you know, to talk with business associates or employees?"

I thought about it. "Good question. Tell you what, develop a list of people you might want to contact. We can go over the names and figure it out. Sound good?"

"Yes." She had that determined look on her face again.

We traveled uneventfully, talked about inconsequential matters having nothing to do with either the case or our improbable relationship. The Spider enjoyed the open road, and she purred comfortably along. The sky was blue; trees and landscapes green. It was a pleasant seventy degrees or so, still with low humidity, the off-and-on rain in the last few days having purged moisture from the air. It was one of those days that made it difficult not to be content, maybe even happy. But that creeping, skin-deep feeling of unrest was coiling up my neck. The feeling that never seemed to leave until some kind of ugliness presented itself. Maybe it was the case, maybe being on the precipice of a new personal entanglement, or it could be something unrelated to either. Whatever it was, the truly grand day had nastiness hiding in wait. No doubt.

"Are you okay?" Lucy was staring at me.

I realized that my hands were white, knuckling the steering wheel; my shoulders were bunched up, and I was scowling. I tried to relax, made what looked like a smile, and replied, "Yeah, yeah. Just thinking about the case." I didn't look at her.

"If you are sure. You just seem a little tense."

"Guess I am. I'll be OK."

We were entering the outskirts of Concord. We were starting to encounter the usual traffic. I slowed down accordingly, checked the mirrors and pulled into the right-hand lane, and put my turn signal on. We turned, merged into a less-congested street, and headed toward my office. Reaching the street, I pulled around the building and into my parking niche.

"Lucy. Let's go in and finalize our plans for the day. But before we do that, I want to forewarn you that I'll be asking Jewels to work with you on the contact list. The three of us will go over the names, but if there is someone who seems questionable in any way, we will strike the name for now. Some people should be approached in person, not by phone, and that will require some preparation, some planning. Okay?"

"Of course. It's much as I expected. So what will you be doing after we develop the list?"

"I'll make a couple of calls myself, and if those calls are productive, I'll go visit with some folks. Car-rental place, probably, and after that, who knows? But it may take some time." She nodded.

We walked into the office building and up the back stairs.

I opened the door, Lucy walked through. Jewels had a big smile and said, "Good morning, Lucy. You, too, TB." She had that knowing face, the one that said volumes about what she wasn't saying out loud.

Lucy said, "Good morning, Julie."

I said, "Good morning. Anything new that's happened? You know, with the office? The Adamo case, in particular?"

Jewels batted her eyes, reached into her letter tray, and handed me a single sheet of paper. I read it, folded it, and said, "Thanks. Any coffee left?" She pointed to the coffee maker, which clearly had half a pot steaming away. "Oh yeah. Good."

I half turned to Luce and asked, "Coffee?" She nodded.

Jewels stood and said sweetly, "Why don't you two go in your office, TB, and I'll bring the coffee in." She walked two steps to the coffee maker.

"Thanks, Jewels. Yeah, we'll be in my office. I'll leave the door open." Jewels ignored me, still grinning.

I turned the lights on as I walked through the door. Luce sat in the right-side chair, her chair newly adopted, presumably. I walked around my desk and sat, putting the folded paper to the side.

"Was Julie acting kind of funny, or was it just me?"

"Not just you. Yeah, she was acknowledging in her subtle-as-an-iron-anvil fashion that we were coming in together. In the early morning. Together."

"Oh. I see." She covered her mouth and giggled, which perfectly synched with Jewels entering with a tray of coffee. Jewels softly placed the tray on my desk, within easy reach of both of us. She left, closing the door behind.

I shook my head wearily, and Luce giggled some more. She said, "How charming is that? I mean, really?"

"Yeah. Charming. Exactly the word I would have chosen if we were errant teenagers!"

"Oh, come on. She's just a romantic who is clearly protective of you. She obviously cares about what goes on in your life. That's not a bad thing."

"I guess not. Okay, the day isn't getting any longer, let's get to work." I reached into my desk, extracted a yellow legal pad, and handed it to her along with a pen. "Start building your contact list. Leave enough room for some quick notes for each name. I need to ask Jewels about this little treasure." I held up the folded paper. "I'll be back in a few minutes." She nodded.

Closing the door to my office, I held the folded note up and asked Jewels, "When did this guy come in?"

Jewels referred to her notes and said, "At four ten, yesterday afternoon."

"What did you tell"—I glanced at the note—"Detective Joseph Foster?"

"Nothing. I said you were away on business, that I expected you back sometime today. He asked for you to call him back 'at your convenience.' That number." She pointed to the note in my hand.

"Did he say what he wanted?"

"Nope. He was polite, professional. What's going on? A problem?"

I thought for a moment and said, "I have no idea." I sat in Jewels's side chair and pulled her phone over in front and punched in the number. It rang a few times, and a female voice responded, "Lieutenant Foster's office. May I help you?"

Lieutenant. Okay, fairly high on the food chain. "Yes, this is Detective Thomas Stone calling for Detective Foster, please." Jewels was watching me, eyebrows raised, no smile.

"Joe Foster here. May I help you?" Sounded like a cop. Flat tone, tired.

"Yes, this is Thomas Stone. You visited my office yesterday."

"Ah yes, I was hoping to have a sit-down with you, Mr. Stone, concerning the break-in at the office of Attorney Benjamin Katz. Sooner than later."

"I can certainly do that, Officer Foster. I should be back in my office later this afternoon, if that works for you?"

"It's *Lieutenant* Foster, and that won't do. How about you come in here this morning. Soonest." The flat, tired tone had magically turned to irritation.

"Well, *Lieutenant*, I have a business to run and clients to serve. My appointment schedule is pretty tight this morning. I'm afraid this afternoon is the *soonest* I can manage."

Big exhale, then the voice changed again. This time, conciliatory. "Look, I am investigating this break-in, and I would like to speak with you regarding some of the particulars. I know that you have been asking questions around the building. That is what I'm interested in. Does that help?"

I smiled. "Actually, it does. But I still can't meet you until this afternoon. Here is my secretary. She will schedule you with an appointment. Oh, and it's not *Mr.* Stone, it's *Detective* Stone. Hang on a second, and I'll transfer you." I hit the hold button, grinned at Jewels, and said, "He may be a bit brusque, but schedule him for three thirty or so."

She rolled her eyes, waited for a few moments, then said, "May I help you?" She listened, listened some more, then said, "One second, please. I'll check." She put the call on hold. "TB, didn't anyone ever teach not to poke the bear?" She waited again, then she answered, "I can squeeze you in at three thirty. What name should I put down?" She pulled the receiver away from her ear, and I could hear yet another tone of voice clearly enunciating his current displeasure. "Well, I have a job to do also, *Lieutenant Foster*. Detective Stone is very busy, I can't just change his schedule at a moment's notice. Do you want the three-thirty appointment or not?" She listened. "That will be fine. Have a nice day." She hung up. "Sensitive for an *important* lieutenant." She sniffed and wrote his name in her register. Once again, I recognized that with Jewels, *my cup runneth over*. Not to confuse metaphors or anything…

After filling in Jewels on the plan, including her assistance, we both went into my office. Lucy had put together a list of fifteen names. She was waiting. I looked at the list and deleted three names only (Tony, Marco, and Gianna Adamo), explaining that it was too soon to bring them into the mix.

"If it makes sense to speak with them at some point, it should be done in person. With these others, a quick phone call may be enough. If you sense that the call is somehow suspicious, try to schedule a meeting."

Lucy asked, "How hard should we push?"

"Don't push. You are gathering information. Jewels, maybe make up a list of questions for both of you to use, a script. You've done this before. And if anything truly strange comes up, call me right away, okay?"

They both nodded.

***

I headed over to the DMV, where my friend Bob Cantrell worked. Bob had a domestic problem a few years ago that I assisted him in resolving. Afterward, he promised to help me out if I ever needed it. Over the three years or so since, I took him up on it a few times. Today, with any luck, he could help again. I pulled into the parking lot shared with some other offices, grabbed a lightweight dark-blue sports jacket, put it on, walked to and through the swinging doors, crossed over to the counter, and beheld three lines of tired folks waiting for assistance. I sat in a nearby chair, texted Bob, and sat back. Five minutes passed, and Bob walked up to me, smiling.

"TB. Good to see you! Come on back." He led me back through the cubicles to his office. We sat. "How are you? What's it been, more than a year, right?" He was a big man, comfortably heavy, balding, and friendly by nature.

"About that. I'm fine, you know. Older, not much wiser. How about you?"

"No complaints. The kids are both in high school, and Shirley is happily staying at home these days. All good."

"Shirley quit teaching?"

"Yes and no. She took an early retirement, so she has benefits and a reasonable monthly income. She also tutors part-time from home. Some virtual, some in person. Not a bad gig for her, and it's great for the kids."

"How's Eddie doing?" Eddie was the domestic problem I helped with. He had gotten tangled up with the wrong crowd and began doing drugs. I managed to extricate him from the crowd.

"He's fine. Grades are good, plays HS ball. He's actually being recruited by some schools. He's throwing a fastball between eighty-five and ninety consistently with control. And his slider is scary!" He grinned and pointed to a picture, one of several, on his desk. Ed was in uniform, happy as a kid could be.

"That is great, Bob. Say hello to him for me."

"I'll do that. Stop by sometime. We can take in one of his games maybe. Believe me, you won't regret seeing him in action."

"I'd like that." I leaned forward. "Bob, I need your help again. I need you to run this Mass plate number. The guy driving this car broke into Ben Katz's office and stole some files. He also assaulted Ben's secretary, sent her to hospital, and I'm trying to track him down."

"Cops involved?"

"Yes and no. They don't have this license plate number, so it's unlikely they will pursue the case from this direction. If they had the number, they'd use their own resources, anyway." He was looking at me questioningly. "I'm working on a case, and the break-in was tangential to the case. If it weren't for that, I'd let the cops deal with it. I want to track down this guy because he has information I need. Plus, he assaulted Ben's secretary, Doreen. She's a friend, so there's a personal reason, as well."

Bob nodded and began typing at his PC. After a few minutes, his printer began whirring. He reached over and retrieved a single sheet, glanced at it, and passed it to me. I read it. The car was, as I had suspected, a rental from a branch of a Boston agency. The name, phone number, and address of the agency were given.

"Excellent. Thank you, my friend." I stood up, folding the sheet. "Very much appreciated."

"Anytime, TB. And please come over to the house sometime soon. Eddie is pitching again on Saturday, at home field, one thirty. I know he would love to see you. No pressure…"

I laughed. "I definitely will keep it in mind. One thirty. If I can, I'll call and let you know, okay?"

"Okay. And good luck with the case."

11

Sitting in my car, in the DMV parking lot, I studied the info sheet Bob retrieved. It was a Boston-based agency, but the branch releasing the car was located in Lawrence. That was a break; I could be there in less than an hour. Great!

The DMV was located on Hazen, so I jumped to the Franklin Pierce and then across the river to I-93 south. Traffic was moderate, so I should be at the rental agency before noon. Another nice day for driving, though going into Mass was always a pain for me, with all the strip malls and billboards and general clutter that went with a much-larger population. To be honest, the southern part of New Hampshire, at least along the interstates, wasn't much better. Anyway, at least Boston wasn't on the agenda. Yet.

The rental place was just a few blocks off I-93. I pulled into the parking area, saw the office not far from where I settled my Spider. I had the car, license, and suspect photos in a folder. Also, Ben had given me a hospital picture of Doreen's shaved head, showing the ten new stitches closing an ugly gash. I might need all the photos or maybe none of them, depending on how cooperative the rental folks were. I walked the distance to the office slowly, taking in the interior office layout through wall-length windows. There was a long reception counter, centered, with passage on either side to the rear of the office. At the counter, standing, were two middle-aged women who were both dealing presumably with customers. Behind the counter were four desk cubicles, two occupied with men, one with an older woman. Behind the cubicles was a small private office with glass walls on two sides. A bald middle-aged man with a tie was working a stack of paper. The tie gave him away as the boss.

I walked confidently through the door, up to the counter between two customers. Reaching into my jacket, I pulled out my PI license, the one issued by the State of Massachusetts, flipped open the official-looking leather folder, and flashed it at the clerk on my right. Her tired face became instantly alert. She said, "May I help you?"

"Yes, please. I need to speak with your manager. Immediately." With a practiced motion, I slid the folder back in my jacket.

"That would be Mr. Danby. Let me call him." She did then said, "Please go on back." She pointed to the office behind her.

I smiled officiously. "Thank you."

I walked back to Mr. Danby's office, all eyes following me. He was waiting, holding the door open for me. I entered and said, "Mr. Danby, you are the branch manager, is that correct?"

"Yes. Please have a seat, mister?" He was polite, suspicious, and uncomfortable.

I pulled the inexpensive desk-side chair so it was perpendicular to Danby's chair. "Thomas Stone. I'm investigating a break-in and assault of an office building in Concord that happened three days ago." I held up the manila folder. "Maybe you've heard about it?" This I said while leaning in toward him, eyes hard. I waited.

"No, no. But how can I help you, Mr. Stone?" He fidgeted with a pen on his desk.

I held his eyes for a bit then opened the folder and extracted the picture of Doreen's wound, handed the photo to him, and waited for a reaction.

"Oh my! That's terrible. I'm not sure how that concerns me, but anything I can do—"

"I need some information." I extracted the picture of the license plate, held it up but facedown, and said, "Understand, Mr. Danby, these pictures are highly confidential. As I'm sure you know, Concord is New Hampshire's state capital, and many of the buildings are secured for a reason. Someone broke into a building in the central part of the city, and it is essential, before I show you this photo, that you agree to maintain confidentiality. Can I count on you?"

"Yes, of course." I stared at him for a moment, nodded, and I placed the photo on his desk. He looked at it carefully, lifted his head, and said, "A Massachusetts plate. Should this mean something to me?"

I sighed, retrieved the photo, and said, "Mr. Danby, this is a plate from one of the cars you rented to the perpetrator. I obviously want to know who that man was and any information you can give me regarding the rental." I waited.

"I see." He relaxed, happy that it was nothing personal. "Well, normally, we don't release that sort of information, but under the circumstances…" He turned to his PC, tapped a couple of keys. "Could I see that picture again?"

I handed it to him. He tapped a couple more keys, used his mouse, studied the screen. While he was busy, I looked around his office. A poster of Bob Marley was push-pinned to the wall behind his desk. Interesting. I looked at him somewhat differently, smiling to myself.

He tapped keys again, and two sheets of paper came out of a printer located on a small table behind his desk, just below Bob, curiously enough. He handed the papers to me. Name, address, phone number, insurance purchased with the rental, emergency-contact name and number. On the second sheet, boilerplate material, as well as his signature, the date, and the name of the agent who rented him the car. Also, a blurry picture of his Mass driver's license.

"I looked up. This should prove helpful. This rental agent, Mrs. O'Neil? Is she here, by any chance?"

"Yes. Why?" Now that he personally was off the seeming hook, suspicion kicked in.

"Because I would like to talk with her, unless, of course, you remember what this Terrence Hampton looks like." I raised my eyebrows wearily.

He held my gaze. "I see. He reached for his phone, hit a button. "Janice? Could you please come into my office? Thanks."

I looked out his door window and saw the older woman in the left-hand cubicle get up. I said to Danby, "Will she agree to confidentiality?"

He nodded. "Let me speak to her first before I introduce you."

Mrs. O'Neil knocked lightly on the door. Danby waved her in. "Janice, please sit down." She sat on the remaining empty chair, equidistant between Danby and me. She sat primly, hands folded on her lap. Gray hair, neat, short. Lightly tinted glasses. Pantsuit, flat shoes. Tired face with intelligent eyes.

"Janice, this is Mr. Stone. He is investigating a crime committed up in New Hampshire that has, well, sensitive government security concerns associated with it. It is necessary that all discussion of this crime be kept in strictest confidence. Do you understand?"

"I think so."

"That means no one is to know about this discussion. Coworkers, your husband, no one. Right?"

"I understand." She became alert.

I cleared my throat and said, "Mrs. O'Neil, I want you to try to remember this person. You rented him a car a few days ago." I handed her the agency contract information sheets.

She took a minute or so, glanced back up, and said, "Yes, I remember him. He was in a hurry but polite about it. I remember he paid in cash, which is always unusual. He rented the car for a week, so I suppose he still has it. The plan was for him to drop it off either back here or possibly Boston. He wasn't sure."

"Interesting. What did he look like?"

She thought about it. "He was medium height, medium build, but he seemed…his motions, the way he walked and moved in general, seemed athletic? Just unusual." She lifted the papers. "As I'm sure you read, his age is on the driver's license, and for a man who is forty-one, he just seemed much younger."

"Anything else? Distinguishing characteristics?"

"Yes, actually. He had a tattoo on his left hand, Oriental, as I remember. He also had one of those faces? The kind that is memorable because it is so undistinguished. Plain, an everyman kind of face." She thought for a moment. "That's pretty much it."

"Thank you, Mrs. O'Neil, you have a good memory. That was very helpful." I stood, she stood, we shook hands. She turned to Danby, who smiled, nodded, and thanked her. She left, closing the door behind her.

Still sitting, Danby looked at me and said, "So what sort of investigator are you, Mr. Stone?"

I reached over to his desk, where Mrs. O'Neil had placed the printed records. I picked them up and inserted them in my manila folder. I retrieved a business card from my jacket and put it on his desk. I said, "A private investigator, specializing in these sorts of investigations." I smiled.

He stood, surprise on his face. I reached out; we shook hands. I thanked him, saying, "I appreciate your cooperation. I now have a couple of leads I didn't have before." I turned to go, then I turned back around, pointed to the Marley poster and paraphrased, "Don't trust people whose feelings change with time. Trust people whose feelings remain the same, even when the time changes."

Danby stared at me for a blink, then he grinned like a kid.

Checking my watch, it was 1:35 p.m. I sat in my car, still in the rental-agency parking lot, looking over the information already gathered. I knew more about him now than I did before. The tattoo verified that he was the right guy. The physical description was helpful, but Mrs. O'Neil's intuitive description was better: "polite," "everyman face," "athletic," "younger than his given age." This was no amateur, not even a typical hood, more like an operative of some kind. The photo ID he used was obviously fake, so whatever he was, he wasn't without resources. And the speed with which he breached Ben's office suggested that he might have been readily available for clandestine activities. More and more, this whole business smelled like spy work. I knew the stench. I reached for my *special* cell phone, swiped it on, and tapped the preset icon.

"Hello, Mr. Stone." Ernie's voice.

"Hi. A couple of questions. First, what's the connection between the break-in of Ben Katz's office and your problem with slippery tech? Second, did you run the intruder's pic through facial recognition?"

"If there is a connection, you just found it. That may be fortuitous. And second, yes, I did that right after you left. No hits. That alone raises a flag, don't you think?"

"A flag? Yeah, understatement. How is that possible?"

"As you know, I'm sure, our database is extensive, and our real-time video surveillance is as good as it gets.

Theoretically, he could be an operative recruited, trained, and put into play without any digital trail. I say theoretical because it would have required raising him from a child in a highly protected environment for the sole purpose of operating anonymously. Either that, or he was plucked, as a child, from some part of the world that is completely off anyone's grid. Think about it. If he is somewhere between thirty and forty years of age, his handlers, when they first recruited him at birth, really, would have been at least thirty years behind today's tech. The sophisticated digital capture of personal information was decades away. Understand?"

"I think so. There is no logical reason why such a level of complete anonymity would be required back then, so why worry about it? Today it would make sense, not back then. Spy work is largely reactive. Okay. So it seems this guy is *special* in ways that are largely unknown. That's just terrific."

"What can we do for you right now, TB?"

"Not sure. But now that you have the guy's face on record, could you set up your surveillance so it will trigger an alarm if his face pops up somewhere? Then let me know?"

"It's already done. Anything else?"

"Don't think so. Oh, maybe one thing. The car the guy rented hasn't been returned. Any way to trace it?"

"Sure. Do you have the make, model, color, and such?" I gave it to him and said "bye."

One more reason I hated covert crap back then and now. Trying to anticipate what the bad guys were up to, when they were engaged in shit that lacked any kind of predictable pattern—it was way beyond frustrating. Give me an honest criminal anytime.

I sat in the car, considering my options. Until I had a lead on the bad guy or his car, there wasn't much to do here. Back in the office, maybe the ladies had made some progress. If so, then at the very least, I could plan for some interviews with some of those folks. I turned the key, and the engine turned over sweetly, encouragingly. I told myself that it would all work out. And my head almost had my heart convinced when the phone sounded. Looking, I saw that it was Jewels. "Yeah, Jewels."

"TB, how far away are you?"

"Just leaving Lawrence, why?"

"We found some interesting possibilities, you know, with the calling?"

I turned the Spider off. "Like what?"

"Well, we were over halfway through Lucy's list, and nothing seemed the least bit interesting. Then Lucy called a manager at Adamo Corp. in Manchester, a man named Walter Hinds. At first, it seemed like another dead end, but then Lucy, per script, mentioned concern about Abe's death *right after* telling him about the break-in, again per script. The guy got quiet, long enough that we thought he had disconnected. Then he came back on and sounded very different, irritated. He told Lucy that she needed to accept what had happened and stop stirring things up for no good reason. So Lucy tried to deflect by saying that the investigation was primarily aimed at the break-in, that she was just helping a friend, and she thought that he, Walter, might have heard something about it, you know, through the grapevine. He paused again then said all he knew about it was what some people at the office were saying. He then excused himself brusquely and hung up. What do you think?"

"That is interesting. Okay. It's about two o'clock now. What time is that cop coming in, Foster?"

"Three thirty, and you really should be here. You already have him pissed off."

I smiled and replied, "Well, you helped in that little matter. Maybe he could be assuaged with a little of your famous charm?"

"Like I said, you better get back in here." She hung up.

I had to laugh. For some strange reason, I actually felt optimistic about the case. Well, more so anyway. Sometimes that was how it went: dead end, delays, frustration, and then a hint of progress that brought perspective back. Don't get me wrong; there was no light visible down that tunnel, but at least there was no light in the rearview mirror. In this business, that meant a promise of light up ahead.

I fired up my green Spider and started the journey back home.

***

When I walked into the office, according to my watch, at exactly 3:20 p.m., Jewels gave me her anxious face and, pointing to my office, mouthed soundlessly, "He's here." I acknowledged her gesture by pointing to my office in mimicry and mouthed, "Oh no!" She lost the anxious face, put her hands on her hips, and said out loud, "Your three thirty is here, TB." Then made a rude gesture.

I walked over to the coffee maker and poured a cup then continued on into my office, closing the door behind. I said, "Lieutenant Foster. Nice to meet you." I extended my hand.

Foster stood, extended his hand, and said, "Detective Stone." He sat back down.

"I see Julie has taken care of the coffee for you. Need a freshener?"

"No, thanks. I'm good. Tell her the coffee was excellent. It was."

I smiled. "She'll be pleased." I sat, leaned forward, and said, "Now. What can I do for you, Lieutenant?"

He cleared his throat. "As I mentioned on the phone this morning, I'm investigating the break-in at"—he referenced a small notepad on his lap—"121A John Stark Plaza. When I questioned some of the folks in adjacent offices, they all seemed surprised that 'two detectives' would need to question them. All of them were under the impression that you, Detective, were representing the police department. Were you?"

"No. I did not tell anyone that I was a police detective. I guess I must look like a policeman. Kinda flattering, actually." I smiled.

He stared at me for a moment and said, "Okay. Let's forget about that for the moment." He cleared his throat again, flipped the page in his notepad, and said, "If you are investigating this incident, and I know that you are, after discussing it with Attorney Katz, what exactly is the scope of your investigation?" He waited.

Interesting. Obviously, there was more to his involvement than the surface of it would indicate. "The scope. Curious question, Lieutenant. Ben Katz, a good friend of mine, as is Doreen, his secretary, hired me to look into it. Frankly, and with all due respect, I'm a little surprised that a detective lieutenant would be assigned to a simple robbery, even one with an assault victim. You and I both know that something like this, in the city, would only rate a uniformed officer or two. Why so much talent?" Wide-eyed and curious was I.

"You haven't answered my question. With all due respect, please answer my question." A hint of official impatience.

"Of course. My *scope* is to find out who broke into Ben's office, stole some of his files, and not coincidentally, hit my friend Doreen over the head. Secondarily, to find out why the assailant stole the files in the first place." I waited.

He stared at me some more. "This morning, regretfully, I was rude on the phone to both you and your secretary. For that I am sorry." He cleared his throat once again—maybe a tic? He continued, "I was upset at the time because I had just been assigned the case by my boss, the chief of police. I have a desk that is overflowing with paperwork and, more to the point, unsolved, active cases, including a homicide. When the chief called me, I asked him the same question you just asked me. His response was decidedly unfriendly and uninformative." He paused, cleared his throat (definitely a habit), and said, "So I can't answer your question. Wish I could."

I relaxed. This guy was pretty much in the dark. I said, "Fascinating. Hey, how about you call me TB, most do." What the hell.

He gave me a blank look, thought about it, and smiled ever so slightly. "I can do that. People generally call me Joe. Let's do this again." He extended his hand. We shook.

We continued discussing the case, tacitly agreeing to share our respective investigations. His info set included forensics (and that added up to zero); witness reports, Ben, Doreen, and various secretaries that collectively added up to nothing; a copy of Melissa Archer's check-in log, which ostensibly showed nothing. Melissa's eyewitness description of the guy was almost the same as what she told me. His conclusion was that the culprit knew what he was doing. His plan, he shared, was to have Melissa come down to the station and go over his collection of mug shots. Of course, I knew that would be fruitless, but I couldn't very well tell him I knew that without giving away my spy buddies. I shared with him Ben's list of clients whose file folders were stolen, suggesting that it was likely a connection could be made. I felt duplicitous, of course, but I couldn't risk, again, Ernie's gang. We parted amicably, each assuring the other that we would stay in touch.

After he left the building, I immediately called Ben and filled him in. I asked him to forewarn Melissa, as well.

***

I walked out to Jewels's desk and asked her about Walter Hinds, the odd call. She repeated what she had already said earlier then added, "Maybe Lucy will have something additional, she knows the guy, apparently."

"Where is Lucy, by the way? I thought she would still be here."

"She went downstairs to the café to get us a couple of sandwiches. She'll be right back." She gave me one of her looks and asked, "Miss her, TB?"

I ignored her, and just then, as if on cue, Lucy walked in holding a bag. She saw me; I saw her. We smiled, and it was nice. Then Jewels smiled, saying, "Thanks, Lucy. I'm starving!"

Lucy responded, placing the bag on Jewels's desk, "Yes! Same here."

Jewels said, "How about you, TB? Are you starving?" She was intently focused on opening the bag, then she said, "Oh. There are three sandwiches. How about that. Two for you, Lucy?"

Lucy replied, "No. I thought Tom might have skipped lunch, so…"

I said, "Thanks, Luce. Good instincts. How about we go in my office, the three of us, and figure out what was going on with Mr. Hinds? More room in there." I scooped up the sandwiches, all still wrapped, and headed for my office. Lucy opened the door for me.

We sat. I distributed the sandwiches and three little bags of chips. Jewels said, "Coffee, anyone?" She stood. "I need some." Lucy and I nodded. Jewels stepped out.

Luce and I looked at each other, a long, mutual look. She reached across the desk and squeezed my hand.

I returned it then let go. Jewels came back in with three mugs, two in one hand. She put the double-handed mugs between Luce and me then set her cup down, grabbed her sandwich, and looked over the tuna fish at both of us, in turn.

"Okay," I said. "Go over the call, Luce. But first, who is this Walter Hinds guy?" I took a bite. Pastrami, yes!

Lucy put out her hand up to her mouth, finished chewing, and said, "He's one of Marco's old school chums. He's involved in marketing somehow, probably managing it. Not sure. But he and Marco are pretty close. He and his wife and kids show up at Tony's for dinners on a regular basis. At least that's the way it was before, you know..." She paused. "Probably still is that way. Marco doesn't really have any other friends like Walt."

"Okay. So go over the conversation, and as you do, let your mind open up and see if anything pops that you haven't thought of before."

"You mean use my active imagination?" She looked at me, with a soft smile.

"Exactly." I held her look for a moment.

She ran through the conversation, glancing occasionally at Jewels for agreement. Nothing popped until she reached the part where he said that all he knew was office gossip, nothing more. She stopped, tilted her head for a long moment, and said, "That's kinda odd. Walt is notorious for being impatient with idle gossip. He even says, famously, that gossip is airborne poison. It seems unlikely that anyone in an office that he oversees would

162

share gossip with him. Maybe it's meaningless, but that's all I can think of." She took a last bite of her sandwich.

Jewels said, "Sounds like duplicity to me, doesn't it?"

Lucy nodded. "And that is also out of character. I have always thought him to be a pretty honest person. Anyone can lie, but for him it would need to be for a very good reason."

I said, "Assuming he was lying, what does that do for us?"

Jewels made a face and said, "It tells us that the phone conversation was uncomfortable for him, and for more than just Lucy's obsession with the accident." She glanced at Lucy. "His perception, not mine. Right?"

"Right." Luce patted Jewels's hand, turned to me, and said, "Now what?"

I leaned back in my chair, swiveled a couple of times, and replied, "We follow up. Let's get some details about Mr. Hinds: his economic status, family life, work status, any extramarital interests, everything. The two of you can do a lot of that from this office. In the meantime, I will pursue the anonymous break-in assailant. I now have enough information about him to draw a profile of sorts. Who knows? Maybe with both of our digs, we can angle for the same buried treasure."

12

It was four o'clock and too late to go into Boston, but I could shoot down to Manchester, book a room near the Adamo complex, and plan the next step from there. But first, I needed to go home and check on Doc. Poor guy probably thought I had abandoned him.

Pulling into my drive, all appeared normal. I parked in front of my house and walked up to the front door. I unlocked the door, closed it, and reached to shut off the alarm, surprised to find it already shut off. I lifted the flap and discovered that it was dead, no power. I flipped the lights on but, again, nothing. Then I looked into the living area. It had been tossed—cushions, books, drawers, papers, and everything else strewn around, broken, trashed. Also, I just realized, no Doc to greet me. He could be outside on a hunt, but usually, he would hear the car and come back in the house, through his cat-sized doorway, and greet me. All this struck me at once. I stepped back out on the porch, reached up above the door, released the hidden panel, and extracted my Beretta. I stepped back inside and slowly started through the house. The kitchen area was clear. I opened the fridge, and it was still cold. I stepped over to a coat closet, leaned against the wall by its side, and in one motion, opened it, dropped to one knee, and peeked around the opening. Nothing. Slowly I stood, alert to any sound. Softly I walked down the little hallway between the kitchen and the utility room. Again, dropping to one knee and leading with the Beretta, I leaned into the room. Nothing. The room had a closed door that led into the garage. I stepped to the door, paused, listened. The bolt was recessed, so it was unlocked; it was always locked. The door was hinged to swing into the garage. I turned around, moved slowly back into the main living area, and started up the open stairway to the loft and the bedroom. I peeked above the landing, into the open loft area. Nothing. I stepped into the open area, walked softly to the bedroom's open door, knelt, and looked. Nothing. Turning, I went back downstairs, went to the front door, and crouching, walked around the perimeter of the house. The garage had two small windows, one on the far side and one in the rear. The far-side window was closest, so I peeked over. It was just light enough to see the interior. In a corner, nearest to the utility-room entrance door, behind a pile of cardboard boxes, was an unfamiliar shape. Something.

I dropped down to a squat, grabbed the Beretta in both hands. From his location, he was obviously expecting me to open either the utility door or the overhead garage door. Considering my options, I stood back up into a crouch and went to my car, retrieved the garage-door remote from the glove box, and headed back to the front door. The intruder knew I had to enter through one of the two doors, so either way, I would be in his line of fire. I quietly walked back to, and then into, the utility room. I knelt on one knee, took a deep breath, and clicked the remote garage-door opener. As soon as the door started rumbling upward, I dropped the remote and, holding the Beretta in my right hand, twisted the doorknob and rolled into the garage. I hit the concrete, heard a muted double shot (the sound of two rounds hitting concrete next to me), and followed with my own double. This was immediately followed by a flurry of motion in my target corner. Lying prone, I took in a man, bent over and still. The garage door was still ascending. It was the only sound. The door clicked into place. No sound. Slowly I stood. Beretta in both hands, I approached the corner. The garage was now fully alight. No movement from within the jumble of cardboard and the intruder. One of his arms, I couldn't tell which, was extended from the jumble. He wasn't moving. I stepped to the side somewhat and waited. Nothing. A box and its contents, an old kitchen clock, some pewter figurines, some towels, and other junk were obscuring his head and his shoulders. I kicked at the box. Still nothing. I waited. Reaching with my left hand, I pulled the box off him, revealing his head, shoulders, and most importantly, a Glock 19 with a silencer. With my right foot, I stretched for the Glock and kicked it aside, well out of his reach.

Kneeling, Beretta still pointed, I twisted him over. He flopped on his back, bloodstains soaking his shirt. Two holes, one on the upper-right chest, one below it, maybe four inches. I looked at his face. It was the guy. The same guy who broke into Ben's office. Checking his pulse, I was surprised to find that he was still alive. The floor around him was covered with blood, but he was alive. I stood, reached for my cell, and called 911.

***

Immediately after calling 911 and ordering an ambulance, I went back to my car and found Lieutenant Foster's card. I called him, told him what had happened. He said he would be out soonest.

I started back to the garage, and Doc came trotting up, rubbed against my ankles, and meowed plaintively. "Hey, Doc. Where have you been hiding, pal?" I picked him up, scratched his neck for a couple of minutes. I took him back in the house, but as soon as I entered, he yowled and jumped out of my arms, headed for the couch, burying himself under a throw pillow. Of course, his backside was sticking out, tail switching. I chuckled.

I left by the front door and went back to the garage. I could hear a siren, far off but getting closer. The guy hadn't moved. I leaned down, checking his pulse again. Slow but steady. Standing, I turned slowly, taking in the garage interior. Everything in place, except the corner with the guy. Guessing, but probably, I thought, he ducked in here when he heard me pull in the drive. Considering how he tossed the place, he must have been searching for something. Then again, it could have been just to scare me. Or, and maybe most likely, it was his intention to kill me, and the tossing was a cover so that it looked like a burglary gone wrong.

The ambulance siren was screeching up my driveway. I stepped out and waved them closer. The driver and his fellow EMT piled out and rushed to the garage. I pointed them to the guy. They began doing their thing.

I heard another siren, close. A civilian car pulled in, a portable red light attached to the driver-side roof pulsing. Lieutenant Foster stepped out, looked around, and walked toward me. "TB. What's going on here?"

"Joe. The EMTs just got here and are tending to the guy I was telling you about—the guy who broke in. Nothing else has been touched."

"What's his status?" He was tight, all business.

"Still breathing, but he caught two in the chest. One here, the other here." I touched my own chest area, showing him.

He walked into the garage, knelt next to the EMTs, looked the situation over, then stood back up. He carefully examined the garage, taking particular notice of the gouges in the concrete floor where the two slugs had hit. He walked back over to me and said, "I'll talk to them before they leave."

Two uniformed cops were walking hurriedly to us. The older cop of the two, stripes on his sleeve, addressed Joe. "What's the situation, sir?"

"Hi, Keller. I think we're in pretty good shape here, with the perp, but we should take a look at the residence. Why don't both of you go inside with Mr. Stone here, the resident, and examine the place and get his preliminary statement. I'll talk with him myself after this guy"—he pointed to the garage—"gets hauled to the hospital. Also, call the station, and arrange to have someone meet the ambulance at the hospital. I want someone there with him until I say otherwise. Okay?"

"Yes, sir, Lieutenant. Mr. Stone, we will follow you." I held Joe's eyes for a moment; he nodded.

I led the two cops toward my front door, but halfway there, the EMTs came out with the guy on a stretcher. Joe walked over to, and then with, them, getting an assessment of the guy's condition. He was satisfied with what they told him and came back to us where we were waiting.

"Change of plans. You two go to the hospital with the ambulance, one inside just to make sure all is okay. I don't want this bozo to be alone until he is under guard at the hospital. Okay?"

"Yes, sir." They hurried to the ambulance, the younger cop climbing in after one of the EMTs. The ambulance, siren screaming, ran down my drive. The police car followed, flashing lights blinking.

Joe said, "They have done what they can, and so far, he's holding on. Both slugs are still in him, so his survival is iffy. After the docs do their thing, we'll have a better idea."

We walked into my house. Joe shook his head. "The guy did quite a job here. Is anything missing?"

"Not that I know of. Unless he has something squirreled away in his clothes, I don't know what it would be."

Joe walked through the mess and motioned to the couch, looked at me, and raised his eyebrows for permission to sit.

"Oh, sure. Let me clean it off." I picked up a bunch of strewn books and a small ivory Buddha statuette, put them on a nearby table. I grabbed a cushion, Joe did the same, and we replaced them on the couch. We both sat.

Joe pulled out his small notebook, sighed, and looked at me, not unsympathetically. "You okay?"

"Yeah. I think so. It was a close call. It'll probably sink in later, but right now, I'm okay."

"Tell me about the shooting." He waited.

I gave him the detailed version, leaving nothing out, including the actual exchange of fire. He wrote, thought about it, then wrote some more. I asked him, "I could probably make us some coffee, if you want?"

"No, thanks anyway. That was pretty crafty, you know, running the garage door up and all?" Calm, patient face. Still a cop's face.

I shrugged and said, "I'm just glad it worked."

"Yeah, it did. Now tell me the rest of the story."

I looked at him, assessing, then said, "I'm not sure, but my guess is that he was here to take me out. The silencer is kind of a giveaway. Burglars generally aren't even armed, let alone with a silenced Glock 19."

"Exactly. And you, of course, have no idea who this guy is? Or why he might want you dead?" Now his expression was all cop, all suspicion.

I frowned, spread my hands, shook my head. "If the guy survives, maybe he will tell us."

Joe sighed again, ran a hand over his face, and looked down at his notebook. "Look, TB, I like you. You seem to be a straight-up kinda guy, but this is bullshit. That dude you shot was a pro, and you know it. The piece, silencer, two rapid-succession shots, and he damned sure wasn't a burglar. What aren't you telling me?"

"I really don't know why he wanted to kill me. Honestly. Again, I don't know who he is. But..." I paused, considering how *much* to tell him and maybe just *how* to tell it.

"But what?"

"The break-in at Ben Katz's office has something to do with this. I'm pretty sure the guy I shot is the same guy who broke in."

Joe cocked his head. "Yeah? And just how can you be sure?"

"Did you get a good look at the guy's left hand? The tattoo. That's how." I watched his face. Puzzlement.

"Didn't the receptionist tell you about the tattoo? At Ben's office building, when you were questioning people?"

"No. You tell me." Voice flat, angry flat.

"She saw the tattoo on his hand the day before the night he broke in. She saw it when he signed the register. I questioned her quite a while, if that's any consolation."

"Okay. Well, if it is the same guy, and I'm not so sure it is, lots of folks wear tattoos these days."

I explained, "It was an Oriental letter or maybe ideogram. A single tattooed mark usually represents something. Well, something other than pure decoration. Maybe a group? Organization of some kind? I don't know." I stopped and waited for his reaction.

He shook his head. "I'm beginning to understand why the chief put me on this case. Anything that's this screwed up always seems to find a home with me." He stood, stretched, and said, "Listen. I can't just ignore this connection, or at least this presumed connection, much as I would like to do just that!" He walked over to the window, gazing intently into his own head.

"Sure you don't want that coffee?" I smiled.

He turned around, grinned. "No, no. I need to go back in town and check out the status of your victim. And after that, I'll hopefully be able to get something other than coffee to drink."

I chuckled. "I hear that. Oh, and something both of us have been missing, what with all of the flurry."

"And that would be?"

"How did our guy get here? He didn't walk. At least not all the way from town. Might be worth exploring to see if we could find a car."

He thought about it, then he said, "That makes sense. Tell you what, I'll do some quick checks along the main roads as I travel back to Concord. You check the back roads around here—you know them better than I do. If either of us gets lucky, we call the other. If not, I can send some uniforms out to do a more thorough job. Sound good?"

"Yes, sir. I like it."

"And, TB, I don't want you to go anywhere I can't reach you. Understood?" He was serious.

"Absolutely, Lieutenant. Could you do me a favor?"

He made a face. "What's that, *Detective?*"

"When you get to the hospital, get a quick picture of that tattoo. Maybe I can find out what it is, what it signifies."

He nodded. "Good idea. And as soon as you find anything, let me know, yeah?"

"You got it."

***

As soon as Joe's car was out of sight, I called Ernie. Maybe he would have a better chance of locating the guy's car if I brought him up to speed. Plus, he should be informed about the shooting. When he answered, I gave him a brief but accurate summary of events. He asked about the consequences, for me, of the shooting and told him all was well as of now. I asked him about his search for the guy's car, but he had nothing new. His thinking was that the guy probably hid it somewhere or maybe drove it into a lake. He was something other than positive about finding it now, after so much tracking. I gave him all the info I had gotten from the Mass car rental agency so he could add it to the database: false name, address, etc. He thanked me; I thanked him. Hung up.

I went into the house, changed from shoes to hiking boots. I picked up and straightened some of the mess the anonymous guy had left me. I sat down for a minute to regroup. Doc jumped on my lap. I scratched him. It finally surfaced: I just shot someone. He might live, but probably not. It wasn't the first time, not that that helped. The feelings that welled up were ugly and bitter and overwhelming. Doc yowled and jumped down. I realized that my scratching had become less than gentle, and that made the ugliness even worse. I stood up, ran out the open front door, and vomited over the side of the porch. And then some more.

After a time, I went back inside, sat again, and Doc jumped up, having forgiven me.

**

I headed out the door to find the guy's car. There was a dirt road, more of a two-furrow path than a road, a half mile or so back in the woods. I started jogging then increased my pace to a moderate speed. I ran back here often, so I knew where all the logs and gullies were located. In less than ten minutes, I had reached the dirt road. I stopped, hands-on-hips breathing. Looking around, I walked up the road toward the highway a quarter mile or so. Nothing. Then I doubled back and started walking back. I reached my original starting point and continued on for another few yards and spotted a clump of leaves and brush just back from the road, behind a tree. It appeared irregular, unnatural. Wading through the brush and around the tree, I pulled some branches away from the clump. A tire, then a frame, then a motorcycle emerged. Cleaning the rest of the mess away, I lifted it. An old two-stroke bike, perfect for on- and off-road riding. Smiling to myself, I pushed it away from, then leaned it against, the tree. Who needs a car when a bike is more practical? Joe could send someone out to pick this up. Might yield something useful when his forensics team checked it out. I started back home.

Sitting on my couch once again, I called Joe, told him about the bike and how to find it. I asked him about the guy. He said the guy was recovering from surgery, but the docs thought he had a good chance of pulling through. He also said he had a pic of the tattoo and was about to send it right before I called. I thanked him, and we disconnected. A minute later, my phone beeped. I opened the text then the pic. It was Oriental, possibly Chinese. I didn't recognize it. I called Ernie on my "top-secret spy phone."

"Yes, TB."

"Ernie, you can call off searching for the car. Our guy was riding a bike, a motorcycle. It's hidden back in the woods behind my house. The Concord police are sending someone out to get it. If they find anything, I'll let you know. But I do have something you may be able to help with. The guy had a tattoo on the back of his left hand. It appears to be a Chinese symbol of some sort. How should I send it to you? Right now, it's on my personal cell."

Silence for a few seconds, then he said, "Okay. Send it to this number." He gave it to me. I sent it. I waited. "I just received it. Nothing I recognize, but I'll have it investigated and let you know. Anything else?"

"No. Well, my cop friend tells me the guy will likely recover. So we may have someone to interview."

"That's good news! Now you will be able to ply your trade, yes?" He seemed pleased.

"Let's see what happens with him first. Interrogation, at least the way I do it, requires a fully responsive subject, not a doped-up, half-dead guy in a hospital bed. So we shall see." I had mixed feelings suddenly.

13

I checked my phone. It was close to six. I was wrung
out, thirsty, hungry, and I sorely needed to reassess
everything that had happened in the last several
hours. I should just stay put, wait for any phone calls,
and relax. I stood, stretched, then noticed that my left
leg hurt. I rubbed the area around my knee where I had
hit the concrete before the short-lived gunfight. I don't
know how the hell he's still alive, but he is. That was
something. I walked to the fridge and grabbed a half-gal-
lon milk container and chugged what was left. Opened
the cupboard, pulled out some peanut butter and bread.
Made two sandwiches, one plain and one with dill-pickle
slices. Then I looked through my wine rack and found a
bottle of German Riesling, opened it, and poured a glass,
thinking that if any wine went with peanut butter, white
German wine was it. I went back to the couch, flopped
down, and tore into the food and drink.

Twenty minutes or so passed, and my personal cell
jangled. It was Lucy. "Hi, Luce."

"Hello yourself. How are you?" She sounded
concerned.

"I'm okay. It has been a busy afternoon."

"I heard. Julie is here with me, and she heard from someone, a friend from the hospital, that there was an incident at your place?" Now the concern had an edge to it.

"You could say that. Could you put me on speaker? So I can tell both of you what happened?" I heard the faint echo and told them the story, leaving nothing out. I finished by saying, "Listen, I'm sorry I didn't call either of you earlier, but it has only been half an hour or so since I returned from the woods. I'm just starting to recover from all of it, you know?" Nothing but quiet.

"TB, don't worry about us. Are you really okay?" Jewels had her mama-nurse voice working.

"I think so, Jewels. Don't worry about me. I'm doing a little R and R tonight, and I'll be rested and ready by tomorrow morning. How did you guys do, researching Mr. Walter Hinds?"

Now it was Lucy who answered, "We have quite a bit of information. More than either of us expected to find." She paused, then she said, "Tom, I..." The rustling sound of whispering and someone moving.

Then Jewels said, "Lucy just left for the ladies'. You are such a dumbass, TB." This with a soft voice. "Listen, the information we gathered can wait until tomorrow. How about you take some downtime, and we'll see you tomorrow. Lucy is staying with me tonight. Okay. See you then." She disconnected.

Once again, not surprisingly, I felt like shit. I knew why Luce was upset. I was not sure what else I could have done. I called as soon as I could. Probably should have talked with Luce when she first answered, but...

but nothing. That was what I should have done. If *I* had learned that *Luce* had almost been killed and then I found out about it over a speakerphone call…yeah, being called a dumbass gave me more credit than I deserved. But what did it really mean? How long had we known each other? Not long enough. *Tommy, you are deep into this thing, and you need to figure it out.* Why did that little voice in my head always sound like Ben? Yeah, I needed to figure this thing out. I poured another glass of the Riesling.

***

I just climbed out from my morning shower, and my spy phone jangled. I wiped my head and my face quickly. "Yeah, Ernie."

"TB. I have some good news, I think. The tattoo imprint is indeed Chinese. It roughly translates into 'loyalty,' though not exactly. The symbol has an odd addition that suggests something more, something private, possibly indicating 'loyalty oath' or even 'death pledge.' Whatever the case, it is unique. The letter or, more properly the symbol without the oddity is fairly common, but with the addition it becomes very personal. My source tells me that she has never seen anything quite like it before. So what do you think?"

"Interesting. Consider: the guy is a highly trained operative, seemingly of European descent, has no tangible record of his existence anywhere, and has an esoteric Chinese symbol tattooed on his left hand. Why would someone who has so been so carefully kept anonymous for thirty to forty years wear a Chinese tattoo in such a visible way? It doesn't make sense." I waited, suddenly suspicious that Ernie knew more than what he was divulging.

"Yes, I was wondering the same thing. So I asked that very question, not of my Oriental languages expert, but of a social psychologist. He didn't have a concrete answer, but he offered a couple of possibilities. First, the symbol might be an outward sign of membership in a cultish group. The visibility of the symbol isn't intended for the outside world but, rather, for other cult members. Something like gang tats, but less obvious. The tattoo is very small and could easily be kept discreetly hidden from anyone who shouldn't see it."

Okay. It's less likely Ernie isn't hiding anything from me, I thought. At least not yet. "And the second possibility?"

"Well, this one seems a bit less credible but in some ways more compelling. He suggested that maybe the guy just wanted something that was his own, a personal statement. If so, what an ironic symbol to use, though the psychologist thinks that might be exactly why he used it."

"How so?"

"Well, if he was conflicted about wanting to be his own man but still wanting to be loyal to his handlers, what better symbol to use?"

"I can see that. You are right, Ernie. I think this could be valuable information. Thanks." And I meant it. This was just the sort of knowledge that could give me some leverage during an interrogation.

"You got it, TB. What's next on your agenda? Any closer to ferreting out who's behind the probable tech breach?" He sounded anxious.

"Perhaps, but it will take some digging. When I get dried off and grab some coffee, I'll be going into my office. My secretary says she has dug up some interesting information on a key player within the Adamo corporate group. And before you panic, she knows nothing whatsoever about your piece of the investigation. As far as she or anyone else is concerned, I am only looking into Abe Adamo's death. Okay?"

"Panic? Ernesto Delgado, panic? Never."

"Uh-huh. A spook is a spook, and you guys are either smug and certain or freaked and panicking. Give me a break." I smiled to myself.

He made a derisive sound and said, "I think I have just been insulted. A fine *Cuban* lad like myself, sprung from a proud tradition, would have challenged you to a duel in years past, you know that."

"Right. Well, when this is all over, you and I will figure out some way for you to get satisfaction for this injury to your honor. I'm thinking batting cage at high noon." Now I was grinning.

"You are on. How did you know that baseball is my second love in life?"

"You are Cuban, right?"

"Proudly so. The batting cage it is, my friend."

***

I reached the office, parked my car, and sat for a few minutes, collecting my thoughts, and my thoughts were swirling. First, new information regarding both sides of the investigation; second, an interrogation looming, something I hadn't done officially for several years; and third, Luce. The first two just required some time and energy to untangle. Luce was another matter. How did I honestly feel about her? How did she feel about me? This wasn't tangled; it had never been untangled. I couldn't fix it or shelve it or, it seemed, ignore it. I could shoot some stranger in my garage without hesitation, but I had no idea what to do with Luce. Even framing the problem as a problem didn't feel right, because... I didn't know why. Damn!

I got out of the car, walked slowly to the side entrance, and opened the door. Each ascending step felt heavier than the last. I reached the landing. I opened the door, walked down the corridor to my office. I read the sign, Stone Investigations. Yeah, some investigator. I needed to have my head investigated. I opened the door. Jewels was sitting in her usual place. Luce was sitting in the side chair. When I stepped in, they both looked at me. Then they looked at each other. Then I looked at each of them in turn and said, "Hi." Simultaneously, Jewels stood up, and Luce looked down at her hands. I didn't move, still holding the door, mouth open, brain in neutral.

Jewels said, "Good morning, TB. Excuse me, but I have to powder my freaking nose." She was using her "Why do I put up with you?" voice. Then Luce and I were alone. I said softly, "Lucy? Are you okay?"

She sat still, looking at her hands. Then she looked up, eyes glistening. "Tom, I'm so sorry!" Corny as it sounded, she burst into tears.

I hurried to her, knelt, and putting my hands over hers, said, "Luce, sorry for what? Don't cry."

She said, with difficulty, "Because you were almost killed and it was my fault!" She continued crying. I suppose sobbing would be a better description.

"Because you hired me? Lucy, it's what I do. I don't like it, but it sure as hell is not your fault, so just get that out of your head. Okay?"

I reached up on Jewels's desk, retrieved a bunch of tissues, and pressed them in her hands. She took them, wiped her eyes and her nose, and said, "I'm sorry. I never act this way."

"Stop saying that, Luce." I laughed. "Frankly, getting shot at is a hell of a lot easier than seeing you cry!"

She looked at me, smiled, and said, "Julie is right—you can be an ass." We both laughed.

I stood; she stood. I turned around, started to walk over to the coffee maker, and heard her call my name. I turned, and she was in my arms. We held each other, and then, like the proverbial ton of bricks, it hit me. Yeah, it really hit me.

"Luce, I don't want you to be hurt because of me. I never want you to hurt. At all. Do you understand?" She pulled away from my shoulder, lifted her head, and nodded. We saw each other, both silently acknowledging what was happening. Then we kissed.

Reluctantly we both parted. Luce straightened her hair, and I got my coffee, and then, as if on cue, Jewels walked in. She glanced at me, glanced at Luce, and said, "Finally. Now can we get back to the investigation?"

***

We grabbed coffee and went into my office. Jewels laid a manila folder in the middle of my desk. I flipped it open. I said, "Before I scrutinize this, how about you two give me the summary version?"

They looked at each other. Lucy indicated with a sweep of her hand that she, Jewels, should start. Jewels nodded and began. "Mr. Hinds is married, as we already knew, but not happily. Talking to a couple of acquaintances, Lucy found out that Hinds's wife, Jennifer, moved into her own apartment a few months ago. Rumor has it that old Walt has had a girlfriend on the side for at least a year, maybe more. So there's that. Tangential to their separation, Jennifer has racked up some serious debt in the last year or so—tens of thousands of dollars. I'll explain how we found that out in a minute. Also, Jennifer now has a boyfriend of her own, or that's what Lucy's acquaintances believe. No one has seen him in person, so who knows." Jewels turned to Lucy.

Luce cleared her throat and said, "This next part is a little strange, and it may be meaningless, but you said to get everything, so..." She looked up. "Hinds has made some moderate investments recently, well, within the last few months—the details are in your folder. He has had a portfolio for years, nothing uncommon there, but these more recent investments are in companies whose home is found in China. That's the new part. Compared to the rest of his investments, mostly blue-chip companies, some safe bonds, and such, these Chinese companies are not that well-known. They all seem to be tech companies, not certain exactly what kind of technologies, but definitely unlike anything else in his portfolio."

They looked at each other. They looked at me, and Jewels said, "That's it. What do you think?"

I thought about it. It all seemed to be coming together, especially Ernie's part, which was why I was thinking about it. What do I disclose to the ladies? What made all the pieces fit into the puzzle was the part I couldn't disclose, at least not now. "Well, for the sake of argument, let's assume that Walter Hinds is dirty somehow. We know he has personal issues, and we know he has been accumulating debt through his estranged wife's excesses. We also know that he has been purchasing stock in companies that may or may not be involved with Adfam Tech. So if a dirty Walter Hinds needs money and he is willing to bend the rules to get it, might he not offer his services to some folks interested in paying for tech that he could supply?" I shrugged.

Lucy considered it, then she said, "Hard to believe Walt would do that. But even if he did, why would that have anything to do with Abe?" Jewels and I shared a knowing glance.

I said, "One possible connection? What if somehow Abe found out? If Hinds was dirty and Abe was onto him, maybe Hinds shut him up." I waited for Lucy to respond.

She shook her head, then she said, "I can't believe that. For a couple of reasons. First, if Abe suspected that Walt was peddling proprietary tech, whatever the reason, he would go directly to his brother Marco and let him deal with it. And second, maybe, just maybe, Walt could steal from the company, but murder someone? No. Never." Face set, certain.

"All of this is conjecture, and we don't have proof of anything, but the trail seems to be leading to Walter Hinds. For whatever reason. Agreed?" I waited.

Lucy thought about it, patted her hair, and said, "Yes. Agreed."

I looked at Jewels. She nodded.

"Okay then. We need to push Mr. Hinds and see what happens."

Jewels went back to her desk. Luce and I smiled at each other. We both knew that something was happening between us, and even though unspoken, we were both eager to explore the new landscape. Unfortunately, we had work to do, plans to make.

This was Friday morning, and as with all Fridays, most working folk anticipated the weekend and thought about what they might or might not do. Catching up on those never-ending home chores or day trips with the family, always something to do. It seemed likely that Walter Hinds would be no different. This was a perfect time to observe him, from a distance, and figure out what he was up to, if anything.

"Luce, would you feel comfortable joining me in pursuit of the uncomfortable?"

Eyes twinkling, she responded, "Uncomfortable can be fun sometimes. It depends."

"So true. But in this instance, what I have in mind is gathering information from Mr. Walter Hinds, by up-close-and-personal observation. It may not be comfortable doing so."

She made a face and said, "The short answer is yes, but only if we can defer the first instance for another time."

"As you wish. Who am I to argue with the charms of a truly beautiful lady?" Corny but sincere.

She cleared her throat softly. "Okay, then. So what do we have to do?"

"If we take off now, we can be in Manchester at or near his office. I assume you know where that is?"

"Of course. We can be there, traffic permitting, in less than an hour." She stood, then she said, "Come on. Let's go. We can be set up before lunchtime. I assume we want to be in a good spot to keep an eye on the building?"

"Yes, ma'am!" I gathered up the papers from their inquiries, stuffed them in the folder, and we left my office.

I explained to Jewels what we were doing, asked if we could swap cars for the day, and she nodded and grinned like a kid at Christmas. She, of course, knew that my Spider was way too conspicuous for a stakeout, and this wasn't the first time we'd swapped. I made a face and told her to be good. She grinned even more, and we exchanged keys. Luce and I were off.

14

T raffic was fine. In forty-five minutes, we were scouting out a vantage point from which the main entrance to Adamo Corporate could be easily, but discreetly, observed. The building was one of several within the Adamo chain of buildings. Apparently, the family owned the entire property, though some of the buildings around the outskirts appeared to be dedicated to NH State and/or Manchester City interests. Clearly, Adamo interests and both local and state government interests were entwined. A sobering thought. The same kind of sobering thought that might cross your mind before swatting a large wasp's nest on your porch. Well, except that wasp stings were rarely lethal.

We circled for a couple of minutes, and Luce pointed to a row of cars with nameplates, on decorative stone posts, in front of each. She said, "See that dark-blue Mercedes? Three cars from the right? That one is Walt's."

Although we were now several rows of cars behind "executive row," our vantage point was perfect. I pulled into a space that was partially hidden by a clump of bushes but still, by judicious maneuvering, allowed an easy, unobstructed view. Jewels's sedan was a pretty good vehicle for anonymous observance, particularly when far away with some cover. I turned off the engine. It was exactly 11:10 a.m.

We waited. We talked. I had binoculars so I could scan the entrance easily. Luce had described Walt for me, but so far, there was nothing. At 11:55 a.m., people started exiting, one and two at a time. At 12:20 p.m., he emerged. Standing alone on the steps, hands on hips, he looked around. Then he walked to his car and slowly backed it out. I gave him a minute, noting which way he turned, then began the tail. We followed him to a small restaurant a couple of miles away, located on a quiet side street. I pulled off to the side, across the street from the restaurant. He drove around the front of the building and disappeared. In a couple of minutes, he walked back into sight, accompanied by an attractive thirtyish blond woman. They entered the front door.

Luce said, "A blond cliché. How appropriate."

"At least we know your rumor source is reliable. That's good. Listen, I'm going to go find his car and put this"—I held up a small tracker—"on his car. I'll show you how it works when I return. Hold the fort." Frowning, she nodded.

I walked across the street, angling away from the front door just in case they had a view. Coming up from the side, I spotted his Mercedes parked in a space next to a bright-blue SUV, probably his girlfriend's. I leaned down and attached the magnetic tracker under the driver-side rear wheel well. Then, extracting my notepad, I copied his plate number and then hers. I walked back to our car.

"All okay?"

"Oh sure. Let me show you how it works." I pulled my cell out, swiped it into life, and tapped an icon. It took a few seconds to activate, then a gridded map popped up with a small red dot blinking in the center of the map. Luce, leaning close, watched. "When he leaves, the map will automatically plot his course. It operates from a satellite mapping feed recording the real-time journey and then storing it in the cloud. Wherever my cell is, I can know where he is relative to my location. It provides distance between the two points, as well as geolocation. Now watch." I tapped the screen, and the image enlarged 25 percent. Tap, and another 25 percent. "Slick, huh?"

"Very. A little Big Brotherish, but useful, I suppose. Where do you get something like this?"

"The tech has been around for some time, essentially the same as the GPS you have in your car, but this particular application was developed by the military a while back."

"But where did you get it?"

I squinted at her then said, "From a friend I served with in my military days."

She smiled softly. "Someday you will have to tell me about your military career."

"It's a long story, but yes. Someday."

"Are you aware that almost everything you say to me is cautious and generally deflective? Deflective of what I don't know. Maybe you can explain that to me someday. Maybe even on the *same* day." She had her innocent-big-eyes face on, and how could I possibly resist?

I opened my mouth to respond, and she said, "No. Don't say anything right now, just think about it. When you are ready, let me know." She smiled and looked back at the restaurant entrance. "Hey! There they are."

I looked. "Sure enough." They walked around the building, his arm around her waist. We waited. Her car emerged into view, then his. She waved at him in her mirror and pulled out. He followed her until the street then went in the opposite direction, presumably back to Adamo Corp. When he was out of sight, we left. I handed my phone to Luce so she could keep her eye on the little red dot.

"He's turning left two streets up. Obviously, he's not going directly back to his office."

"Interesting. Let's see where Mr. Hinds is going on this beautiful Friday afternoon."

I turned at the correct side street, in a mixed residential/apartment house area. It wasn't exactly an upscale neighborhood, not the sort of neighborhood where a Mercedes boat like his would go unnoticed. He was still out of sight, but we maintained our distance.

"He's turned again, this time to the right. Keep driving. Okay. Make the next right turn." I slowed, but there was no street as such. The turn appeared to be a drive into a small apartment complex of sorts. Two rows of two-story apartments buildings, one row on each side of the drive, maybe twelve buildings per row. The buildings were basic, unadorned, each painted in a different faded color. I drove slowly, looking for the Mercedes. Luce said, "There!" She pointed. The car was one of many cars scattered throughout the complex, some parked on the drive, hugging the low curbs; some halfway up on the broken sidewalk; and some, like the conspicuous blue Mercedes, parked in a parking lot at the end of the drive, a sort of functional cul-de-sac. I pulled over to the right, tucking behind a tired old Jeep. The Mercedes was empty. Apparently, our executive was visiting someone in one of two apartment buildings abutting the parking lot. Probably the house on the left since his car was parked closest to that one. The building was labeled 1021 Lyme St.

I smiled at Luce. "We wait some more. Too bad we didn't have time to stock up on snacks."

She smiled back. "Water would be nice. Maybe some fruit."

"Ah. Not really a chips fan? Doughnuts even?"

She made a face. "Italian pastries, perhaps. Holidays, special occasions. Doughnuts? No."

I chuckled, reached for my phone, and dialed the office. Jewels answered. I asked her to check for all the names in the apartment house address and to call when she had the list. I knew she would probably have the info before we left the complex. Jewels was that efficient.

Luce was checking out the area with my binoculars. I asked, "Anything?"

"Not really. I thought maybe I could see in the windows, you know. Might get lucky and see Walt. Too much reflection from this angle." She started to hand them to me but stopped. "Wait. Look at the entrance."

I took the binoculars and focused on the entrance. The door was half-open; someone started to come out but hesitated. Then Walt walked out with another man in tow. Walt's friend was maybe thirty, slim, dressed in jeans and a brown polo shirt. He was Asian, maybe

Chinese. They walked to the Mercedes and stood beside it, talking.

"That's interesting," said Luce, "I know that guy. He was an acquaintance of Abe's. I met him at a gathering, a party of sorts, a year or so ago. It was a business celebration. I can't recall his name, but he had purchased a property here in Manchester for some sort of manufacturing start-up. Marco was also involved, so I'm guessing it was some kind of computer operation. Just a guess."

"Luce, you are my hero! This lead is starting to pay off." I leaned over and gave her a quick kiss on the cheek.

She grinned. "I like being a hero. If I put on a cape, what else might you do?"

The two of them chatted, well, more like a mild argument, but after a few minutes, Walt got in his car and drove away. His friend watched him go, then when Walt was out of sight, he pulled a cell out of his pocket, listened for a moment, then said a few words, tapped the screen, and put it away. He walked back to the apartment house.

"What now?" Luce asked. "Do we follow Walt or stay here?"

I considered our options for a few seconds, and my phone rang. It was Jewels. "Hey, Jewels. Got the information? I'm putting you on speaker."

"Yes. Hi, Lucy! There are twelve apartments at that address, six up and six down. One is empty, eleven occupied. They are numbered 1A–6A, lower level, and 1B–6B upstairs. I am texting you the names and corresponding apartments now."

"Okay. Got it, Jewels. Give me a second to check it out." I did. In 3A, the name was John Lu. All other names were either female, couples, Hispanic, or decidedly Anglo. "Jewels, I think we have what we need. Do me a favor, and run info for the occupant in 3A. Get everything you can but discreetly. Okay?"

"Got it. I'll text you. Be careful, you two."

Luce and I both said goodbye.

"Okay, Luce, let's see where Walt is by now." We opened the app, and it appeared that he was heading back to work. "All right. Hard worker is our Mr. Hinds. We'll keep the app open and track him just to make sure. Let's see…it's two thirty-five now, so…"

"Tom! Look." She pointed to the parking lot, where a familiar bright-blue SUV was pulling into a slot. Sure enough, Walt's girlfriend got out. How curious was that? She looked around, quickly surveilling the area, and then walked to the entrance of John Lu's apartment house. Luce and I looked at each other.

I said, "Now that's unexpected. I wonder what those two have in common, well, other than Walt."

"My guess is that whatever it is, Walt is unaware of it. She shows up ten minutes after Lu makes a phone call, and that call came immediately after Walt left."

"I think we need to investigate this busy lady, yes?"

"No doubt. Where do we start?"

"Well…" I reached for my cell, tapped the appropriate app, and another screen popped up with the familiar red dot flashing rhythmically, only this dot indicated the parking lot directly in front of us.

"Aren't you sneaky. You tagged her car, as well."

"Yes, I am, and so I did. I also have her license-plate number. A New Hampshire plate, so a quick call…" I dialed up Bob's cell number. "Hey, Bob, it's me again."

"I don't hear from you in months, and now, twice in a week? What's up?"

"I need another license-plate run, if you can."

"Same case, I assume. Shoot." I gave him the number. "Give me a couple minutes."

I put the cell on mute and told Luce who it was. She nodded and pointed to the entrance where our lady friend was exiting with Mr. Lu. They both got in her car.

"TB, the name is Gloria Simpson, 132 Biscayne Drive, apartment 222, Manchester."

"Thanks, Bob. I have to go right now. I'll catch up with you soon."

"You gonna make that ball game tomorrow?"

"Ah. That's right." I looked over at Luce. "Could I bring a friend?"

"A friend? Sure. A lady friend, perhaps?"

"I'll meet you at your house. Gotta go, Bob. Thanks again!"

While I was talking with Bob, Gloria and John had pulled out of the apartment complex. After they drove out of sight, I followed. Luce, monitoring the location app, guided me as we followed. We made several turns, drove all the way across town and then past the city limits, into a large industrial park. The SUV had stopped somewhere in the park, but the map only showed the main drive and a couple of larger cross streets. We drove slowly. The way the app worked, the closer we got to the red dot, the smaller the map, so we could eventually find the location by process of elimination. But then again, with two sets of eyes, it was easier to just look for it.

We drove around the main circuit, with no luck, then we started on the side streets, extending from the main oval-like spokes in a bicycle wheel. On our third street, we found the vehicle parked in front of a building at the end of the street on the left. It was new construction, though obviously operating in some fashion, judging from the company sign, reading Cutting Edge Tech Inc., and the open, active loading dock. A single-story building was fronted by a small parking lot holding a dozen or so cars, then a sidewalk running perpendicular to the building, running up to the main entrance. Along the sidewalk, on either side, was additional parking. Although there were six angled parking slots on either side, only four slots were being used. One of them held our SUV.

We continued to a widened turnaround at the end of the street, circled, and then drove back down the street. I took a left and another left and drove down the street next to our friend's. I parked on a wide spot, so our car angled in such a way that we had an unobstructed view of the Cutting Edge Tech facility. The physical distance was approximately 150 yards, so with binoculars, we could observe everything. Plus, not unintentionally, I positioned the car so we had some shade from a nearby set of trees.

"This must be the start-up company I told you about. I wonder what they do."

"Yeah, it's obviously new. I don't know what they do, but they must be manufacturing something. Look at the shipping dock over there. Very busy. Let's see if we can find out what they are making in this place." I called the office. "Jewels. I have some more research for you. A new company, Cutting Edge Tech Inc., located in an industrial park just outside of town, north side. Find out everything you can. Maybe even call Ben. Thanks. Let me know."

"All right. Let's see… It's almost four o'clock, so we'll give our friends in there until five o'clock, maybe a little after, to emerge. One way or the other, we will be leaving at five o'clock. Okay?"

"Okay with me. What will we learn by remaining here? If she leaves, will we follow her?"

I stretched. My shoulders were tight, and my stomach was growling. "What will we learn? Maybe nothing, maybe something. Hard to say. And if she leaves, we can see where she ends up by following her. If we hadn't followed her here, we wouldn't have known about this place, so again, who knows? Make sense?"

"Yes, it does. I'm just starting to feel the weariness of the last few days catch up. Also, I could use some coffee." She smiled tiredly.

I reached over, ran the back of my hand over her arm, and said, "Same here. Another hour, and we can relax for a time."

"Whoops! Looks like she's coming out." Luce was pointing to the entrance. She handed the binoculars to me.

Sure enough, Gloria was walking to her car. She got in, backed out, and headed toward the park entrance. We waited, then I followed at a distance.

"Interesting that Lu remained. We shall see where Gloria goes at least, and then when we have more info on Cutting Edge, we can decide what to do with Mr. Lu."

We followed Gloria, weaving through back streets, until she reached a tidy-looking small single-story house in an eastside suburb. The yard was nicely landscaped, as were all the yards in the subdivision. Although the houses weren't showy, they all appeared quietly expensive. Unfortunately, there was really no place to unobtrusively surveil. I drove past the house, took the first right, and drove back out of the neighborhood.

"We're not watching her?"

"No, I don't really see any point right now. We don't have a good place to park without being obvious, and that's not what we want to do right now. Sometimes it makes sense to surveil in the open, you know, to see what can be stirred up. But not here, not now."

"I see. Better to be circumspect, yes?" Eyes twinkling, Luce patted me on my leg.

"Yup. Instead, let's order some food and go to my place. I'll introduce you to Doc, my faithful companion."

"Yes. Your cat." Again the twinkling eyes.

I cocked my head and glanced over at her questioningly.

"Julie told me about Doc. She called him your *familiar*. Intriguing description, to say the least."

"Jewels has quite the imagination. Doc is his own person, not an extension of my shadow side or any other part of me. He is a friend, though." I was smiling but also realizing that telling Luce this sort of thing was surprisingly easy, comfortable.

"Interesting." She looked out her side window and said, "So what kind of food do you want?"

"Whatever. You choose."

"Chinese? Is that okay?"

"Absolutely. Here." I handed her my phone. "Look for Chinese Gardens, and use my name. We can pick it up on the way. It's on the north side. We should be there by…six o'clock."

She called, ordered a mixed platter with extra egg rolls to go. When she mentioned my name, after a pause, she chuckled. Then told them we would pick up around six o'clock.

"What was the little laugh about?"

She chuckled again. "Mr. Yuan." She raised her eyebrows, looking for confirmation. I nodded. "He said that I should tell you, Mr. Stone, that he was happy I called for you and that he would include his TB special with no charge." She giggled. Yes, giggled.

I shook my head, chuckling. "The first meal I ever had in my house, several years ago, was takeout from Yuan's restaurant. Bachelor that I am, I would probably have starved without Yuan's food. Actually, he has a home only a few miles from mine. We have become friends over the years. You haven't lived until you've eaten barbecued Chinese food!"

"What's the TB special?"

"You will find out soon enough. Patience, grasshopper."

We pulled up in front the Chinese Gardens at 5:50 p.m., having made pretty good time. The parking lot was packed, as usual, on a Friday evening. I opened my door, then I turned to Luce. "Coming in or no?"

"Try to stop me. I know your secretary, of course, and I feel like I even know Ben and Doreen, even though we have never met, but to meet a friend who has nothing to do with work? How could I possibly not meet Yuan?" Her expression was, dare I say, inscrutable. I was beginning to think Lucia Nardone had an infinite number of facial expressions, all intriguing and most charming. What was I getting myself into?

"Okay. Let's go then."

We walked into the restaurant. It was noisy, lots of children, laughter, chatter. The takeout counter was close to the front, with a short line of people queued up. One of Yuan's daughters, Emily, was ringing up the orders. She was home from college for the summer and, thank you, Lord, though going into her senior year, hadn't acquired the condescending attitude that seemed to infect many of her generation of kids. We waited in line.

I heard Yuan's voice calling my name from behind. I turned, and Yuan was a few paces behind us, smiling his smile, arms extended. He reached me, grasped my right hand in both his, and said, "TB! Good to see you!"

I smiled, then I said, "Yu, how goes it?"

He nodded, looked around the dining area, and said, "Not bad tonight. And Emily is back working the counter, so all is good." He caught Emily's eye, and he and Emily smiled at each other. Then he looked at Lucy, assessing her in his own way, gave her a quick bow, and said, "Introduce us, TB. Where are your manners?"

I introduced them. Yu reached out and, again with both hands, held her extended right hand formally yet gently and said, "I am very pleased to meet you, Ms. Nardone."

"And I you, Mr. Yuan. TB speaks highly of you." She gave him that smile, full force.

"Ah. TB is being extravagant then, but despite that, he is a good man." He gave her another bow, which for Yu was unusual.

I said, "Okay, now that you two have met, where's our food, Yu?"

Yu pretended not to hear, leaned in close to Lucy, and said softly, "Your order is ready, Ms. Nardone, and please forgive TB's lack of proper manners. It's one of his many flaws."

He looked at me, waved his hand dismissively, and turned motioning toward the kitchen area, where his youngest son, Sylvester, was waiting. His son stepped out of sight then almost immediately came back out carrying two large plastic bags. He walked over to us, handed me the bags, and said, "Hello, Mr. Stone."

"Hello, Sly. Thank you. How are you tonight?" Sly was in his early teens. A good kid who tended to Doc when I was gone for any length of time.

"I'm okay. Pop keeps me hustling, but that's okay." He looked over at his father, who smiled softly at his youngest.

"Sly, this is my friend Lucia."

Lucy took a step closer, smiled, and said, "Hello, Sly. May I call you Sly?"

"Yes, ma'am. Everyone does." He shook hands with Lucy politely, saying, "Very nice to meet you."

I said, "What do I owe you?" I looked at Sly then back at Yu.

Sly glanced at his father then said quietly, "Pop told me to put it on your tab. Enjoy it." He grinned.

I knew enough not to question it, but I nodded and thanked him. Then I said, "And thank your father for me, please." Sly looked over at his father, made a quick nod, and turned back, walking back to the kitchen.

Yu said, "It was very nice meeting you, Ms. Nardone. I hope you enjoy your meal. Well, maybe not the TB special, but the rest of it."

"Mr. Yuan, first, please call me Lucy. And second, what exactly is the TB special?"

"Well, Lucy, I think I'll let TB explain the special to you. After all these years, I still can't understand it." He chuckled.

We said our goodbyes, and Luce and I made our way back to the car.

We pulled into my drive. Instead of parking in the garage, I positioned the car as close to my front door as possible. I stopped, shut it down, and sat in the dark for a moment, remembering the previous day. I felt Luce squeeze my hand. I turned. Her face was very close, and she had a sweet, flowery smell. She kissed me on the cheek, then my chin, then my mouth. And suddenly I forgot everything but her, and that was exactly as it should be.

15

The next morning, after waking up together and realizing that we were still capable of loving each other but quietly and comfortably, giving more than taking, and the morning somehow agreed with us, we were at peace. Then Doc jumped on the bed, letting us know that despite our moment, he was still the most important member of the household. We laughed; he didn't. I climbed out and followed Doc to the kitchen, where I fed him. Then I took a quick shower, put on some old jeans, and a faded Phillies tee.

While Luce was showering, I threw together some breakfast, most of it from leftover Chinese. I found some green peppers in the fridge and one tomato that was almost not too ripe. Anyway, I blended my aged veggies with Yuan's in a large frying pan, and well, it smelled pretty good. A little black pepper, a hint of salt.

Luce came up behind me, put her arms around my waist, and said, "Smells good. You seem to know what you are doing…"

"Hah! This is leftover, and mine is but to warm it up. If it turns out to be palatable, we can thank Yuan. If you want to contribute to this, why don't you make us some toast to go with. The bread is over there"—I pointed to the old-fashioned bread box—"and there should be some butter in the fridge."

She kissed me on the neck. "Yes, sir. I can do that." And she did.

The food turned out to be pretty good. As we ate, unselfconsciously watching each other, making silly small talk, she asked, "So last night, after...you know."

"Yes, ma'am, I know." I grinned.

She smiled, looking down then up. "Well, I had forgotten all about asking an important question." She invented another face, something between tease and curious, with a hint of coquette.

"Maybe by that time it was a little late to ask your question."

"No, not that question, whatever *that* might be. No, my question is, which of those dishes was the TB Special?"

"Ah." I got up, walked to the fridge, retrieved a half-full container, and put it on the table, in front of her.

She looked at it, sniffed, and said, "Egg Foo Young? What's so special about it?"

"It's cold now, so the true, flavorful essence will be somewhat reduced, but give it a taste."

She did, thoughtfully chewing. "Hmm. It is different. I taste pork, of course, and soy, peppers, and something else. The texture is unusual. What is it?"

"At the risk of spoiling the aha moment, the TB Special is pork Egg Foo Young with apple slices and white grapes. Not all that special." I said the last mock apologetically.

She returned a blank look then giggled. "So what's all the fuss? Yuan made it sound like it was going to be a taste-bud tragedy."

"Yuan is a purist. When I was a little kid, the only way I would eat eggs was with apples and/or grapes cooked in. My mom always made a fuss about how good it was. It became a habit, and I still prefer eggs with…"

"Apples and grapes. The TB special." She shook her head. "Well, you haven't tried one of my Italian omelets. You will forget all about apples and grapes." This time a smug face.

"Maybe. But how can I possibly convince Yuan to make my egg foo young with garlic and zucchini?" She made a face.

"Luce. It's Saturday morning. How would you like to take in a ball game this afternoon?"

"A ball game? Baseball?"

"Yeah. A friend of mine, Bob, has a fifteen-year-old son, Eddie, who is playing today. I promised that I'd attend the game. Up for it?"

"Sure. But I have to get back home to change, you know."

"No problem. We can meet Jewels, swap cars, then head up to your place. Plenty of time."

***

On the way back down from Luce's, I called Jewels. She gave me as much information as she could find on John Lu and Cutting-Edge Tech. Records indicated that the company was registered three years prior but opened operations only ten months ago. It was listed as a wholly owned subsidiary of a company located in Silicon Valley, whose origins were a little fuzzy, with a long list of owners going back to the early '80s. John Lu, even more mysterious, was officially labeled a private consultant currently working for Cutting Edge Tech. Interesting.

I asked her to do research on Gloria Simpson and, if possible, have something for me when I got into town to swap cars. She asked, sweetly for her, if I would consider letting her hang on to my Spider over the weekend. I thought about it, considering the relative anonymity of Jewels's vehicle, and agreed. So I told her where Lucy and I would be in the afternoon, just in case we were needed. To her credit, Jewels didn't make any snarky comments about that. I really did need to consider giving her a raise.

Then, to be safe, I called Joe Foster's cell. It rang a few times, then Joe answered, "TB. What's up?"

"Hey, Joe. Just following up. Anything new?"

"Not really. We still don't know who the guy in the hospital is. We even ran his face through our contacts at Interpol, but nothing. How about you?"

"Maybe. I tailed a couple people who might be tangled up with the break-in, but nothing definitive yet. As soon as I get more, I'll let you know."

"That's good. As *soon* as. I'm getting pressure from above, especially concerning Mr. No Name in the hospital. You know, the guy you shot twice?" He sounded impatient and irritated, then he said, "They want to know why I didn't pull you in at least for questioning. I told them why, but bureaucrats can't be bothered with a cop's reasoning. But that's my problem, at least for now."

I smiled to myself. "I appreciate what you are doing, Joe."

"Yeah, well, how about you give me something concrete to work with and appreciate me after we figure this mess out?"

"You got it, my friend. Keep in touch. Oh, and if anything changes with our pal in the hospital, let me know. Okay?"

"You will be the first." He disconnected.

16

We left Luce's place around ten thirty. As we got into Jewels's car, I thought it was a shame I didn't have my Spider, after all. Luce was dressed for a summer's day and a convertible. She was wearing white shorts, a light-yellow blouse, with a darker-yellow tie thing holding her hair up. Fashionable sunglasses on top, tan deck shoes on the bottom, and some tasteful jewelry in between, she was a tanned vision. She scooted over close and scratched my leg with those manicured nails and said, in a throaty voice, "Let's go to a ball game."

I inhaled sharply. "Yes, ma'am. Whatever you want." I put the understated sedan into gear, and I took her out to the ball game.

It was around eleven thirty when we knocked on Bob's door. Eddie answered the door, with a big grin, took one teenage-boy sort of look at Lucy, and the grin faded. He just stood in place, mute. I waved my hand in front of his face, mockingly, and said, "Eddie! May I introduce you to my friend Lucia Nardone?"

Eddie woke up, and the grin returned. Lucy extended her hand. "Hi, Eddie. Just call me Lucy. Nice to meet you."

"Hi, Ms. Nardone, I mean, Lucy." Then he stood for a moment, happy to be introduced, and then noticed me. He said, "Hey, TB. Come in, come in." And we entered the Cantrell residence.

Bob came striding into the room, smiling. "TB! Hey, man, glad you could make it. And you did bring your friend. Excellent!" He turned to Lucy, held out his hand. "Bob Cantrell."

Lucy took his hand. "Hi, Bob. Nice to meet you."

"Come in here, the kitchen, you two. Shirley's in the middle of fixing lunch. You guys haven't eaten yet, I hope?"

I said, "No. Not since breakfast."

Luce discreetly elbowed me. I looked at her frowning, raised my eyebrows, and mouthed, "What?"

She mouthed back, "Breakfast?" And I got it. Shrugged and grinned. She elbowed me again but harder.

In the kitchen, Shirley was setting the table. She looked up, smiled, and said, "Hi, TB." Then she walked around the table and extended her hand to Lucy. "Hello. Shirley Cantrell. Welcome to our home, miss?"

"Lucia Nardone. Lucy, please." They shook hands warmly.

"Please, won't you sit down? It's only some sandwiches, but Eddie doesn't like to eat anything heavy before a game, so I try to make it simple."

Lucy said, "Sandwiches sound good to me. And this salad"—she pointed to a large salad bowl in the middle of the table, filled with several kinds of green, cucumbers, tomatoes, bits of cheese, and other things I didn't quite recognize—"is incredible!"

Shirley smiled. "I'm a salad person, actually. So many different ways to make them."

"Oh, I agree!" And the two of them were off discussing all the ways.

We all sat. Bob looked over to Eddie, nodded, and Eddie made the sign of the cross, and we prayed. It was nice. Luce reached over and squeezed my hand.

The food was great. As we were preparing our sandwiches—a variety of cold cuts, sliced roast beef, cheese, fresh tomatoes, and some sort of wrinkly dark-green lettuce—I asked Shirley where Gillian, their eleven-year-old daughter, was today. She said Gill was staying over with a friend. We chatted for a time about the kids, and then Shirley asked Lucy how the two of us had met.

Lucy gave me a glance then said, "I went to see Tom for business reasons, to get his help, and one thing just led to another. Actually, we are still getting to know each other." She smiled, looking at me.

Bob said, "Funny. That's how we got to know TB also. What's it been now, four years?" He looked to his wife for confirmation.

She nodded. "About that, Gill was six and Eddie almost eleven, so maybe closer to five years. TB really helped us out, and here we are. We all just hit it off. I was teaching back then, and my mother was staying with us, watching the kids when we weren't home." She looked at Eddie fondly. Ed was oblivious, lost in his roast-beef sandwich.

She caught Lucy's eyes, gave her a conspiratorial smile, and then said, "So how much time do we have, Bobby?"

Bob checked the wall clock. "We should leave in fifteen minutes or so. Ed needs to warm up. He's pitching today."

Eddie's attention suddenly focused. "Yeah, Dad, the game starts at one thirty, and I need at least forty-five minutes to get ready. You know."

Shirley said, "I have an idea. How about you three men leave for the school right away, take TBs car, and then Lucy and I can meet you there around one fifteen or so? That way, you three can talk baseball unimpeded." She looked at Bob then me.

Bob said, "Works for me. TB, Eddie?" We both nodded. I looked over at Luce.

Luce smiled. "Yes. I can help Shirley with all of this"—she lifted her hands, taking in the table—"and we can talk about salads, not baseball, necessarily."

I squinted at her, then I said, "Okay." I checked my watch. "We should go then?"

Bob and Eddie simultaneously pulled their chairs back. I gave Luce a peck on the cheek and pulled my chair back. Eddie dressed in his uniform, grabbed his gear, and we left.

***

When we arrived at the ballfield, Eddie took off, loping over to a cluster of kids scattered around the field, warming up. Bob and I walked over to the bleachers, finding a nice spot about halfway up. Bob said, "From here we can also watch Eddie warm up. I'm his father, but I'm telling you, the kid can pitch. He's fifteen and will continue developing. He loves the game."

I could see Eddie seated on the ground, stretching, right leg extended; pulling on one foot; touching his head on his knee, then the next leg. Back and forth. Then he and another kid helped each other do some sit-ups, then iso exercises. After all this, Eddie stood up, did some running in place, then walked over to an area that was laid out like an open bullpen. The other kid turned out to be his catcher. They began the process. Eddie started out slowly, warming up his shoulder and throwing arm. After maybe a dozen pitches, the catcher started giving him signals. After a couple of pitches, a slider that ended up outside, and a high, moderately fast pitch that dropped over the plate in a nice curve, the catcher extended his index finger once and then patted his left leg. Bob elbowed me, grinning.

Eddie wound up and threw a fastball. The ball popped into the catcher's mitt with a sharp sound. The catcher gave the same signal twice more, each pitch hitting his mitt over the plate, on the inside, assuming a right-handed batter. I looked over at Bob and said, "Holy shit!" Bob chuckled.

The next three signals were similar, but the catcher tapped his right leg. All three pitches came in low with velocity and on the outside. Then some off-speed pitches, but Eddie still used the same wind-up and arm movement. The kid really looked good!

This went on for over half an hour, then the coach called all the kids over to him.

The stands were almost full by this time, and the opposing team was still on the field, warming up. I was looking around, expecting to see Lucy and Shirley, but not so far. We had saved spots on either side for the ladies.

I asked Bob, "How much longer?" He checked his watch.

"Ten, maybe fifteen, minutes. Don't worry, they will be here right on time. Shirley has it down to a science. This is how we always do it." I nodded.

The other team, dressed in blue and white, were jogging toward their dugout. Their jerseys read, "Nashua." I asked, "These kids any good?"

"They have a winning record, not as good as ours. We are ranked second in the state. We should win this one, but you never know. They do have one kid, Billy Murphy, who leads the state's Division 1 in hitting, .382, and as of today, he has fifteen homers. He's the second kid who will be scouted today. Coach Williams told me that Boston College may be here today."

"Impressive. How old is the Nashua kid?"

"He's a senior this year. Big kid. Looks like a wrestler, but quick."

"Not to be in any way disrespectful, but is the scout here to see the Murphy kid?"

Bob looked at me, grinned. "Yeah, him too. Murphy is good, but Eddie is better than good and not yet sixteen. You know?"

The kids and the coaches were lining up for the national anthem. Before they were all in place, Lucy

212

and Shirley walked up and sat down. I smiled at Luce. "Thought you were running late."

"Were you worried?" Her eyes were twinkling.

The PA announcer suddenly broke in. "Ladies and gentlemen, welcome. Won't you please rise for our national anthem." We all did, and the recording began playing. Here with friends, baseball, beautiful day in New Hampshire. The recording ended, and everyone clapped. The stands were full, maybe 400 to 450 people. Life was good.

Our kids took the field, and Nashua's first batter strode toward the plate, stopping a few feet before the box, taking a couple of practice swings, stretching the bat over his head. All this while Eddie was winding up and throwing a few pitches to his catcher, getting a feel for it. He caught the ball nonchalantly, rubbed it in his glove, then stood waiting for the batter.

The batter walked into the box on the right, waved his bat twice, tapped the plate once, then took his stance. Eddie waited for the signal, quickly nodded, stood for a moment, then wound up, left leg elevated, and then he threw a fastball low and inside. The batter hesitated then let the ball pass. The ump pumped his fist and yelled, "Strike!"

The batter stood back, swung his bat with one hand, then stepped back into the box and took his stance. Eddie got his signal, wound up, and threw another fastball. This one high center, but definitely in the zone. The catcher's mitt cracked with the impact. "Strike!"

The batter stood back, looked at his bat, then over to his dugout. Received his orders, presumably to swing this time. He stepped back into the box, even more intently, and crouched into his stance. Eddie reared back, threw a changeup. The batter anticipated another fastball and swung quickly, and the ball hit the catcher's mitt with a gentle thud. "Strike 3!"

The batter, shaking his head, walked back to the dugout. The same routine, with another right-hand batter and one left-hander, followed. Eddie mixed up his pitches, showing a slider that was pretty good and a curveball that could be hit by a batter who guessed correctly. But his main strength was a very fast fastball with command of the plate. The top of the inning recorded three strikeouts.

I turned to Bob. "Wow! Eddie's arm speed, the way he steps off, his release—everything! You were not overselling him. He is, well, good. Can he hold this pace?"

Bob grinned. "Just watch the game, TB."

Our guys got one hit, one walk, but no runs in the bottom of the first. Then it was the second inning. The kid who batted first was Billy Murphy. He was well over six feet, lanky but muscular, and he walked like he owned the game. From the right, he stepped into the box, planted his feet, bat resting on his shoulder. He stood there, face like stone, eyes unblinking, waiting for the pitch like a young predator waited for prey. I glanced over at Luce. She was into the game.

Eddie looked down at his glove, rubbing the ball in a circular fashion, a thoughtful fashion, sending the message that in this exchange, he was not the prey. He got the signal, shook it off, got another, and nodded. He wound up and threw a slider, outside and ending just out of the dirt. Murphy started to swing but checked it. Nothing from the ump. A ball.

This time, Eddie threw a high fastball, and Murphy hit it foul, over the left-side bleachers, maybe 325 feet. His swing was impressive, no doubt. The count was 1–1.

Eddie wound up, same motion, same release, same everything except the pitch was high and inside, just missing Murphy's head by inches. Murphy jumped back, almost falling, then righting himself. He looked out to the mound, same stone face, but his body gave him away. His shoulders bunched up; his hands gripped the bat like it might have been someone's throat. The count was 2–1.

Eddie threw a fastball low, a little inside but in the zone. Murphy swung, and you could almost hear the bat whistling as it arced above the ball. I did hear him grunt as he swung. But the ball banged mitt loud enough that I felt sorry for the catcher. It had to hurt. Count: 2–2.

At this point, all spectators, mostly family and friends of the players, stood. Concord cheered for a third strike; Nashua, for a hit. These were the best players for each side, squaring off on the diamond as so many had done over the years, underlining the exact reason baseball fans loved the game. Yes, it was a high school game, and yes, there were fewer than five hundred fans, but it was baseball. And this pitcher and this batter were our two champions.

Eddie, seemingly oblivious to the cheering, looked at his catcher, affirmed the signal, paused just long enough to make eye contact with Murphy, then wound up and threw his fastest heater of the day. I knew it was coming. Everyone knew it was coming. Murphy knew it was coming. Murphy drew back ever so slightly, watching the release. Like a rifle crack in the middle of the night, the ball hit the catcher's mitt. The sound was so loud that it shocked the whole big bunch of spectators into a hush. Simultaneously, the ump double-pumped both of his fists and yelled, "Strike! Yer out!"

With that pronouncement, the Concord fans erupted! The Nashua fans all sat down. Eddie waited for his next batter. But he was grinning.

The game was entertaining, Concord winning 4–0. Eddie went all seven innings, though in the last two he gave up three hits and one walk. All three hits came from off-speed pitches, and two of them were from Billy Murphy. To Murphy's credit, his hits were not accidental. After the game, Murphy shook hands with Eddie, and both kids seemed to respect each other.

As the five of us were walking back to the car, Eddie was somewhat quiet, the adrenaline having drained away. Bob put his arm around Eddie's shoulders as we walked, and he said, "Good game, bud. That was quite a performance with Murphy. The man has some talent, yeah?"

"Yeah, Dad. I was just thinking that there are a lot of guys out there that are as good, and better, than Billy. You know?"

"Ed. Just remember how you dealt with him. He's good, yes, but overall, today anyway, you won that exchange. Think about it. Right now, he's considering exactly the same thing about you. Granted, he got you for a couple hits late in the game, but not with your best pitches. And you can learn from those hits, right?"

"Yeah, you're right, Dad." And Ed was quiet again, looking into his future, a little scared and a little confident. And all of us saw a bit of the same future.

Suddenly Ed's head popped up, and he said, "Mom. Can we have pizza tonight?" We all laughed.

17

We left the Cantrell home, following the usual goodbye ritual. I was surprised somewhat when Lucy and Shirley hugged and Shirley gave Luce a peck on the cheek. Generally speaking, I'm not a hugger, so it always seems awkward to me, but a demonstration of sincere affection is hard to dismiss as convention only. It was just one more curiosity swirling around the person of Lucia Nardone.

We were wending our way through the late-afternoon traffic, aiming for my place, when my cell rang. I pulled it out of the cupholder. "Hello."

"TB, Joe here. I thought you might want to know that Mr. Anonymous is awake and seemingly alert, although not very talkative, according to the docs."

"What do the docs say? Is he still in danger?"

"Apparently not. They took him off the twenty-four-hour monitoring, pulled out some tubes, and downgraded him to intensive care. When I asked if he could be questioned, the doc said some weasely crap about not endangering his recovery too soon but then agreed to give me a few minutes. I haven't talked with him yet because I thought you might like to join me. Yes?"

"Yes. Of course. When do you suggest?"

"As soon as you can get here, I'm thinking. Maybe he'll be more inclined to share his thoughts with us while he still feels vulnerable."

"I agree. Okay, I can be there in half an hour or so. Thanks." I disconnected.

Luce said, "What's up?"

"The guy I shot? Our candidate for breaking into Ben's office? He has been taken off the critical list and is awake. Joe, my cop friend, says the guy can be questioned, so I need to get to the hospital." I gave her an apologetic grimace.

"That's good then. Do you think he will? Talk, that is?"

"I'm not sure. Under normal circumstances, probably, but this guy is a ghost. Who knows?" And I really wasn't sure. I did have a talent for, and experience in, interrogation, but this situation was complicated. He tried to kill me, and he broke into Ben's office, so I could start there, but the rest was blurry. With Joe present, I had to be careful about disclosing all that I knew, and that was exactly the leverage I would use to open him up. And my guess was that he was skilled at evading interrogation.

"Okay. Well, it's too late to drop me off at your place, so I'll go with. How long will it take?"

"Luce. I'm sorry to put you through all of this. I could call Jewels and have her pick you up?"

She gave me a poisonous look and said, "No. I'm not letting you out of my sight. You have a knack for disappearing when things just get interesting. I'm coming along." She sat back in her seat, chin pointed toward the windshield, and that was that.

In fifteen minutes or so, we were pulling into the hospital parking lot. I put the car in park, shut it down, and turned to Luce. "Okay. Come into the hospital, and wait in the cafeteria or one of the lounges. But you can't come into the room when we are questioning the guy. You know that, right?"

"Of course. Let's go in, and I'll figure out where to wait. Patiently. For you."

***

Prior to going upstairs to meet Joe, Luce and I hunted around for a good spot for her to wait. After a few places were rejected for one reason or another, she chose a small waiting room with a few vending machines and comfortable chairs. The room wasn't exactly hidden away, but it was decidedly off the high-traffic-beaten path. And not coincidentally, it was situated directly across the chapel. We hugged, kissed, and separated.

Joe was waiting for me on the second floor. There were two uniforms stationed at both ends of the corridor, monitoring everyone, including me. I gave the officer my name, and he checked over his shoulder with Joe, who waved me in. I sat down on the bench next to him and handed him a cup of coffee fresh from one of Lucy's vending machines. He thanked me, took a cautious sip, and made a practiced face. I shrugged; he took another sip.

"How do you want to handle this, Joe?" I sipped my own coffee.

"Well, we could do it in separate shifts, after agreeing who will do what."

"'Good cop, bad cop' sort of thing?"

He gave me a disapproving scowl and replied, "Assuming that's a serious question, no. Way too predictable for someone like this guy. I was thinking that we could either split up what we would say or maybe how we would say it or both."

"Why would that be more effective than both of us questioning him together?"

"He might respond to one of us, but not the other. You know, better rapport with one or the other. If both of us go in, he's more likely to be on the defensive." He waited for my response.

"Seems reasonable. Also, he doesn't really know you, and he definitely knows me. Different starting points. Okay. Who goes first?" I waited.

He thought for a moment then said, "I should go first. Spend what time I have just probing, seeing how cooperative he is. Easy stuff. Then you go in and follow up on that with a more direct approach. He tried to kill you and failed. My guess is that hasn't happened very often for him. It might elicit a measure of respect."

"Sounds good. How much time will we have? His doc wasn't specific, but I'm guessing not much. I'll play it by ear then let you know when I come out. Also, that window over there"—he pointed to a rectangular window a few feet to our left—"has a view of his bed so the duty nurse can keep an eye on him. If you walk over to the far corner, you can see him, but he has to lift up and turn his head to see you. Might be worth watching?" I nodded. "Oh, and one more thing, are you carrying?" I shook my head. "Okay. Both of the officers at each end are, but just to be safe"—he reached down to his right ankle and pulled out a small .22 subcompact and handed it to me—"eight rounds and one. Okay?" I nodded, checked the safety, and slipped the pistol in the small of my back under the waistband.

"Good luck, Joe." He entered the room.

I walked over to the observation window, noted that the nurse was watching me, and positioned myself so I could see both Joe and the guy. Joe pulled a side chair over to about six feet from the bed and sat. He shuffled through some papers in his folder, took a sip of his coffee, and looked up at the guy. He examined the straps that held the guy to the frame of the bed, both hands and feet. The guy was watching him calmly, maybe tiredly, but totally devoid of emotion.

Joe began speaking. I could make out some of what he was saying, thanks to being able to read lips. Joe's manner was equally calm, but he exuded confidence and authority. The guy took no notice. Joe asked him for his name. No response. Then he read some of the incident report from his folder, including how the guy was shot. Still no response. This went on in kind for another few minutes, after which Joe stood up, moved the chair back, looked at the guy the way you might look at a cockroach in a glass jar, then turned and left.

He went back over to the bench, and I met him there. We sat. He held the folder out to me, but I shook my head. He said, "You're up. But hang on for a minute." He reached into his pocket, pulled out his cell, and made a call. He spoke for a few minutes in monosyllables, saying virtually nothing, then ended it. He looked over to me noncommittally. My cell rang, surprisingly, my spy phone.

Still looking at Joe, I answered. It was Ernie, who said, "Hi, TB. I'll get right to it. Joe knows a little bit about who you are. Not everything, but enough that he won't be surprised by anything you say in your interrogation of the guy. He also has an understanding of what we do here in my building, at least in part. Now listen to me carefully. If, in order to question the guy thoroughly, you need to disclose to Joe what you are doing for us, then do so. Just let him know that it's all highly confidential. Impress that upon him. If you understand, just say yes."

"Yes."

"Okay. Call me when you are finished, one way or the other." And he hung up.

Joe raised his eyebrows and said, "Are we on the same page?"

I nodded, saying, "I think so. We can talk about all of this afterwards." I started to get up. Joe stopped me, and I sat back down.

He said, "You should know that I have the room wired. I'll be listening to you." He turned his head and tapped an earplug. "Okay?" I nodded. Well, that was a surprise. But thinking it through would have to be put off, at least until I finish with *the guy*.

***

Any interrogation is dependent upon three factors: circumstances, information sought, and time allowed. *Circumstances* are always varied but fall into two general categories: location and social setting. *Information sought* may be details regarding, for example, a crime committed. It can also be anticipatory, perhaps the disposition of enemy troops or position of some explosive device. *Time allowed* can be from an hour, as with finding an explosive device, or indefinite, as when trying to establish a terrorist organization. Sometimes, an interrogator looks for all three (acronym CIT) but settles for the most urgent.

The interrogation itself varies, depending upon the subject, who can be completely naive of interrogation methods or skilled in resisting them or somewhere in between. Interrogators are just as varied, though effective interrogators are almost always formally trained. Police-based interrogators are frequently trained by fellow officers, sometimes at advanced academies and rarely (though effectively) at FBI training facilities. Military interrogators, depending upon their branch of service and their assigned duties, learn their skills within designated training sites or schools. Military training focuses on extracting information either in the field, as with Army Special Forces interrogators, or in the rear areas, like Guantánamo, by CIA operatives. Again, CIT dictates the actual event.

It is also true that, like anything else, some people are uniquely, even naturally, capable of interrogation, much like some athletes or musicians are naturals—consider Joe DiMaggio and Miles Davis. After going through MP school then CID and after exhaustive testing, the army, in its infinite wisdom, discovered that Thomas Bradley Stone was a natural born interrogator. It came as a surprise to me, but whatever. Yeah, ever since I could remember, I always seemed to know what other people wanted, what they were thinking, what they were going to do. Nothing mystical or telepathic or any of that stuff, it just seemed natural. Then came the training, the honing and focusing. After that, I was pulled from regular duty and put on special assignment, along with three others, in a military intelligence unit. Each of us was bounced from place to place, country to country, to question and uncover information presumably held by different subjects. It was not glamorous duty. Granted, when the subjects were being held in some American consulate, the food and lodgings were pretty good. But more often than not, I'd be flown into some third-world jungle or desert, and well, the amenities were only just tolerable. The worst part, after years of it, was the inevitable moral ambiguity. I never tortured anyone, and I never witnessed anything like it. But manipulating people into disclosing what was important to them, however ugly it might be, became onerous, sickening. I had always thought of myself as a patriotic kind of person—I still do. But you could only clean so many toilets before you got sick of it. When I left that life, I swore to myself I'd never do it again. But here I am.

***

I walked into the guy's room and closed the door softly behind. I stood looking at him. He appeared to be securely strapped to the bed frame, hands and feet. His eyes were closed; his face, peaceful. Up close, he appeared to be in his midthirties. He had close-cropped brown hair, was tanned, and had central European features. An average kind of a guy. I walked closer to his bed. His eyes snapped open, instantly alert. His eyes were anything but average or peaceful, yet they weren't hostile or emotional in any way. I suppose they might be considered noncommittal or disinterested, but for being weirdly unblinking. The sum total, features and eyes together, told me that he was unlike most people. Instead of looking like an accountant, he looked like a predator. And of course, he was.

Without breaking eye contact, I pulled the side chair, the one Joe had just used, halfway to the guy's bed. I positioned myself far enough away from him that if he sprung at me suddenly, there would be a fraction of a second to respond—the old instincts were kicking in. I sat with the balls of my feet on the floor, my butt firmly pressed against both chair back and seat. My hands placed separately on each leg, palms down, relaxed. When I sat back, the little .22 slid upward just enough. All this took less than half a minute and wouldn't have been noticeable to anyone but a trained operative. The guy noticed.

I said, "We don't have a great deal of time. Your doctors tell us that you are still in critical condition, that it's important for you to rest. So I will be brief. I have a few questions for you." He showed nothing. "Why did you try to kill me?" I waited. Still nothing. "Why did you break into Ben Katz's office?" Nothing. "Who are you working for?" Again nothing.

I broke eye contact and stood up slowly. I walked to the foot of his bed, still a couple of feet away. Making eye contact again, I said, "With all due respect, you can continue saying nothing, and if you hold out long enough, one of two things will happen. Certain of my professional associates will arrange for you to be taken from here and placed in a facility that specializes in extracting information from recalcitrant folks like you. No one ever holds out forever. If you are as good as I suspect, you know that I'm being truthful." He blinked. Otherwise, nothing. "The other possibility is that one of your fellow operatives will manage to get to you and take you out. After all, you failed to kill me, so you failed in your mission." His expression altered slightly. Anger? Disagreement? Contempt? Something.

I walked back to my chair, reached for the .22, and thoughtfully examined it. I said, "Or since you tried to kill me and, more importantly, because you hit my friend over the head, a fifty-year-old woman, no less, I could always dispose of you myself." I checked the chamber, closed it, and pulled the hammer back. I met his stare, seemingly poised. I broke eye contact with him then put the revolver back after softly clicking the hammer safe.

I said, "I'm leaving now, but please understand, from one professional to another, that I'm being straight with you. I don't know your name, but you do know mine. Think about what I have said. If you want to talk, just ask for me." I stood, took a couple of steps toward the door, then turned and said, "Oh, by the way, that's an interesting tattoo you have on your wrist. Chinese. Does your organization tolerate operatives that fail in their assignments?" Now his face subtly changed. Yeah, it was anger. I walked out the door.

***

That evening, after the guy had finished with his chicken broth, steamed carrots, and toast, I walked back into his room, stood before him just out of reach. "Good evening, guy. That's how we refer to you. We know your name isn't William Warren, nor is it Terrence Hampton, so we call you *the guy*. If we had a name, it might help in all of this." No response. The blank face was back. "Ah. So have you reconsidered? Answering my questions?" I waited. Then I said, "Of course, since you have no record of ever having existed and since you clearly are here, maybe your handlers didn't bother giving you a name. I'm assuming you were raised from a child to be what you are. A pretty clever plan. Isolate you from any real family, train you from earliest childhood to be physically adept at killing other people, well, not people like you, but people who are normal. And you were, no doubt, convinced that you were an elite, special kind of person, ready to execute every order, every wish that your masters might want. Your martial arts skills, weapons skills, and absolute loyalty to your cause must have been very satisfying on some level. I wonder if a lifetime of all that would compensate for not knowing your mother or your father or never being allowed to love a woman. Well, maybe women were served to you occasionally, but certainly not a woman who might freely love you. I do admire dedication. But here you are, albeit recovering from two nine-mill slugs I put into you. I'm curious. You were all set, ready to execute your orders, but despite a lifetime of loyalty and dedication to your craft, your unsuspecting prey—that would be me—outsmarted you and outmaneuvered you and shot your ass. A nice double tap to your chest. So here's my question: how hard is it to know that I beat you? That I tricked you? I'm curious." The anger was back.

I looked at him, smiled, turned my back on him, pulled the chair up, and sat down. "So, *guy*, the docs here tell me you are recovering surprisingly quickly. I suspect that you have been genetically altered, maybe before birth even. That would explain a little bit." I laughed. "You know, your masters are going to be really upset that their special asset, their anonymous, unique asset, is now worthless. But my intelligence friends can't wait to get their hands on you. For all kinds of reasons." I chuckled. "You are certainly not worthless to them—my friends, that is, not yours. And since your recovery is speeding right along, it may be only a matter of days before you are hustled off to one or another black sites. Forever."

I looked at him, slowly shook my head, and waited. The anger was fading. He licked his lips. He started to open his mouth but thought better of it, and he returned to the blank but ever so malevolent stare.

"Okay, guy." I checked my watch. "Here's what I'm going to do. I am leaving right now, but I'll be back tomorrow morning. And when I come in, I'll ask you the same questions I did this morning. Three questions. If you don't answer those questions, you will never see me again. Frankly, I have other leads to pursue regarding all of this, so if you elect to remain silent, to protect your masters, I'll still track them down. On the other hand, if you do decide to talk, well, in this country, cooperation is a minor virtue. I can't really say any more, but you get the idea."

I stood, pushed my chair back against the wall. I looked at him with a kind sort of smile and said, "Oh, and by the way, don't bother fantasizing about getting loose and tracking me down. That's impossible. In addition to all of these medical monitors, our cameras and microphones are also monitoring you every minute. The guards have orders to shoot you if anything looks funny, and they really have no sense of humor." I gave him a mock salute, started to turn, and said, "Besides, if by some miracle you did escape from here, I would obviously know about it, and I'll be expecting you. And next time, I will take you out with a nice head shot. That's my favorite."

***

The next morning, after Joe had cleared the way for me with the docs, I stood looking into the guy's room. Earlier, I had reported to Ernie exactly what I had threatened to do with the guy if he didn't cooperate, and I received his blessing. If the guy refused to talk, I'd call Ernie, and within minutes, a couple of black SUVs would show up. The guy would go away.

I walked casually into the hospital room. I immediately moved the side chair away from the wall and sat down. I pulled my cell out; placed it on my lap, where he could see it; and made eye contact. I said, "Good morning, *guy*." He had the usual expression on his face, but his jaw was clenched just a hint. He had made his decision, one way or the other. I said, "Ready for your questions?" He blinked. "Why did you try to kill me?" I waited. His jaw twitched. "Why did you break into Ben Katz's office?" He licked his lower lip. "Who are you working for?" He cleared his throat. I waited for a few seconds then picked up my cell.

In a raspy voice, the guy said, "If I talk, what will happen?" He stared at me intently but not with anger or malice.

I put the cell back on my lap and, with a blank expression and a flat voice, answered, "That depends on what you tell me."

His expression had shifted minutely to one of guarded, somewhat fearful, hope. He said, "I was told to eliminate you. I was ordered to do it. Why the order was given can only be speculation. When I am given an order, I simply follow it."

"Okay. That's a good beginning." I reached for the .22, stood, and walked slowly to his bedside. I put the barrel against his temple and waited. His face became calm, returning to that same dull expression I knew so well. I said softly, "I'm just going to turn back your sheet." I did. His arm straps and leg straps were still firmly in place, hands unclenched. I took two steps back away from him, put the safety on my .22, and replaced it behind my back. "Just making sure you were being sincere. You understand." Of course, there was more to it than that—I was establishing my control over him. A first step.

He gave me a quick nod and said, "Now I have answered your first question. Before I answer the second, please answer mine. What will happen to me?"

His voice, his face, seemed different. All appearances suggested that he had crossed the boundary separating loyalty to his organization from his own self-interest. Now the interrogation could begin.

***

The answer to my first question was a bit less satisfying than I'd hoped; that is, he really didn't know why he was ordered to kill me. He suspected it was because I was getting too close to figuring out what was going on in Adfam Tech, but it was only a guess on his part. He broke into Ben's office in search of any information that might link up to Adfam. Hitting Doreen was, for him, a simple matter of necessity. Most of the information he disclosed had to do with my third question: that is, "Whom do you work for?" That question, interestingly, was the easiest to get. It was almost like a confession for him; it just flowed. Actually, he gave a great deal more than what I was expecting. Of course, his statement was being recorded, so we had something to review later, but it really was an incredible story.

Extracting truth from both intentional and unintentional distortion, delusion, conflation, and conditioning takes time and patience. The *guy* who signed into Ben's building as William Warren knew himself as James

Smith. Apparently, it was the name his masters chose for him when he was a child first entering training in a special camp located somewhere in the northern region of mainland China. Along with four other children known by him as his *family*, he was brought up to think that he and his mates were all abandoned on the streets of an uncaring America. They were rescued by a few compassionate Americans who wanted them to have a better life in the People's Republic of China. And that was how it all began. He and his family, Susan, Sharon, Alan, and Mary, were all educated, developed, and formed into all-purpose clandestine operatives. Their code of honor required absolute loyalty, obedience, and persistence. They learned covert skills, including martial arts, assassin's arts, and the ubiquitous social arts of deception. They were taught American English, all major dialects, and American culture, from street cred to the Hamptons. They learned American history as understood by most Americans. In other words, they could blend in anywhere in the fifty states. They could kill without remorse, steal anything and everything, befriend politicians, stir up a mob, infiltrate any organization, and effectively do whatever their masters ordered them to do.

His direct handler was, not surprisingly, John Lu. At least for this assignment. All James knew about him was that when Lu called, he would answer and follow Lu's direction. He had never met Mr. Lu in person. This was part of the protocol. When his last assignment was finished, his handler then would assign him to the next handler and so on. Apparently, James Smith had been in this country, completely off the grid, for almost ten years. There would be ten years of operational history to debrief. That, of course, would be for our intel folks to do.

After finishing, almost three hours later, James Smith collected himself and said, "So now what?" His face was calm, peaceful.

I looked at him and said, "First you need to spend a little more time here, recovering. When the docs say you can be moved, you will be taken to a place where others will question you in much greater detail. The gentleman I work with arranges all of that."

"The police officer who was here before you?"

"No. Someone else. But don't worry, he's a reasonable person, and your cooperation will make things much easier for you. I can't promise any more than that."

He nodded his head, closed his eyes for a moment, then said, "I'm very tired. But before you go, could I ask you another question?"

I nodded, then I smiled.

He grinned, and with that, suddenly and startlingly, he became human. "Thank you. This is a difficult question for me to ask, and you probably won't be able to answer it, but after all of this is over, could I live in this country? Even in prison, if necessary."

His face was so open and so innocent, more child than man, that I was embarrassed. I cleared my throat. "I don't know, James. I wish I had an answer for you."

18

Afterward, I called Ernie, and we reviewed the interrogation details, including that I was confident James Smith hadn't killed Abe Adamo but that Abe's death was definitely tied up with what was going on at Adfam. I then asked him what would happen to James. Ernie demurred, probably under orders, but he did assure me that he would pass on my thoughts and recommendations regarding James.

Since I still didn't have a name to offer Ernie as originally assigned—that is, who was working within Adfam to allow the CCP access to specific proprietary technology—we talked about some possible next steps. This continued for half an hour or so. Toward the end, I reassured him I was getting closer to putting all the pieces together, and he should not be surprised by what might happen fairly soon. He seemed satisfied.

After Ernie, I called Joe and filled him in. We agreed to link up in person to discuss what James Smith would be doing next and when that might happen. It would be tricky for Joe. We agreed to meet the next morning at nine o'clock in my office to hash it all out.

Next, I called Luce. After the first day, she went back to her home to wait out however long it would take me with the guy. "Hi there," I said.

"Hi, Tom. How are you?" She sounded like home. Funny how that worked.

"Better, now that I hear your voice. Have I told you yet what a musical voice you have?"

"Not that I can recall. Of course, *musical* could mean many things, from dulcet violins to a calliope." Teasing tone. Cute.

"I suppose that's true, but all I hear is how I feel, like listening to Etta James in the dark." I was kidding, but not really. I could hear her processing what I said.

"Did you finish your interview?"

"Yes, but I don't want to discuss it on the phone. Too involved. How about a late lunch?"

"Yes, please. I miss you." She paused. "Could you drive up here? The lake?"

"Sure can. I'll stop off at the office first, bring Jewels up to speed. Give me a couple of hours to be safe."

"Okay. See you then."

***

I stopped off at the office, parked Jewels's car, noting that my Spider was in its usual place. As I was walking up the stairs, everything seemed a little bit foggy. So much had happened since I was last here, even though it had only been a couple of days. I paused outside the office door, then I opened it. Jewels looked up, grinned, and stood.

"TB! Are you okay? What's been going on?"

"I'm fine. Tired, but fine." I sat down in her side chair. It felt good.

She dropped back into her chair. She did one of her visual assessments and, apparently satisfied that I really was okay, said, "That's good. Oh! Before you tell me exactly what's going on, *exactly* that is, I gotta thank you for lending me the Spider! I love that little car!"

"You are welcome. But you were doing me a favor, again. Surveillance is much better in your car than mine, so I have to thank you."

She grinned. "So. Spill it all."

"Well, first, the guy in the hospital started talking."

She stood and walked to the coffeepot and drew out two cups. "Keep going," she said, handing me my mug.

"Well, there's so much. The guy was responsible for the break-in, both Ben's office and my house. We already knew that, but he was just the button man. He disclosed who he was working for, at least in part." I paused, drinking coffee.

"Who?"

"John Lu. Listen, I'm meeting Lucy as soon as I finish here, so I don't have as much time as it would take to give you all of the particulars right now. Here's what I want you to do." And I told her.

She considered what I wanted, cocked her head quizzically, and said, "Kind of unusual. Sure that's what you want to do?"

I thought about it for a minute, then I said, "Yes. I think we are in the seventh inning with this case, and if I'm right, we need to stretch just a bit. It will help us finish up successfully."

She smiled and said, "Okay, coach. You got it."

"Thanks, Jewels. I'd better get going." I stood; she stood.

"One thing before you go, TB." She handed me my keys. "You and Lucy…everything going okay with you two?"

I handed her keys to her and grinned. "Yeah. Yeah, I think so."

"That's good, good. I really like her." And that was, for Jewels, high praise. Almost gushing.

***

It felt good behind the wheel of my Spider, so top down, I let her wind out just a bit on the highway. The odometer indicated that Jewels had clocked seventy-five miles, and surprisingly, that was less than the last time we traded vehicles. She had filled the tank, cleaned both interior and exterior, including the top. I should trade with her more often.

I parked in front of Luce's house, got out, stretched, and walked to the door. She stepped out on the porch and waited for me. I took my time, bending over to mock-dust off my shoes, whistling all the while.

When I reached the steps, she made a petulant face, shook her head, then said, "You can be a pain in the ass. Come here!" So I did.

Afterward, lying next to each other, her right ankle over my left and my left hand over her right, I slowly spun out everything that I had learned from James Smith. Everything I could, that is. She listened, questioning for the occasional clarification. When I finished, she propped up on an elbow, looked at me directly, and asked, "Did he have anything to do with Abe's death?"

I shook my head. "No. He knew about the reported accident because he was told to confiscate any files in Ben's office concerning it. But that was it."

"And you believe him?" Question, not accusation.

"Yes. When I asked him about Abe, it was after he had mentally broken through his lifelong conditioning and loyalty and everything else that supported who he had always been. I don't think he could have lied, about that or anything else. It's likely that sometime in the near future, he will have second thoughts about all of that, but not for a while."

She lay back quietly. After a minute or so, she asked, "How did you get him to open up?"

"Experience. The army trained me, and it was part of my job."

She said nothing. Then she remarked, "They trained you well, it seems."

"Look, Luce, I do what I do. And thankfully, we are closer now to solving the puzzle that is Abe's death than before. I'm optimistic that in the next week or so, we will have answers to all of this. And I'm pretty sure you will be a big part of getting at those answers. But it has to play out. Okay?"

She sat up, put her legs over the side, turned back to me, and smiled. "Okay. I'm sorry, Tom. Everything is happening so fast. And now, as close as we are, I'm almost afraid to find out how it will all end." She stood and walked into her bathroom. The door closed softly.

19

The next morning, we enjoyed a breakfast of strong black coffee, ice-cold tomato juice, and easily the best omelet I have ever eaten (despite the absence of apples and grapes). It was a little before seven o'clock when we finished up, drinking coffee and enjoying each other as the morning sun filtered through latticed windows.

I said, "Much as I hate to say it, we need to be on the road in half an hour at the latest."

"I'm coming with? I have so much here to do, not to mention my office. Not that I don't want to, but is it necessary?" Her expression was difficult to read. With all my supposed instincts, her expressions were still sometimes puzzling.

"Well, it's pretty important. We both need to go into my office for a meeting at ten o'clock. I want to get there earlier to prepare and also to talk with Joe prior to the meeting. Is that okay?"

Her face relaxed just a bit. She reached over and put her hand over mine. "Of course. If it's important. Let me take a quick shower and get dressed."

We pulled onto the highway a few minutes before eight o'clock. The drive was uneventful, and we pulled up

241

to my parking alcove a little after nine o'clock. Walking into the building, with Luce beside me, felt somehow different but in a good way, a relaxed way. At the top of the stairs, by the light, I could tell that Jewels was already in. I reached for the door handle, but Luce pulled me aside, and we kissed, holding each other for a time.

I whispered, "We need to go in." She nodded. We went in.

"Morning, you two. Coffee's on, if you want."

Lucy said, "Thanks, Julie. You want a cup, Tom?"

"Yeah, thanks. Jewels, is everything set?"

She cocked her head and said, "Now, what do you think? Everyone will be here. And Joe should be here in a few minutes. Go look in your office, please. See if it works."

I opened my office door. My desk was pushed back close to the window. Two tables had been positioned together, making one long table. At the end, a large whiteboard hung on the wall. The table had six chairs, three on either side, and one chair on the end nearest the whiteboard. Coffee cups, napkins, and two boxes of doughnuts were strategically placed on the table(s). On the table, in front of each chair, was a blank legal pad and a pencil. On the corner of my desk were three large bottles of water and a stack of cups.

"Jewels, it's perfect. Thanks." She smiled. Lucy handed me my coffee. Jewels walked back out to her desk, and I heard the outer door open.

Jewels said, "Good morning, Detective."

Joe replied, "Good morning. Call me Joe."

I walked out of my office and greeted him. "Hi, Joe. Glad you could make it." We shook hands.

"Coffee, Joe? It's fresh." Jewels lifted her own cup.

"Yeah, that would be great. Just black, please." Jewels pointed to the coffee maker. "Ah. Thanks." He poured a cup in one of the empty mugs.

"Come back here, Joe. I want you to meet someone."

"Joe, this is Lucia Nardone, my client. Lucy, Detective Joseph Foster."

"Ms. Nardone." They shook hands.

"Please, just call me Lucy. Tom has told me a little bit about you. It's nice to meet you." She smiled. Joe returned the smile.

I said, "Lucy, I asked Joe to come in a little bit early so we could talk together prior to the main meeting. I hope you don't mind." I looked at her in a beseeching sort of way.

She smiled at me then at Joe. "Not at all. Julie and I can catch up." She left, closing the door behind.

We sat across the table from each other. "Okay, Ernie told me that you were briefed on 'the rest of the story,' right?"

"Yes, and now it all makes sense. What you did with James Smith was, well, interesting. Obviously, you know something about interrogation. Where did that come from?"

"My time in army CID, mostly."

He looked at me skeptically and said, "Not what I saw. That came from somewhere else."

I just looked at him, then I said, "Maybe someday I'll fill you in, but I can't right now. And that's kind of what I want to talk to you about. Aside from Ernie, who will be attending this meeting, as well, you are the only one who knows anything about 'the rest of the story.' We need to keep it that way."

"Yeah, when Ernie briefed me, he stressed the need for confidentiality. I understand."

"Okay, good. At this meeting, what I will be talking about has all been cleared with Ernie, so some of the side story will be included. But not all of it, so I'm sure some of the natural follow-up questions will have to be deflected."

Joe thought about it, then he said, "Can't Ernie help us with all that?"

"No. As far as anyone else can know, Ernie is just an IT guy who was particularly helpful in getting me the pics that ultimately led to James Smith. And that's the role he will play. In his business, it has to be that way. It sucks, but there really is no choice."

"So no one else knows about Ernie?"

"No one."

He nodded. "I get it. I've dealt with Feds before."

My desk phone buzzed. I stood, reached for the button. "Yeah, Jewels."

"Your guests are starting to come in."

"Okay. I'll be out in just a minute. Thanks."

Joe and I finished up. I told him to get comfortable and I'd bring everyone else in. I opened the door, closed it behind, and put on a happy face.

Ben and Doreen were seated on the small couch that was placed against the wall directly across from Jewels, and Lucy was sitting on Jewels's side chair, turned to face the couch. Ben rose when I came out.

"Morning, you two! Doreen, it's good to see you up and about. How are you feeling?" I walked over to her, reached down.

She took my hand, rose, and said, "I'm fine. I heard you caught the son of a bitch that clubbed me?"

"You could say that, yes!" We hugged. "I'm really sorry you had to go through that." She patted my back and pulled away. She looked at me, shook her head, and looked over at Ben.

Ben said, "Tommy, if you two are finished with your love fest, what's this meeting all about?"

"I'll explain everything after one more person shows up. He should be here soon. How about everyone goes into my office, that's where we will be meeting." I walked over, opened the door, and stood back. They all filed in except Lucy. She waited for me, then she and I walked in.

"Please take a seat, grab some coffee and pastry." Everyone did. Joe and Ben nodded to each other.

I heard the outer door open and walked back over to greet Ernie, who smiled and quietly said, "All set? No problems?"

"No problems. Were good to go."

We walked into my office, and Ernie smiled, saying, "Sorry I'm a little late, but I'm here." He took the last open seat next to Joe and perpendicular to my chair. I left the door open and walked to the end of the table. Jewels had poured me a cup of coffee.

"Okay. First, just to make sure everyone knows everyone else, starting with Lucy here, please introduce yourself and explain what you have to do with this case." I sat down.

"Hi. I'm Lucia Nardone, the client who dragged TB into all of this." She turned to Doreen.

"I'm Doreen Clark, Ben's legal secretary. I'm the one who got hit on the head." She rubbed the back of her head. Everyone chuckled, though somewhat nervously.

"Julie Ellis, TB's secretary. Enough said." This time, the chuckling was unimpeded. She looked across the table to Ben.

"I am Ben Katz, attorney. My office was broken into, and Tommy and Joe have been working the case."

"Good morning. Joe Foster, lieutenant detective, CPD, assigned to the break-in and assault at Mr. Katz's office." He nodded at Ernie, sitting on my right.

"Ernie Delgado, IT operations manager at the NH Memorial Office Building across the street from Mr. Katz. My girlfriend, Melissa, is the receptionist in Mr. Katz's building. She asked if I could possibly help Mr. Stone by checking our surveillance camera tapes for the intruder, and as it turns out, we did find something." He turned to me. "Is that too much?"

"No, Ernie. That's perfect. Thanks."

I stood up again, walked to the whiteboard, grabbed a black marker, then turned back. "Okay. First, thanks everyone for coming in. I want to try something a little different. Since all of you have been involved in this case in one important way or another, I thought it would make sense to fill everyone in on our progress at the same time so we would all effectively be on the same page." And so I did, enumerating key events on the whiteboard.

From the initial case involving Abe Adamo's presumed accident to the (sanitized) questioning of James Smith. When finished, I sat back down, pouring another cup of black elixir from the carafe. The room was quiet.

Ben, not surprisingly, said, "Thanks, Tommy. But what's next? You found the guy who broke in, and he's under arrest. Technically, that takes care of my part of the case, no?"

"Not quite. We still don't know why Smith broke in, though we suspect it has something to do with the death of Abe Adamo. What I'm hoping is that all of us can put our resources together and figure out the rest. Everyone at this table has a vested interest in what happens next. We all have skin in the game, as it were."

Doreen said, "I'm in, TB. I can't speak for Ben"—she gave him a look that contradicted what she said—"but whatever I can do."

Ben, grinning, shook his head. "Of course, I'm in also. Not to repeat what Doreen said, but whatever I can do." He looked out the corner of his eyes at Doreen and made a face that said "Holy shit!" Everyone laughed.

Each member of our newly formed cabal chimed in, including Ernie, who did so with an odd facial expression. I'd have to ask him about it later.

"Okay. Thanks, everybody." I turned back to the whiteboard. "Have you got all of this, Jewels?" She nodded. "All right. I have a suggestion about how to go forward from this point on, but please hear me: if anyone objects or has a better idea, speak up." I began writing names in pairs in a column on the right side: "1st—Ben and Doreen, all legal and personal research; 2nd—Joe and Ernie, Adfam and Cutting Edge; 3rd—TB and Lucy, Adamo family." Then at the top, I put "Jewels, coordinator." I stepped back, checked it, turned around, and waited for a response.

Ben asked, "I assume 'legal and personal research' refers to running down anything having to do with information that can be gleaned from official records? How about unofficial records? You know, like following up leads?"

"As in?"

"Well, suppose we find something 'official' that points to someone who should be questioned off-the-record? Or some contact who is on the margins of respectability that may have a distinct talent for gathering information?"

"I see. Well, as far as direct questioning goes, just be careful. And your special contacts should be used discreetly. When in doubt, let Doreen be your conscience." This drew a laugh.

I looked over the group. "Any other questions? Anything?"

Joe and Ernie were whispering to each other. Joe looked up and said, "Yeah, a couple of things. Both Ernie and I have other commitments, daily and ongoing, that will take up much of our time. But having said that, we both believe that with the help of certain people within our respective teams, we can go forward. If that makes sense, we are on board with our part."

I thought about it and responded, "You two are both professionals, so use your judgment."

Joe and Ernie both nodded. Joe said, "That works for us. I'm assuming that follow-up with James Smith falls into our purview, yes?"

I nodded.

"Okay. One more thing, Jewels will be coordinating. That means everything goes through her, including daily agendas, unforeseen occurrences, hourly updates when appropriate, and contact with other team members. We don't want any surprises. Each of our pairs will be operating separately but not independently. When in doubt, contact Jewels." Everyone nodded. "Anything to add, Jewels?"

"Just be sure to keep me in the loop, night or day. If you need to know what one of the other teams is doing or need to speak with them, contact me first. In fact, please write down my cell phone number, and use it when appropriate. I will always be available. That especially includes you, TB."

I bowed my head, shook it resignedly, and said, "Yes, ma'am." That got another laugh, especially from Ben.

Everyone started talking, kidding around, and finally eating the pastry. I motioned for Lucy and Jewels to join me in the outer office. I sat on the end of the desk and said quietly, "That seems to have gone well. I know some of it came as a surprise to you two, but I hope it all makes sense now."

Jewels nodded, recognizing why I did it. Lucy said, "I assume a good part of it was for efficiency, yes? Too much for the three of us to do?"

"Yes, mostly. Also, each pair is doing what their skills dictate, so not only are the tasks being spread for the sake of efficiency, but for proficiency as well. Hopefully, it will get us what we want sooner and better, that is, with fewer screw-ups along the way."

Jewels said, "And what we want is to find out who killed Abe?"

"Yes. And why." Lucy was twirling her coffee cup and gazing off into somewhere other than where we were. "You okay, Luce?"

She looked at me, half here and half there, then focused, then said, "Just thinking about how far we have come in such a short time. It should be overwhelming, but it's not. Not sure why."

I wanted to say many things to her but held back. Instead, I reached for her hand, and we shared the feeling and the moment.

Jewels cleared her throat, getting our attention. She said, "So what now, TB? Which Adamo will you be pursuing first?"

Luce and I let go of each other, reluctantly on my part. "Good question. I'm thinking Marco, but what do you think, Lucy?"

"That depends. Marco is closer to the heart of this, considering it all seems to swirl around Adfam. But Tony always knows what's going on, or at least that's what Abe always thought. Marco is closer and will be easier to reach."

"Okay, Marco it is. How soon can we get in to see him? This afternoon, maybe?"

Lucy walked over to Jewels's phone and said, "May I?"

Jewels made an impatient face. "Of course, Lucy. Just hit the top left button and dial."

Lucy did so. She spoke, "Yes, hello, Sue. This is Lucy. I was wondering if Marco had time to speak with me?" She listened, then she said, "Marco! How are you?" She listened some more. "Good. I'm fine, but I was hoping I could come in and see you. I have something I need to discuss with you." She listened again for a bit, said yes a couple of times. "Okay. Where?" She listened. "Great. I'll see you there at one o'clock. And thanks, Marco." She hung up.

"Today, one o'clock, at the Tamarind, a restaurant close to his office. Is that good?"

Jewels and I looked at each other, smiling. I replied, "Yes, that will do. But why do we have to wait so long?" Lucy rolled her eyes, those eyes. And once again, I got lost momentarily.

Jewels said, "Okay. I'll let everyone else know, just so we are all *on the same page.*"

20

fter bidding everyone adieu, Luce and I drove off in my Spider to seek out and speak with Marco Adamo. On the way, I called Yuan and asked him to have Sly look in on Doc for me. Yuan had an extra key to my place, and since Sly and Doc were great pals, there would be one less worry. Luce called a neighbor who would watch over her cat. I was not sure exactly why, but I had a vague feeling that neither of us would be home tonight.

Traffic in the Concord-to-Manchester corridor, such as it was, was moderate, so we pulled into the parking lot of the Tamarind at twelve fifteen. It was clearly an upscale restaurant catering to upscale people. The lot was filled with Mercedes, BMWs, expensive sports cars, and even one beautifully restored Bentley parked along the side.

"I've never been here before, Luce. I'm somewhat underdressed, no doubt."

"Don't concern yourself. We will be seated in a private area reserved for the Adamos. Being Marco's guests is all the *attire* required. In fact, when the poor folk seated outside the reserved section see who you are with, they will all rush out to buy designer jeans and polo shirts."

"Hah! You have a cynical streak, Luce. I'm impressed."

"You forget, I was part of the Adamo clan for quite some time. It's difficult not to be a bit cynical when constantly breathing the rarefied air surrounding them. And of all the Adamos, Marco is the most influenced by all of it. Don't misunderstand, he's not a snob, but he knows instinctively how to navigate through the wealthy end of the gene pool."

"I see. We have some time before going in, how about telling me some more about Marco."

She shifted in her seat then said, "Where to start. Okay, Marco, as I said before"—she reached over and squeezed my hand, remembering as I did our discussion in the coffee shop—"is all business. Thinks, feels, eats, sleeps business. I guess the only thing in his world that trumps business is family. The difference for him between business and family is how he deals with them respectively. His business interests are controlled by calculation, pragmatically. His family begins with emotion and ends with emotion. If there is any crossover, I have never witnessed it. Abe was very different in that respect."

"How so?"

"Abe was balanced. Logic and feelings were melded together, not bunkered separately."

"Example?"

"Hmm. Okay, my field is real estate, so that's a business I understand. Before I bought my house, I was talking it over at Tony's before dinner one Sunday. I was describing the house for the family, only Abe had actually seen it, and part of my description included the seclusion, the lake, the way the sunsets glittered and cast gold through the early evening air. Yes, it was a good investment, and yes, it had all of the amenities that I needed, but after experiencing that golden light one evening, I knew it was my house. Understand?"

"Sure. It could become a home because it reflected a part of you."

"Exactly! And Abe knew that truth also, whatever else he thought about the house. Marco, on the other hand, hearing my assessment at the same time as everyone else, asked if I had gotten comps and if the resale value would hold over the course of the mortgage, and some other things that to me mattered not at all. The quality of evening light meant less than nothing to him, though he should have known me better than that."

"I see. I'm curious, what would happen if Marco and Abe disagreed over something? If it had to do with both business and family equally?"

"As I said, I have never witnessed or heard about anything like that. I can't make a guess. Marco loves his family without exception. And he is equally driven by his businesses. I just don't know." She shrugged.

"Interesting. What is he going to think about me showing up with you? Especially after he hears my name and why I am with you."

"I have been thinking about that. If Marco has somehow been involved with any of this, he may already know who you are. Whether he shows it or not will be telling."

"Absolutely. You know him, I don't. We both need to be alert to that first moment when he sees me. We can compare notes after. Okay?"

"Of course. What exactly is the plan? How much do we tell him and ask him?"

"This sort of thing is not unusual for me, and in some ways, the first encounter can be really productive. Once the introductions and small talk are finished, it will be best if you take my lead." I tried to gauge her reaction.

Her face was blank. She said, "Yes, that makes sense. You have the experience, and after all, that's why I hired you in the first place." She smiled. "But, Tom, you don't think Marco would have had anything to do with Abe's death?"

I looked at her, digesting what she asked. "It seems unlikely. But he may know more about Abe's death than he is aware. Again, this is all speculation. Let's just wait for the discussion to play out." I looked at my watch. "It's ten till one. Is he likely to be there yet?"

"My guess is that he is walking through the side entrance right about now. We should give him a few minutes to settle in and then go in ourselves." And that was what we did.

***

When Lucy told the maître d' that we were expected by Mr. Adamo, he bowed, smiled, and led us through the labyrinth of tables, cul-de-sacs, and far too many people for a one o'clock lunch, into a short hallway opening into a section of private rooms in the back. The whole thing seemed unnecessarily elegant, but maybe that was just me. Our guide stopped before the last room, knocked gently, then opened the door. He stood aside, bowed again, then gestured us in. We entered.

Marco was standing, close to six feet in height, slim like a runner was slim, dark hair cut short and brushed back. He was tanned, had dark eyes, and was dressed conservatively and smiling.

Lucy greeted him with a smile and a very chaste hug and a kiss on the cheek. She said, "Marco, it's good to see you. Let me introduce you to Thomas Stone, a friend. Thomas, Marco." Curiously, he held out his hand in welcome to me, as if he expected me all along. I shook his hand, giving a like response to his firm, professional grip.

I said, "Mr. Adamo, very nice to meet you."

He said, "Thomas. Please call me Marco."

I smiled, crinkling my eyes, and said, "Thank you, Marco."

We sat, adjusted our chairs, looked at each other. Lucy said, "Marco, in case you are wondering, Tom is more than a friend." Marco looked away from her, at me, then back to her. "Tom is a private investigator who is looking into Abe's accident." Marco, again, curiously, did not react, as if he knew that all along. "I hope this is not a problem."

Marco studied her briefly then said, "I know you fairly well, Lucy. We shall see if it turns into a problem, but for now, I have no objection." A tight smile, then he looked over at me, holding the smile, holding my gaze, and said, "What exactly has your investigation yielded that brings you to me?"

I broke the gaze, looked over at Lucy, and said, "Lucy, you are my client. Are you comfortable with me disclosing our progress so far?"

Lucy, crafty soul that she was, without missing a beat, said, "Of course." She looked over at Marco. "I should have warned you that Marco is very direct." She smiled.

I said, "Good enough. Well, to be direct, I am convinced that Abe did not die as a result of the accident. In fact, I'm convinced that his death was planned and executed by someone. At this juncture, I don't know who was behind it, but we"—I looked over at Lucy—"are following some leads."

Marco, with his face set, responded, "If you will forgive me, Thomas, our family believe that Abe died in an unfortunate accident. I'll need more than your opinion to accept any of this."

"Of course, I understand your skepticism. Let me tell you just one of the reasons for my *opinion*." And that was just what I did, telling him about the break-in, the material stolen from Ben's office, and then the attempt on my life. I stopped there.

He cleared his throat, drummed fingers on the table, then pressed a discreetly placed button located on the side of the table. He said, "Let's order. I want to hear more, but I also need to consider what you have already told me. Any objection?" He looked from me to Lucy and back to me.

I said, "Not at all." Lucy nodded agreement.

A soft knock at the door preceded a youngish waiter entering, notepad in hand. He stepped up to the table, bowed, and silently waited.

Marco said, "Any objections if I order for the table?"

Luce and I exchanged glances, and I said, "No. That will be fine. Thank you." Seemed a bit formal to me, but when in Manchester, the very hub of all things glittery…

Marco ordered Caesar salad, Parmigiano-Reggiano, and espresso with mignardises. I couldn't pretend I knew what all of it was, but it had an elegant Italian sound, so it would probably be edible.

While waiting for the food, Marco was very quiet, but after a few minutes of awkward silence, he said, "If, for the sake of argument, Abe was murdered, how can I be of help?"

I responded, "By answering some questions."

He nodded. "Go ahead."

"Can you tell us what you know about a gentleman named John Lu?" I said it quickly, watching closely for his response.

His face seemingly showed nothing, but he unconsciously drew his extended fingers on both hands together. "John Lu is one of our clients. He's currently developing a manufacturing operation here in Manchester. We, that is, Adfam, have a partnership of sorts with him."

"What sort of partnership, if I can ask?"

"The usual sort. When his new facility is fully operational, he will be supplying key components for two of our manufacturing sites." He leaned back, studying me.

"I see. Did you supply the capital for his enterprise?"

"I'm unable to understand where this is going. How does any of this relate to Abe's death?"

"We have arrested the man responsible for both the break-in and the attempt on my life. He disclosed during questioning that he reported to John Lu, and it would seem that Mr. Lu ordered both the break-in and the hit."

"Really?" He seemed surprised, though as he expressed it verbally, his fingers contracted once again. That was twice. "Why haven't you arrested him or at least brought him in for questioning?"

"Because we still don't know what motivated Lu's order, assuming the guy we have in custody is telling the truth. Better to find out what Lu is up to and then, hopefully, simultaneously discover how Abe's death is figured into any of this."

Marco looked down at his hands, consciously extending his fingers. Three times. He said, "Well, this is all very troubling. Obviously, I will do whatever I can to help. Any other questions?"

"Yes. Back to Lu's business venture, if you supplied the capital, then it is less likely that Lu received financial support from his home country. Is that a fair assumption?"

He cleared his throat. "Ah, I see. That makes it less likely that Lu is receiving his orders from someone else or, rather, from someone in China. Is that it?"

"Exactly. So what's the answer?"

"Yes. Our agreement involves providing the start-up capital in exchange for a reduced price in component purchases until the capital, with interest, is repaid. Good for us, good for him."

"Okay. Next question. Why were you and your family so certain there was no foul play when Abe ran off the road?" Again, the question was direct, and I watched for a reaction.

Marco sighed, tightly but reservedly, and said, "We had our own investigators look into it. They were thorough. I ordered the investigation with my father's approval. The investigators have been retained by the family for years. They are trustworthy." His hands remained relaxed.

Lucy said, "Yes, Marco, but you now have to see that all of this, the break-in and attempt on Tom's life, followed Tom's investigation into the event. If Abe's death and all of this aren't connected, how else can it be explained?" Lucy was getting wired up.

"Obviously, I can't explain it, Lucy. Until today, as far as I knew, Abe had a tragic accident. Now that seems unlikely. And"—his voice became softer—"you were right to pursue the matter." It seemed a sincere admission.

At that point, a knock came at the door, and our waiter joined by a server rolled a cart into the room. They laid dishes, cutlery, water goblets in front of us, then they served the salad in what appeared to be crystal bowls. The waiter then poured water in our goblets, stepped back, and they both exited. The salad was unlike any Caesar salad I have ever had, with layers of exotic leafy greens, perfectly groomed vegetables, small pieces of fruit, and at least three different kinds of cheese. The olive oil and balsamic were exactly right, enhancing, not overpowering. The bread was perfect. I was a bit surprised that Marco hadn't ordered wine, but honestly, the salad was nicely complimented by mineral water.

We chatted about nothing and everything amiably. Even Marco seemed to enjoy the lunch. After salad, we were served the Parmigiano-Reggiano. I was expecting a parmigiana dish of some sort, but we were served buttered linguini, a wonderfully flaky parmigiana with black truffles, and olive oil. It was incredible. Truffles for lunch! And then, following that, espresso and mignardises. The little desserts were like small tarts, chocolate, raspberry, and others. All in all, the best lunch I have had in years. Even better than tuna on whole wheat.

Over coffee, Marco agreed to stay in touch and let us know if he could think of anything else that might be pertinent. I cautioned him to keep our conversation confidential, and he seemed to understand.

After lunch, we parted ways.

***

As soon as we were in the car, Luce was asking questions—actually, more of a flurry of incomplete sentences punctuated by hand gestures and roller-coaster voice tones. I chuckled and said, "Whoa! Slow down, Luce. Give me one clear question…"

She took a deep breath, grinned, and said, "Sorry. Okay. Was it just me, or did he seem a little evasive? Especially when you mentioned the man you guys have in custody."

"Maybe. Or maybe he was genuinely surprised and just didn't know how to respond. The best way to evaluate the conversation is to look at the whole, not pieces of it. Overall, was what he said consistent? Did he seem nervous, did he hesitate before certain questions, were his body actions, or inactions, consistent with his verbal responses?"

"All right. Let's see, for Marco, he seemed nervous. Like, he kept flexing his hands, even though his face and answers were calm. I also thought it was odd that he wanted to eat lunch right in the middle of it all. Almost like he wanted to interrupt it." She paused, looked at me, and asked, "Is that what you mean?"

I chuckled and said, "Yeah. Exactly what I mean. You're a natural, Luce. Now start looking at the pieces, and put it all together."

She leaned back into her seat, with a satisfied expression on her face, and considered. After a few moments, she said, "Tom. I'm just going to think out loud, so if I say something screwy, tell me, okay?"

"You got it."

"Marco is so controlled, so aware of everyone and everything going on in his world, that it's hard to surprise him with anything. He's like a chess player, always several moves ahead. So the idea that a break-in, not to mention an attempted assassination, by someone tangential to his business interests would go unnoticed stretches credibility. Maybe he wasn't expecting it, but I can't imagine he didn't know about it. That's one thing." She looked over at me.

I said, "Go ahead. Works for me so far."

"Another thing. When I told him that you were investigating Abe's death, he showed nothing, said nothing, really. Almost like he had practiced his response, and that would mean that he knew exactly who you were. And assuming that, then how could he not know about the break-in? The attempt on your life, perhaps not, but the break-in? Someone had to tell him about it, at the very least. Also, now I may be stretching with this one, but in the Adamo family, to exclude wine from any meal except breakfast is unheard of. But the waiter didn't even ask, he just brought mineral water, which means that Marco nixed the wine prior to us showing up. If he thought it was only me attending, well, trust me, wine would have been served. He knew you were coming."

"All makes sense to me. And now it also makes sense to conclude that your friend Marco knows something about all of this that he's not disclosing. What that is, I can't say. Yet."

I called Jewels, gave her a brief summary of our conversation with Marco, and told her that he was likely hiding something. She gave me an update on how the other two pairs were progressing, and then I told her we were heading back to Concord. It was almost three o'clock.

I pulled out of the restaurant parking lot, reached over, and put my hand on Luce's hand.

Luce asked what was going on, and I began. "Joe and Ernie, based on some deep diving by Ben and Doreen, have discovered that Gloria Simpson, our stakeout friend, was a government employee. Apparently, she worked as an analyst for the NSA a few years back, but now she is a private IT consultant. So Joe and Ernie dug even deeper and found out that she has a contract with Cutting Edge, presumably helping them with their start-up. Now get this, she is serving as a liaison between Cutting Edge and Adfam Tech. Joe and Ernie are planning to visit Cutting Edge tomorrow to question John Lu. Joe's police badge gives him entry, so they will, hopefully, be able to see what's going on there. Also, they have an appointment to see Walter Hinds later in the morning. I'm guessing Gloria's name will come up with both Lu and then later with Hinds. That's what I'd do anyway."

Luce considered this and said, "So by noon tomorrow, we will have delivered the message to all concerned that a net has been thrown and we are drawing it in, right?"

I nodded and said, "Absolutely."

We were leaving the outskirts of Manchester, so we would be back at the office in less than half an hour. I stretched, realizing that my shoulders and my neck were tight. I needed to relax, let the stress go. Luce reached over and started kneading the back of my neck.

"Thanks. That helps."

"Tom, do you have any idea yet who actually was responsible for Abe's death? Or is it too soon to speculate?" She continued with my neck.

"Well, I have a pretty good idea who didn't do it, even who wasn't responsible for having it done. I can say that, barring a surprise, it will be one or two out of a handful that I suspect. And before you ask, no, I won't list my suspect list with you. I need for you to be open to all possibilities because that will help me narrow the list down."

"Okay. I'll trust your judgment, but I still don't like it." She watched the strip-mall scenery as we pulled onto

I-93, quiet, with face set. She was impatient, and like her name, morning light was ready to burst forth on the horizon, in more than a couple of ways.

We parked, walked to the office building, and rather than going immediately upstairs, we ducked into the café and got two cups of coffee and one cup of green tea for Jewels. Sid, the owner, as we were checking out, asked, "So did that lady ever find you?"

I asked, suddenly alert, "What lady?"

"Just a lady, kinda tall, blond. Seemed in a hurry to find you." He handed me my change.

"Keep it, Sid."

I gave Luce a look and said, "Come on. Something doesn't feel right." We hurried upstairs and into the office. Jewels looked up, smiling. I audibly relaxed, exhaling aloud as my pulse pounded.

"TB, you look like hell. What's up?" Jewels stood, concerned. Luce was also perplexed and out of breath, hanging on to my arm tightly.

I paused, examined the office, eyes sweeping the space before answering, "Was a blond woman up here? Earlier?"

"You mean Gloria Simpson? Yes. She left a little bit ago" She reached for a card on her desk and said, "She asked that you call her as soon as you get in. Actually, I was just about to call you. Here." She handed me the card.

I wiped my face, out of reflex, and said, "I thought she might be a problem."

"As in dangerous? Didn't seem to be. Impatient but polite and insistent that you call her ASAP."

"Okay. I'll call her in my office. Thanks, Jewels. Oh, here…" I handed her the tea.

Luce followed me into my office, sat in the same chair as she did the first time. I picked up the phone, punched in the number. A somewhat-deep voice answered, "Gloria Simpson."

"Ms. Simpson, this is Thomas Stone." I waited.

"Yes, Mr. Stone. Marco Adamo told me that you might be contacting me, so I thought that I'd see what you wanted. He wasn't very specific, but he did mention that you were a PI investigating the death of his brother. Is that right?"

"That's correct, Ms. Simpson, but I had no plans to contact you."

"Oh. Well, then maybe I misunderstood Mr. Adamo. As I said, he was somewhat vague."

I said, "But now that you have taken the trouble to come up here, perhaps we should talk. Could you come back in?"

"Well, I haven't left Concord yet, so, say, fifteen minutes or so?"

"Great. See you then." I hung up.

"Okay, Luce, let's check my phone app and see where Gloria is right now." We checked. The little red dot blinked, showing her sitting right outside my building. Apparently, Gloria was staking out my office.

"Now there's an interesting turn of events, Luce." She laughed softly.

21

loria Stimpson sat across me, calm, confident, and seemingly ready to hear whatever it
was that I had to say. I held her gaze, looked
down, and opened a manila folder, tilting it back so she
couldn't see the contents, not that she would be particularly interested in the annual leasing agreement for our
office copier. I studied the first sheet, flipped to the second, then closed the folder. I said, "Ms. Simpson, as you
probably know, I am investigating the supposed accident
resulting in the death of Giorgio Abraham Adamo that
happened early last winter." She nodded. "So I guess my
first question has to be, why have you taken the trouble
to drive up here to see me? Granted, Marco told you I
might want to talk with you, but why didn't you just wait
to see if I would actually contact you? Why the hurry?"
I waited.

She replied, "Well, for one thing, I'm curious. Why
me?"

"Forgive me, but you must be an extremely curious
person. Inordinately so."

She smiled broadly and shrugged.

"Okay, it's getting late, and I really don't have any interest in playing verbal tennis with you. Why are you really here?"

The smile disappeared, and she said, "Because I had nothing to do with Mr. Adamo's tragic passing and really only knew him distantly through his brother. So my suspicion is that your investigation is broader than what you are telling me. I'd like to know what your investigation has turned up that includes me." She gave me a defiant, impatient look. She was obviously someone who was accustomed to getting what she wanted. Kinda like a birthright.

I gave her a look of my own and said, "You came here. You wanted to see me, not the other way around." She started to respond, but I held up my hand, stopping her. "I also know that you were parked across the street when I called you. Want to tell me why you were staking out this office?"

She shifted in her chair and said, "Okay, Mr. Stone. I was hired by Tony Adamo, not Marco and not John Lu. My job, ostensibly, is to serve as a bridge between the two companies, and I'm sure you already know that. What you don't know is that Tony Adamo hired me to keep an eye on both companies because he has received some reliable information from an outside source that John Lu might be stealing tech from Adfam and then passing it on to the Chinese government. His source also believes that there is someone in Marco's organization that is feeding this proprietary tech to John Lu. I'm telling you this because your investigation is interfering with me finding out the truth. Got it?"

I studied her for a few moments then said, "Interesting. Are you also connected with the Feds in some way?"

She made a wry face. "No. Tony Adamo, just as I said. And, Mr. Stone, I strongly encourage you to focus on the death of Marco's brother and leave it at that. It may prove an easier path for your original investigation."

"That wouldn't be a threat, would it?"

"Not in the least. Just good advice." She stood. "Unless you have any more questions for me, I will be going."

"Actually, I do have one more question." She raised her eyebrows and waited. "Did you know that John Lu used a hit man to try to kill me?"

I think I caught her by surprise. "No, I didn't know that, but thanks for telling me. It might help in my own investigation." She walked out.

I waited until I heard the outer door open then close. I lifted my receiver and said, "Did you get all of that, Jewels?"

"Sure did. I'll give you a transcript in a few."

I turned off the intercom and thought about what Gloria had said. The more all this seemed to clear up, the murkier it got.

I picked up my spy phone and rang Ernie. He answered, "This is Ernie. May I help you?"

"You're not alone?"

"No. But I have a couple minutes."

"Okay, I'll make it short and direct. If, after you hear it, you elect to share it with Joe, and I would encourage you to do so, let me know."

"I understand."

I proceeded to pass on everything I had just learned about Gloria, including her working relationship with Tony Adamo. Then I said, "Will you pass it to Joe?"

"I probably will be free in half an hour or so. Will that be soon enough?"

"Yes. It's the cell, right? Don't want him to know that you have a special phone just for little old me?"

He laughed. "That's certainly true." He waited.

"Okay. I'll wait for half an hour then have Jewels give you guys a call. Good?"

"Yes, that's perfect. See you soon." He disconnected.

I opened the door and walked out. Luce stood and asked, "Everything all right, Tom?"

"Yeah, I think so, but I have to give it some time. This jigsaw puzzle is coming together, and we now have another piece that fits somewhere, but I'm just not sure exactly where it fits."

She reached out, rubbed my upper arms, and kissed my cheek. "You'll figure it out."

Jewels cleared her throat and handed me the transcript; her eyes were soft. I made a face at her and said, "Thanks."

She shook her head, made a derisive noise, and asked, "So. Do you want me to call everyone and let them know about Gloria's little visit?"

I looked at my watch. "Yeah, but give it another half hour or so before you do. In fact, how about you two come in my office. I want to do a quick review." We went in.

"Jewels, could you please do the whiteboard this time around?" She nodded, grabbed a marker, and stood waiting.

Luce and I sat across from each other. I said, "Jewels, make two columns. The first headed 'Abe's Accident,' the second, 'Adfam Issue.'" She did, effectively dividing the board in two. "Okay, now let's do some old-fashioned brainstorming and consider everything we know about the case, whatever it might be. Then figure out which column should best receive the individual elements." We all looked at the board.

Luce said, "What if something fits in both columns?"

"Then pick the column that's best served, and if it seems equal in weight, then use the time of occurrence for your choice."

Forty-five minutes later, the board looked like this:

Abe's Accident	Adfam Issue
Lucia visits Stone PI	L & J call potential suspects
Ben researches accident	Robert Hinds suspicious
Ben's office breeched	TB & L stake out Hinds
Doreen assaulted	Gloria discovered
TB questions secretaries	John Lu discovered
Pics of culprit found by Ernie	Cutting Edge Tech discovered

Joe enters picture	JS reports to Lu
TB & L visit	TB & L Qd
accident site	Marco Adamo
TB tracks culprit	B & D find out
	Gloria is former NSA
Culprit tries	Gloria shows up,
to kill TB	threatens TB
TB shoots culprit	
Culprit Qd by	
Joe & TB	
Culprit named	
James Smith	
Summary Meet/	
Groups formed	

While we all studied the list, I couldn't help thinking that we were missing something, but nothing came to mind. Yes, little things, but they were all subsumed within the items listed.

I asked, "Anything else? Lucy? Jewels? Okay. Looking at the list, is there anything that emerges? Any questions that haven't been asked?"

Jewels said, "Are we sure that the two are connected? I mean, obviously, the people involved are, but was the accident, the murder, a result of whatever is going on at Adfam or just coincidental?"

"Good question, Jewels. What do you think, Lucy?"

Luce thought a moment then said, "Well, what if what's going on at Adfam is a result of the murder? You knew, the other way around. If we know that, wouldn't our suspect list be affected?"

"Interesting. Well, the list, the way it has formed, is a pretty fair timeline, as well as an incident list. So what came first? We know John Lu and Cutting Edge precede the accident. We don't know when Gloria showed up, but we do know that Tony hired her. I wonder if it was before or after the accident. We need to find out because the timing could very well tell us which came first, accident or Adfam issue."

Jewels said, "Okay. I'll go update everyone regarding Gloria's visit, and I'll have Ben and Doreen find out about Gloria's start date with Adfam?" She waited for my response.

"Yeah. Caution them to be especially discreet."

***

The three of us had ordered food from the café downstairs and were tucking into it when Jewels's phone rang.

"Stone Investigations. May I help you?" She listened, got a big grin on her face, and said, "Hi, Joe. Yeah, fine." She looked up at me then said, "Maybe. TB and Lucy are sitting here. I'm putting you on speaker." She did.

Joe spoke. "Hello, guys."

Simultaneously, Luce and I said, "Hi, Joe."

"Listen, after that last update from Jewels, we decided to wait before trying to see Gloria, you know?"

"Yeah, Joe, that makes perfect sense. How about the other two?"

"We did visit John Lu and then, later, Walter Hinds. Well, actually, *we*, Ernie and I, visited John Lu. But I saw Hinds by myself. Ernie had some emergency back at his office."

"Anything major? For Ernie, that is?" I was thinking maybe it had to do with our investigation, but Joe might be erring on the side of discretion.

"No, I don't believe so. Just some IT matter that required his presence."

"Ah. Well, so what happened with Lu and Hinds?"

"Boiling down the interview with Lu, we didn't learn much that wasn't already known. When we brought up James Smith and all of that, he seemed to know nothing about it. No surprise there. However, he is definitely worth watching. Call it instinct. At this stage, I'm more inclined to trust James Smith than John Lu." He paused, then he said, "Walter Hinds is another matter. Very nervous, contradicting statements regarding knowledge of the break-in, and for an executive with a big outfit like Adfam Tech, he seemed poorly informed about his business. Actually, I wouldn't be surprised if he doesn't do something that reveals his complicity."

"Complicity?" I wasn't entirely sure what Joe meant.

"Yeah. He's tangled up in something, but there's not enough evidence to say what. Maybe the break-in, maybe the attempted hit on you, I don't know. But I'm having a couple of my plainclothes guys tail him. They are staked out right now at his building."

I said, "Okay, Joe. Keep us informed if Hinds does anything. Thanks."

Joe said, "Julie, could I speak with you for a second?"

Jewels hit the button, taking Joe off speaker, and said, "What's up?"

Luce squeezed my arm and motioned for me to go with her. We went into my office, and she shut the door behind.

"What's going on, Luce?"

"We need to let Julie and Joe talk." She made a face that said "Wake up, dumbass."

"What? Oh! Jewels and Joe? Seriously? That's kinda sudden."

She gave me another look, very much like the previous one, but punctuated this time with a headshake. "Yeah, sudden. That kind of thing never happens…"

22

Luce and I were on the way to her house, talking loosely about the case and what might happen next. We were about fifteen minutes from the Lake Sunapee turnoff, when I noticed a couple of young boys wrestling, fighting, really, in the front yard of an older, somewhat-dilapidated house. It was just a glancing impression as we drove by, but something about it caught my attention. Why?

A few minutes passed, things were quiet, and I realized Luce was watching me. I looked over at her and said, "What?"

She smiled, saying, "You missed our exit."

I looked around and realized that yes, I was past the exit, and apparently I had gotten lost in thinking about those two kids.

"Where have you been? You have been gone for ten minutes or so. I was starting to worry."

"Huh. I'm sorry. I was just distracted by those two little kids fighting back there. You know, in that yard."

She cocked her head and said, "I must have missed that. But take this next exit, and I'll guide you back." I turned, followed her direction, and we got back on her road, the lake road.

She said, "Are you going to tell me what you were thinking about? That was just a little bit weird, the way you zoned out." She smiled, but she was also perplexed. Someday I'll figure out how she manages to say so much with one facial expression.

"Hmm. That's complicated. Let's get settled at your place, and then I'll explain." She nodded.

We pulled in, parked, and were walking up to her front door, and I heard a bird cry. I looked up, trying to see it, and did as it pulled away from a copse of trees. It appeared to be a hawk of some kind dangling a small animal, maybe a young rabbit, in its talons. I tapped Luce on the shoulder and pointed to the hawk, saying, "Do you have a nest of those birds around here?"

She turned and looked to where I was pointing and said, "What bird?"

"You missed it! He was just there, above those trees. He veered off towards that wooded area over there. I think it was a hawk."

"Yeah, there are a few around. Maybe there are some nesting in the woods. I don't really know." She unlocked her front door, hitting the light switch as we entered. There was an audible pop, and the light bulb blew. She said, "Oh no! I just changed that bulb last week."

And then it happened. The boys fighting, the hawk and its prey, and now the light bulb. Another convergence was forming. I walked over to the couch, sat down, and stared out the front window. I sensed Luce sitting next to me, and then in my mind's eye, I was back in Hanover, walking past the Baker-Berry Library, and in a little park across the street, two boys were fighting, yelling at each other, and punching wildly. Over the sound of their fight, I heard a hawk screech as it plunged and picked up one of the boys, carried him off, and then the overhead sun suddenly dimmed. I looked up and could see that an eclipse was in process, darkening everything until it was almost night. Then I came out of it.

Luce was shaking me. "Tom, Tom! Are you all right?"

I turned my head and looked at her. "Yeah, yeah, I'm fine. Not to worry."

"What happened? You just went into a trance or something. You scared me!" And I could see that she was frightened.

"Well"—I laughed, in a reassuring sort of way— "you just got a genuine demonstration of what I told you earlier that I would explain. You know, in the car, when I missed the exit?"

She nodded and relaxed a bit. "Okay. So explain. Please!" And I did, although verbalizing it somehow reduced it to something that experientially it was not. Since Ben was the only other person who ever got an explanation, at least an honest one, I was unaccustomed to putting it into words. But that was okay. Sometimes it was too weird even for me.

"Is it like a vision? Whatever that is…"

"Not really." I thought about it for a bit then said, "Do you remember that night at your place, the first night, when we were talking about actively using imagination?" She nodded. "It's that, but even more like a waking dream. You know that dream you sometimes have right before you wake up in the morning? You know exactly where you are and recognize that you are dreaming, but the dream still continues. You talked about that? Remember?"

"Ah. I see. Yeah, that's an odd experience, a little bit like watching a movie." She nodded, understanding somewhat.

I watched her as she processed it. Then she said, "But why do these dreams happen to you? It's not really..." She was a hint embarrassed.

"Normal? Yeah, I know. But it isn't a hallucination or a prophetic vision or anything like that. It's a subconscious process emerging, letting me know on a conscious level that a problem or puzzle is, well, answerable. And since this has been happening in one way or another for most of my adult life, I know that my solution is somehow tied up with the event. The *event* is brought on by certain occurrences in my real-life environment, and generally I know something is forming."

"So what precipitated this particular dream? Do you know?"

"Yes. In this case, the two little kids fighting, then the hawk diving down by the lake, and when we stepped in here, the light bulb popping when you switched on the lights. The events frequently come in threes."

She held my hand in both of her hands, staring at me but thinking about what I had said. "Tom, do you believe that this dream will help you, us, solve this case?"

"All I can say is that based on previous experience, previous dream events, it may help. If it helps, it will be by pointing us in the right direction. We still need proof to get a proper result, and that requires time, persistence, and doing what we have been doing."

She smiled. "Okay, so what do we *do* next?"

I extracted my hand from hers, gently reached behind her shoulders, and drew her to me. Sometimes, a demonstration was better than an explanation.

23

The next morning, over espresso and Luce's special omelet, my phone rang. Jewels said, "Good morning, TB. I received some news this morning from Joe and Ernie that you need to hear."

"Morning, Jewels. Good news or bad?"

"I'm not sure. That's why you need to hear it." I heard someone in the background, then her receiver was muffled. She returned with "Joe and Ernie have decided to bring Walter Hinds in for questioning."

"That is news. I thought they were going to be watching him for a while. What changed?" Again the muffled phone. Then I heard the phone change volume.

"Morning, TB. You are on speaker now."

I looked up at Luce and grinned. I said, "Good morning, Joe. What's going on?"

"This morning, I got a call from one of the guys staking Hinds out. We have a bug on his home phone, and it seems he made reservations for a flight to Beijing. For noon today."

"I see. Yeah, kinda hard to tail him there. Any idea why he's leaving? Anything happen?"

Joe sighed. "Not really, other than what you already know. Personally, I'm guessing things are starting to get too hot for him and he has decided to leave before it's too late. I told my guys to watch him until he starts for the airport, then pick him up. James Smith's testimony gives us enough to drag him in."

"What does Ernie think about all this?" Ernie's interests were somewhat different from Joe's.

"He doesn't like it, but he also agrees we can't let him leave the country."

Then Jewels said, "What are your plans today, TB?"

"Not entirely sure, but maybe it's time to meet Tony Adamo. What do you think, Luce? Could we get in to see Tony today?"

She thought about it for a moment then said, "Maybe. I can call and see. If not today, then soon, if that's okay."

I said into my phone, "Lucy thinks we might be able to see him today. I'll let you know as soon as we know. Other than that, we don't have anything concrete, so let me know everything, Jewels."

"Will do, TB. Tell Lucy I said hello. Bye." She disconnected.

Luce said, "I got part of that…"

"They are picking up Walter Hinds. Seems he booked a flight to Beijing for noon today. We can't let him do that."

She nodded. "Was Joe there? At the office?"

"Nope. Jewels was calling from her apartment. She wanted me to say hi for her *and Joe.*"

Lucy beamed.

Lucy called Tony Adamo at his home. His secretary answered, and Lucy asked if Tony might be able to see her and a friend today. As Lucy's luck would have it, he could. She was told to show up anytime, but if possible, the afternoon would be best.

Later that morning, while Luce was in the shower, I called Ernie on the spy phone. We discussed all that had transpired in the last couple of days, pros and cons. I told him about the upcoming visit with Tony and what I would definitely discuss with him, as well as what I hoped to learn. Then Ernie informed me that some of his associates had picked up James Smith earlier that morning. He didn't know exactly where James was taken but that he would be treated humanely during interrogation. Lastly, we discussed the fact that we still didn't know for certain who was giving Adfam Tech's proprietary info to the Chinese government. Yes, it was probably Walter Hinds, but maybe there were others involved. I reminded him that I still didn't know who killed Abe Adamo, but we were closing in. We clucked about that for a while then agreed that I would call him ASAP after meeting with Tony.

Later, Luce and I walked down to the lake. When she bought the house, she also joined with a few of her neighbors in an association that gave her access to Sunapee's shore. Technically, the association rented it from the township, but practically, it was theirs to use exclusively as they wished, with certain provisos, of course. We brought coffee, a couple of wide-brimmed hats, and canvas beach chairs.

We found a dock jutting out, devoid of neighbors, and that gave us a perfect view. We set up shop out toward the end. The midmorning sun glistened on the water, making bright-white flashes as little ripples randomly skittered across the surface. There were a few boats in the distance, seemingly stationary, maybe with folks fishing or maybe just enjoying the laziness of it all. From our spot, we could see most of the lake's length, although the tail extended at an angle another few miles beyond the wider section. On our left was a tapered small lighthouse on a little peninsula, and to our right, the tree line hugged the shore and climbed up the hills, where it met the bluest sky possible.

"Luce, this is absolute perfection. I can't imagine a more beautiful place." She reached over for my hand, not saying a thing. We watched as human activity slowly, naturally began to form along the shore and on the lake itself. It was so quiet that we could hear voices, laughter in the distance.

Later, Luce said, "I come out here just to be." I could understand that.

Even later, checking my watch, I asked, "How long does it take to get to Tony's place?"

She replied, "Maybe an hour and a half, most on 89. A little longer if we take the scenic route."

"Well, it's almost noon. We should probably think about getting ready," I said, reluctant.

"If we must. I haven't been this relaxed in…a very long time. I could stay right here, with you, until dark. And then we could go back to the house and make food, drink wine, and talk about all the things we didn't do today. And when the moon shines into my bedroom window, we could make love. Wouldn't that be better?"

Then she looked at me with those eyes that were increasingly becoming my center.

"Better, yes." I kissed her hand. "However, duty calls."

We stood, grabbed our stuff, and walked slowly back to her house.

24

On the way north, I asked Luce, "Anything I should know about Tony? I know you gave me a fairly detailed bio, but what about personal sorts of things? You know, foibles, likes and dislikes, political preferences, all that."

"I can try," she said, "but it's easiest just to think of him as *old country*. Tony still takes the notion of family honor seriously and ranks it higher than almost anything. Politics are meaningless to him, as such, unless they intrude into his world. Then, like everything else, he takes it personally. I mentioned before that he admired Frank Capra enormously. If you consider Capra's sense of decency and fair play shown so simply in all of his movies, then you will understand how Tony likes to operate. However, he is not naive, and he recognizes that the ideal is rarely reflected in business matters. In business, Tony is pragmatic. That might sound like a contradiction, but it isn't where Tony is concerned. He can function perfectly well holding two or more contradictory notions in both head and heart. In short, he loves his family, life in general, and this country intensely. And he operates his business interests, many and diverse as they are, with cold precision. He is generous and patient with friends but ruthless with enemies. Does that help?"

"Yes, it does. Can I ask you a sensitive question?"

She smiled. "Of course."

I considered how to frame the question, then I asked, "You have been persistent, insistent that Abe didn't die as a result of the accident, and I know Tony disagrees with you, so are you still his friend?"

She cocked her head and looked at me. "Yes. I loved his son. I was almost his daughter-in-law. Why would you think it could be otherwise?"

"Actually, I pretty much thought that, but I just wanted to be sure. I need to know what he is likely to think about me. It's important because it will determine in large part how I question him. And I am convinced that Tony, whether he knows it or not, holds the key to this whole case." I studied her reaction.

She frowned. "Really? You don't seriously suspect that Tony had anything to do with it? Abe's father?"

"No, no, of course not. But what he knows, I believe, will reveal who is responsible."

She thought about it. "Okay. I'm curious about this but trust you know what you are doing." She paused, then she said, "Anything else you want to know? About Tony?"

"Yeah, what does he do for fun? How does he relax?"

"Let's see, aside from family, he's a big football fan, *calcio*, that is. He's a proud American, but not where football is concerned. With the World Cup, it's the Italian national team, the Azzurri. He likes to cook, though it's a family joke that his skills are limited in that regard.

Maria, his daughter, is the real chef. Everyone in the family, including Tony, laud her talent in the kitchen. He also listens to opera, no surprise. He has a large sound room with perfect acoustics and state-of-the-art equipment. His collection of opera—on vinyl, mind you—is incredible. How's that? I can't recall anything else. Oh, and Tony makes wine. He could probably live without all of his other diversions, but not his vineyard."

"Perfect. Thanks. Again, just as with Marco, follow my lead with the questioning, okay?"

She nodded. "Tom, see that exit up there? Take it. Then turn right, and then in a few miles, take 118 north. Tony's place is maybe half an hour from Hanover, but it takes a few different roads to get there."

I did so. "What's his place like? Nice, I suppose."

"You could say that. His land covers several square miles and extends over the river into Vermont. Most of the Vermont side is undeveloped."

"How does that work, being in two states?"

"Two separate deeds. His home is in New Hampshire, so his personal taxes are paid in NH. He pays property taxes to both states. That's about all I know. He has lawyers who take care of all the details. He has an entire law firm that deals with the business concerns." She was starting to get tense, her words edged.

"How far to the turnoff?" I asked.

"Another ten minutes or so. Watch for Route 118 N." She sighed. "I'm starting to wonder if this was such a good idea. What will Tony know that Marco doesn't? I don't know how Tony is going to react to you, let alone the questioning."

"As I said earlier, he may know nothing more consciously, but I'm pretty sure he will disclose something that will help us even though it may seem meaningless to him. Consider, he owns the whole company, so surely, he receives reports from all of the various divisions, including Adfam Tech. He knows I'm working for you, and he also knows about the break-in and the attempt to kill me. It would be impossible for him not to know. Besides, remember that Gloria has been working for him, reporting to him. He knows exactly what's going on."

"I suppose you are right." She stared out the window.

"There's something else bothering you, yes?" I waited.

She said nothing for a moment, then finally stated, "It's you. I was engaged to Abe, and Tony was very, very happy about it. And now I come waltzing in with you! What will he think?" She was on the verge of tears.

"I understand, I really do. But he doesn't know how close we are. And even if he does, it's been almost a year since Abe's death. It might be a little sad for him, but if he cares about you—and it sounds like he does—then he will accept it."

She was quiet again. "Up here, Tom. The turnoff."

I turned on to Route 118, accelerated slowly, then said, "Is there anything else, Luce? If so, just say it."

She looked at me, grabbed my hand, and said, "I really do love you, Tom. Is it wrong that I still love Abe?"

I didn't answer immediately because I had no idea how to respond. Finally, I said, "I guess I don't believe that it's a question of right or wrong. It's a hard situation. I do know that one of the reasons I love you is because you are an emotionally complicated person. Grappling with something like this is just who you are. You could no more ignore it or bury it or not feel it than the tide could ignore the moon. I can tell you that I will love you through all of it. That's the best answer I can give you."

She put her head on my shoulder.

***

Luce had been quiet for the last few miles. I asked, "Are we getting close? I'm not all that familiar with this area. I know we're somewhere close to the National Forest, but beyond that..."

"Yes, about a mile more and turn on 25 north. This is beautiful up here, isn't it? Unspoiled."

"Sure is. I can't imagine living anywhere but New Hampshire. Sounds corny, huh?"

"Not a bit. Tony told me once that when he first came up here, from Boston, he knew that he had found his home. I think that's when I knew he and I would get along. You know, on a personal level." She was smiling. "Tom, take this next hard road up there on your left."

I did. "Now how long?"

"You just turned on the Adamo family property. We will be at the house in five, ten minutes."

We were driving through a forest with pines so tall the road winding before us was intermittently dappled with shadows, then dim gold, then shadows again. On the right, we passed a small lake or maybe a large pond, glistening blue, isolated, with no cabins or boats or anything man-made. Hunks of granite showed along the

hillsides, reminding me that human concerns were min-
iscule by comparison. It all just felt right.

I could see a space, open sky, and thinning trees start
to appear before us as I climbed a gradual incline. Then
one last turn and a small valley emerged, green and gray
and brown, with a small creek running down the little
hill; we were descending. The road ended about halfway
down on a small plateau. From the plateau, three different, narrower roads ran to left, right, and center places
down into the little valley. The center road terminated
before what had to be the main house. I stopped to take
it all in.

It felt like we had somehow been transported to
Tuscany. The house was built around a traditional watch-
tower, with wings jutting off it in three directions. The
walls of the entire structure were made of varied shades
of brown stone set in beige plaster. Windows and doors
were all inset with dark wood and crisscrossed frames for
thick bluish glass. Most of the structure was two stories
but for the tower, which was three. The tower sported a
oval-topped, deeply set large window, obviously designed
originally for observation. The roof was covered with
rounded, oblong orange-brown tiles, extending uni-
formly over all sides by eighteen inches or so. Small trees,
each individually inset with decorative stone and brick,
grew up along the walls, some taller than others, no two
the same. Between the trees were large clay pots holding
bushes and some flowers. Several additional buildings,
all following the same design, stretched from either side
of the house. And to make the Tuscan illusion even more
credible, behind the house, running up the back valley

hill, was a vineyard! A small vineyard but beautifully, lovingly kept. In fact, a gentleman wearing a straw hat was tending the vines.

I turned to Luce, who was grinning at me unabashedly. She laughed and said, "You should see your face! So you like Tony's little place?"

"Oh my god! This is Italy! We just left one reality and entered another."

I put the car in gear and drove down to the house. Crushed white stone made up the parking-area surface, bordered by shrubs and a low, stained wood fence. It was located approximately twenty yards in front of the house. I pulled up next to a walkway on the right side. On the left side was a medium green BMW M3. My Spider was a proud little lady, but the Beemer was something else. I looked it over. "Who belongs to this beauty, Luce?"

"Not a clue. The family doesn't use this parking area." She pointed to a long building adjacent to the main house. "Family parking is back there."

"Let's go in, Tom." She took my hand, and we headed down the path.

She rang the bell. I noticed that perpendicular to the walls, variegated, irregularly shaped stone tiles set in concrete extended eighteen inches or so from the house. The bushes and small decorative trees that were visible from the hilltop were set in this beautifully crafted skirt. It all fit nicely and suggested great care for both proportion and function. Yet with all these touches, it still seemed rustic and old-world.

The door opened. A middle-aged man, not tall, but stocky and fit-looking, took us in and smiled. He said, with a pronounced accent, "Miss Nardone, welcome! Please come in." Opening the wide door, he stood back, ushering us in with his arm extended and a quickly bowed head. We walked in.

"Good afternoon, Bruno. It is good to see you. This is my friend Thomas Stone. Tom, Bruno."

"I extended my hand, saying, "Good afternoon. Nice to meet you."

He took my hand, shook it, and returned with "Very nice to meet you, sir. Please follow me." He led us through the entryway, into a large sitting room, then over to a doorway that led into a wide hallway that appeared to run the length of the house. The back wall was decorated with paintings, potted floor plants, a couple of tapestries depicting various stylized scenes of vineyards and olive groves and rolling hills of green and brown. Here and there were dark wooden chairs, small tables, and shelves with interesting-looking statuary. The outer wall had windows running the entire length, with approximately six feet between them. The windows all had thick fabric curtains of muted green-and-blue patterns; most were closed, but a few were parted, revealing an outer courtyard. Directly across our doorway was an open double door leading into the courtyard. Bruno led us across the hall and through the doors. He gestured toward an area to our right and said, "Mr. Adamo is waiting for you." He gave another quick bow and exited.

The inner walls were exactly the same design and composition as those of the structure's outer walls, and of course, above the courtyard was open sky. Several balconies reached over the courtyard, permitting the floor area some shade and, presumably, protection from rain. The inner courtyard, or atrium, perhaps, was bordered with marble perhaps eight feet out from the walls, and within that rectangle was a central pit of sorts, stepped down seven inches or so. This inner area was surfaced with mortared, patterned stone, and covered with variously sized and variously shaped pots containing a bewildering assortment of plants, some flowering, most not.

Lucy led me to one corner where an older man sat on a dark rattan sofa. As we approached, he stood, greeting us, arms wide. He said, with a big, open smile, "Lucia!" He hugged her, and she him. She gave him a kiss on his cheek. He held her by her shoulders at arm's length, looked at her with genuine fondness. "Why is it that every time I see you, I fall in love again!" He laughed, then he looked over at me, smiling.

"Tony, this is Thomas Stone, my friend. Tom, Tony." I reached out; he took my hand, nodded, and shook firmly.

"Please. Sit." He motioned to the sofa, then when we were seated, he sat on an accompanying chair, first placing it so he could face us. "Something to drink? Espresso, iced tea? Or perhaps some wine? The wine is from my own vineyard…" He raised his eyebrows, opened his hands in invitation.

Luce looked at me. "Tony's wine is always very good." Then in mock secrecy, she whispered, "We wouldn't want to insult him!"

I laughed and said, "Well, it's a little early for me, but how can I refuse?"

Tony said, "Good man." He stood and said, "Excuse me. I'll be right back." He walked back into the main house.

I asked, "He went for the wine himself?"

"Of course. Besides, it's his wine, made effectively by his own hands. We are his guests, and it's just old-country manners and graciousness." She smiled. "You two will get along."

All this, the house, the location, Tony himself, and the simple joy that Luce felt coming back into this world, made my objective for this visit surreal. Investigating murder, especially of Tony's son, should take place out there far away from this timeless sort of beauty. Driving down into this valley, so far away from the world's frantic and silly needs, had changed my focus from one of objective information gathering to subjective openness to a sweeter reality. If it could be described more clearly, I would do it, but my focus was truly altered, and in a weird way, I was helpless to go back. My years working in intel had hardened me, inured my senses in so many ways. What was it about this place, this moment that drilled down below all that ugly conditioning?

Tony returned, carrying an unopened bottle of red wine. He handed the bottle to me, smiled, then walked over to an inlaid dark wood cabinet and opened the doors. He took out three glasses and a simple corkscrew then brought them to the low rattan table in front of our sofa. He said, "Would you like to do the honors, Mr. Stone?"

I grinned like a kid and said, "Of course, but please call me TB. Most of my friends do." He bowed.

The label was an off-white with a dark-brown silhouette of the house, this house, below which was the vintage date, five years ago. I peeled off the foil then stood and inserted the corkscrew, twisted it, then gently rocked the cork out. I smelled the cork, reflexively, then put it down on the table. I offered the bottle to Tony, but he refused and indicated that I should continue. I did my usual sampling routine. It tasted of fruit, earth, and something else I couldn't identify. "Wonderful, Tony. Very different but somehow very Italian. Could I ask what varietals?"

He smiled. "Of course. A grape primarily from the Piedmont region, Nebbiolo. Over the years, and thanks to the efforts of some good people from the University of New Hampshire, I have managed to get a hybrid developed that can prosper here in New England. The wine itself is a mixture: 80 percent Nebbiolo-H and 20 percent Cabernet Franc. You like it?"

"Very much. What happens to it with a bit more aging?"

"I don't know yet. After all of the experimentation, this is the best result, and it is only five years old. I hope that it will age well." This he said with modesty.

"I can't imagine that it won't." I reached down and poured a glass for Luce and Tony then myself. I sat back down. Luce patted my arm.

We drank, enjoying the wine and the company. After topping off each of our glasses and finishing the bottle in so doing, Tony said, "Now. I know that you are here for more than my adequate red wine. What can

I do for you?" His face was relaxed but serious. He was waiting for me to speak.

I looked at Luce then Tony. "As I'm sure you know, I am a private investigator. Lucy and I have been checking into the presumed accidental death of your son." I watched his reaction. There was none. I continued, "We are convinced that it was not accidental. As a result of my investigation, again as you may be aware, an attorney friend of mine who was researching the accident had his office broken into and his secretary assaulted. Following that, an attempt on my life was made. During the attempt, the culprit was stopped and is now in custody. Questioning him revealed that he was directed by John Lu, a business associate working in conjunction with Adfam Tech." I waited for Tony to respond. This time, he nodded. I continued with the entire story, leaving very little out. After the telling, I said, "So now that you are brought up to speed, I'm wondering if there is anything that you know about any of this that might help in finishing our investigation." I crossed my legs, put my hands in my lap, and waited.

Tony held my eyes then looked over at Lucy. He cleared his throat then said, "As you have suggested, TB, most of what you have related today, I already knew. It is clear to me that something is going on at Adfam, and as you know, I have someone in my employ who is looking into it: Gloria Simpson. Her efforts have revealed the duplicity of John Lu, as well as the likely disloyalty of Walter Hinds. All of that will be dealt with." He stood up, stretched, then said, "But none of this means that my son died of anything other than an unfortunate accident." He sat back down.

Tony was certainly a gentleman and charming in an old-fashioned Italian way, but he was either stubborn to the point of denial or intentionally sandbagging. I said, "With all respect, how do you reconcile the simple fact that some fairly benign, completely legal inquiries into Abe's accident resulted in a robbery/assault and an attempted murder? Just that." I waited, uncrossed my legs, and waited some more.

He responded, "All circumstantial. Let's assume that Walter Hinds learned of the inquiries then mentioned it to John Lu simply because it was a probe into the affairs of my family. Lu wants to know why Ben Katz, a very well-known attorney in government circles, is curious about a highly publicized accident that was seemingly forgotten about. Both Hinds and Lu have much to hide. Isn't that a plausible reason?" His turn to wait.

"Perhaps a reason for some counterinquiry, but attempted murder? I suggest to you that while your latter reason is plausible, my former reason is much more compelling. If it hadn't been, I wouldn't be sitting here today. Besides, the inquiry results were dodgy, the accident scene itself was suspect, and if Abe's death were *not* an accident, everything that followed would be consistent with a cover-up." I waited.

Tony sighed, spread his hands wide, and said, "Okay, TB. Your reasoning is sound, and I will have to give all of this some thought. Marco called me earlier this morning and familiarized me with the discussion you and Lucia had with him. He said that you were persistent, and that you are." He stood, walked to one of the larger potted plants, and broke off a withering leaf. He inspected it then turned back to us and said, "While you are still here, why don't you let Lucia give you a tour of the grounds. It's a beautiful day. I would join you, but I need to make some business calls, and I'm afraid that my afternoon will be full. For that I must apologize."

We both stood. I thanked Tony and again complimented him on his wine, as well as his hospitality. Lucy hugged him. We said our goodbyes. As if by magic, Bruno entered through the courtyard door and motioned for us to join him. We did.

Bruno led us to the outer door, opened it, and waited. Lucy thanked him then told him that Tony had suggested that we tour the grounds before departing. Bruno offered to assist us, but Lucy thanked him and declined.

We stepped off the porch, and Lucy motioned turning right, in the direction of the winemaking facility, as well as the vineyard. We walked past the main house and started to pass the long multicar garage. One of the doors was open, and glancing inside, I saw something that made me stop. I pulled Lucy into the garage and said, "Look at that."

She did then asked, "Why? I never would have guessed you to be an off-road-truck guy…"

"Luce! Take a close look at that truck."

Puzzled, she did. Then she remembered, "The accident! Across the road…"

We walked over to the truck. It was a full-size four-wheel pickup with oversize knobby tires and a long light bar on top of the cab roof. It was obviously outfitted for both off-road driving and rough terrain. I climbed up so I could reach the driver's-side roof then the lights. From my perch, I couldn't see the top of the light bar, but I could reach it. I ran my hand over the top, and it was rough to the touch. I dropped back down, walked behind the truck, climbed into the bed then up on a mounted toolbox, then hopped up on the roof. I reached into my pocket, extracted my phone, and took several pics of the light bar. I jumped back down, and we examined the pics. Clearly, the light bar had scraped something. I flipped back through my cell library and found the pics taken at the accident scene. And as suspected, the two taken under the granite overhang looked very much like they could have been made by the light bar on the truck. I looked back up at the bar. The spotlight covers held by the bar were painted the same shade of blue as that of the truck itself. And seemingly the same shade of blue as that of the scrape left on the granite overhang.

"Don't you find that interesting, Lucy?"

She nodded, held my gaze, then said softly, "This is Bruno's truck. He uses it for hunting."

I walked around to the front to see if anything else might be suspicious, like maybe where Abe's car was pushed over the embankment. I knelt and carefully examined the heavy dull-black brush guard. Aside from some knicks and bugs, it was unscathed. However, the design of the guard was such that just pushing another vehicle probably wouldn't show anything. Maybe the other vehicle could be damaged, but probably not even that.

I checked the bumper, headlights, grill, but all seemed fine.

"What now, Tom?" She was obviously shaken by the discovery.

"Let's continue with the tour then leave. We need to figure out our next move before we do anything. Okay?" She nodded, and we did.

25

We had just left Tony's property when my phone sounded. "This is TB."

Jewels said, "Hi, TB. Want an update?"

"Yes, ma'am. I'm putting you on speaker so Lucy can hear it. Okay, shoot."

"Joe arrested Walter Hinds and took him in for questioning. And according to Joe, and I quote, 'He folded like a bad hand.' He confessed to passing tech info to John Lu for money and the promise of protection by John's Chinese-owned company."

"Wow! That was quick. Joe did the questioning?"

"Yes, he did! He wanted me to pass on to you that—again I quote—'I don't have TB's style, but I can usually get the job done.' Joe's a talented guy, huh?" Uncharacteristically, she sounded proud. Luce and I exchanged a quiet smile.

I said, "Jewels, did Hinds say anything at all about the break-in or attempt on me?"

"Joe is convinced that Hinds knew nothing about it, not even that John Lu initiated all of it. His relationship with Lu has been somewhat one-sided."

"Okay. Anything else, Jewels?"

"Not really. How did you two do with Mr. Adamo? Learn anything new?"

"Our conversation with Tony isn't over. We planted some concerns in his mind regarding his son's accident. He will be getting back in touch. However, we did learn something totally unexpected. We found a truck, one of those tall off-road four-wheelers? Well, the light bar on top of the cab had a scratch on it that matched a scrape found at the scene of Abe's accident. We have pictures. The truck belongs to one of Tony's employees. Pretty damning evidence, even if circumstantial."

"Interesting. I'll be sure to pass it on to everybody. Anything else?"

"Not yet. For the time being, I think we will wait for Tony to call. I'm curious what he will say about these latest findings." I waited, then I said, "So, Jewels, you and Joe? Any update on that situation?" My tone was teasing, but I was curious.

"The *situation* is progressing. That's all I can disclose at this point." Her tone was equally teasing.

Luce said, "Julie, just ignore Tom. In the short time I have known him, I've already learned that sometimes, ignoring him is the best tactic."

Jewels laughed then said, "Good advice, but then you don't work for him."

"Really? You could have fooled me." Luce looked at me with a grin.

"Okay, you two, time to say goodbye. This case isn't over yet. Say hello to everyone for us, Jewels. Bye."

I said, "That's good news. About Hinds confessing. But it still doesn't tie anyone directly to Abe's death."

Luce nodded, paused, and asked, "Tom, do you think Bruno himself might be involved in Abe's death? It's hard to believe. Bruno has been with the family since he was just a small child. He and Abe were playmates."

"I don't know. Could anyone else have taken the truck?"

She considered my question, then she answered, "I suppose. It's always parked in that building, along with family personal vehicles. Another worker, maybe, or even someone in the family."

"I think our next conversation with Tony will be key. For now, let's get back to your place. I'm tired and hungry." She took my hand in her hand. We drove.

26

The next morning, Luce and I drove down to the office. I wanted to talk with Joe and Ernie both, though not necessarily together. Joe could give me a full briefing on Walter Hinds's confession interview, and hopefully, Ernie could give me an update on James Smith and what was happening with him. For some perverse reason, I actually cared what might happen to him. Before going into Concord, I swung by my place to check on Doc. I missed the little guy, and I knew he would be looking for me. Sly was very dependable, and he and Doc were friends, but still.

We pulled into my drive, and Doc was sitting on the front porch, watching us drive up. We walked up, and he came off the porch, circled my legs, and flopped down with his legs up in the air. He rolled back and forth, expecting some personal attention. I knelt and rubbed him, talked to him, and he loved it. Luce watched the reunion with a big grin. After a few minutes, I stood up, unlocked the door, and the three of us entered. It was good to be home.

***

Next morning, we were back on the road. A light rain started just before we turned off into the alleyway where my parking alcove was located. I parked, and we hurried up to the building. The air had that musty odor that preceded the clean smell of rain-washed streets and buildings. We entered the stairwell, damp and sticky rather than truly wet, and prior to climbing up to the office, we hugged. Nothing monumental, but somehow, just being able to embrace each other made the dismal weather, and the likelihood of another difficult day, almost sweet. Almost. We intentionally bumped each other as we climbed the stairs, you know, affectionately.

Jewels greeted us when we entered, "Good morning, you two. Coffee is on, so grab some and sit down. I have some news." So we did. Then we sat.

"What news?" Luce asked.

"I just got a call, literally minutes ago. Your visit with Mr. Adamo must have made an impression because he wants to come in to follow up on your talk yesterday. He is in town and asks if it can be this morning. He's waiting for a return call. I told him I would arrange it if possible." She sat smugly, waiting for a response.

Luce and I looked at each other. I said, "Okay, then. Yeah, call him back. Tell him we can meet as soon as he gets here." I looked at Luce; she nodded.

Jewels made the call. Tony would be here within the hour.

I said, "Something tells me that our investigation is about to ratchet up a couple notches."

***

Tony came in accompanied by a fit-looking tall man in his midthirties. Tony smiled tiredly and extended his hand to me. I took it; we greeted each other politely. He turned to Jewels, who was seated at her desk, and said, "Hello. Are you the young lady who arranged for Mr. Stone to be here?"

Jewels smiled and said, "Yes, sir." She stood, reached over her desk, and shook his hand. "Julie Ellis, Mr. Adamo. Very nice to meet you." She could be charming when she wanted to be. And she wanted to be. Tony seemingly had that effect on people.

"Well, thank you, Ms. Ellis. I know it was short notice. I do appreciate it." Julie beamed.

Tony turned to Lucy, smiled, and they did their usual quick hug. He then turned back to me, gestured toward his associate, and said, "TB, this is Andrew, my driver and friend." Andrew nodded. I nodded back. Tony said, "I hope it's all right for him to remain here in your office while we talk?" Andrew was standing by the door, hands folded in front. When he came in, prior to Tony coming in, he visually scanned the office—doors, windows, the whole room. He was wearing a lightweight, unbuttoned sports jacket, loose dress slacks, and the kind of soft-soled shoes that made standing, and running, for that matter, bearable. I had assessed him when he came in. He was a professional.

"Of course. Coffee, Andrew? Could you get a cup for Andrew, Jewels? Thanks." She did. Andrew thanked her, took a sip, then put the cup on a nearby filing cabinet.

I invited Tony into my office. Before we went in, Andrew walked across the room, stuck his head and shoulders through the doorway, then entered and once again stood by the door. He moved so quickly and efficiently that it seemed perfectly normal. Then Tony, Lucy, and I followed.

Tony turned to Andrew. "You can stay in the outer office, Andrew. I'll be fine."

Andrew nodded. "Yes, sir." And he left, closing the door behind.

Tony looked at me, somewhat sheepishly, and said, "Andrew is obviously more than my driver. When I travel, he provides a measure of safety. I apologize for any inconvenience."

"No apology necessary. He seems to know what he's doing."

Tony, who was seated next to Lucy in front of my desk, reached into his jacket pocket and extracted an envelope, holding it up. He said, "After our last discussion, I decided to visit my son Marco in Manchester. I wanted to speak with him directly with regard to all of this…turn of events. I left home early this morning having arranged for Andrew to accompany me. Marco and I met in his office at Adfam rather than our corporate offices in Concord because, frankly, I wanted to see what was going on there. Last night, after speaking with Marco, I called Gloria for an analysis of the situation, as well as her educated opinion about any linkage between the unfortunate business at Adfam and Abe's death. I mention all of this because it is pertinent to this"—he held up the envelope—"letter." He cleared his throat and asked, "Would it be possible to get a cup of that coffee I smelled out there? Lucia will tell you I live on the stuff!"

"Oh, of course. I should have asked earlier." I buzzed Jewels and asked her to bring in a tray. Tony smiled at Lucy, reached over, and patted her hand in a distinctly fatherly manner. I knew he was stalling with the coffee request, and a feeling somewhere between curiosity and concern was beginning to form. I caught Luce's eyes and she was feeling the same thing.

Jewels brought in the tray, put it on the side of my desk, and began pouring the coffee. "Just black, please, Ms. Ellis," Tony said. She handed him the first cup. She fixed our cups the way we liked, handed them to us, then left. Tony sipped the coffee. Unbidden, he smiled, nodded, and said, "Wonderful! She must be Italian!" We laughed.

Tony took another sip then carefully set his cup in the saucer and put it on the corner of my desk. He cleared his throat and began. "I'm afraid that what I have to say next is not going to be pleasant, not at all pleasant." He handed the letter across the desk to me. "Please open it, TB." I did, carefully.

"I'm sorry, Tony. I don't speak Italian. I don't know what it says." I started to hand it back to him.

"Before you hand it back, please look at the bottom of the next page. Can you read the signature?"

I looked; the letter was handwritten, but I could make out the signature. It was signed by Bruno. I handed it back to Tony and said, "Bruno. I assume the man I met yesterday?" I looked at Luce. She was looking at Tony.

"Yes. Bruno. This morning, while I was talking with Marco, I received a call from my wife. Apparently, Bruno hadn't shown up for breakfast, and later in the morning, she went to check on him." He stopped, shaking his head. "Bruno took his life sometime last night. A pistol."

Luce sat upright. "No! Bruno? Why? Tony, what's going on?"

Tony stood, reached for her. They held each other, Tony patting her gently on her back. She pulled away from him, crying now, and still holding his hands, asked, "What happened?"

Tony gently guided her back into her chair. He sat, looked up at me. At this point, I was standing by Luce's chair. Tony smiled sadly and said, "You should sit back down, as well, TB. For the rest of this, perhaps you could pull your chair around here? Next to Lucia?" I did.

"I will translate part of this letter for you, but not all of it. As Lucia may have told you, Bruno was like a third son to me, and some of what he says is very personal." He read the letter silently then said, "In effect, Bruno apologizes for being a disappointment to me and the rest of the family. He goes on in that way for a bit, then he explains why he…took his own life." Tony stopped, then he said, "Now this will be hard to hear. I almost didn't come over to your office this morning because I wasn't sure I wanted to share any of this without thinking it through. But after our discussion yesterday, I realized that it was unavoidable." He reached for his coffee cup, took a sip, made a face, then grabbed the carafe and warmed it up. "When I received the call from Gianna, I remembered the letter left for me at the door. I didn't open it at the time because I was in a hurry. Bruno frequently leaves messages for me regarding the estate, so I thought nothing about it at the time. Anyway, after getting over the shock of it,

I remembered the letter, but even then, I didn't open it. Marco and I had been deep into our discussion when the call came, and I think the shock for Marco was even worse than it was for me. Bruno and Marco were the best of friends, growing up. They always looked out for each other. Abe was a little younger than the two of them, so Marco and Bruno fell in together. I decided to spare Marco any more pain." He stopped again. "This is hard for me. Bruno confesses, in this letter, to pushing"—he had a catch in his voice—"my son's car over the embankment. Then he waited, making sure that Abe couldn't escape his car." Tony put his head down, shoulders shaking, and he cried. Luce put her arm around his shoulders, looked up at me where I was now standing over him, her eyes wet, and she shook her head in disbelief.

In a few minutes, Tony gained control and sat back up, patting Luce's arms. The office was very still. I could hear traffic outside the building and faraway kids laughing and my desk clock ticking. We waited for Tony to speak. He did, holding the letter up.

"Bruno says he did it for the family. That was his reason. For the family. He must have been crazy. I don't know because it makes no sense." He stood up, and for the first time since my meeting him, he looked like an old man. He spread his arms, his face took on an openly tragic expression, and he said, "And now you know what happened to my son. And so do I." His arms dropped to his side, shoulders slumped, and he shook his head, over and over. He walked to the door, we followed, and he turned before going, and said, "Goodbye. Thank you for everything, and I mean that."

Tony started to open the door, but Andrew opened it first, and Tony walked out.

After they left, for a time, we were quiet. Jewels held her tongue for a while, recognizing that something uncomfortable had transpired, but finally, she said, "TB. Can you tell me what happened in there?" I told her.

"My god, that's terrible. That poor, sweet man."

27

It rained most of the next day. A rain soft but continual. After informing everyone of the events regarding Bruno and the accident, it seemed like the case was resolved. Bruno killed Abe for reasons unknown but obviously personal to him. We might never understand exactly why, but then, is murder ever truly understandable? Even when the mechanics are known, the means and the motive, in a larger sense, there is never any reasonable, lawful justification. So for want of a more satisfying rationale, we all more or less accepted Tony's pronouncement upon reading Bruno's letter: *he must have been crazy*.

I was sitting in my office, feet propped up on my desk, looking out the window at the rain. Ernie was satisfied that Walter Hinds was guilty of passing proprietary military tech to the Chinese. Apparently, Joe's wresting of a confession from him was enough to charge both him and John Lu, who had served as intermediary for Hinds; the FBI had swooped down, arresting him for espionage. Ernie was a happy guy. So there was that.

Tony had assigned Gloria Simpson the task of cleaning up the mess between Adfam and Cutting Edge. The Feds had put locks on the doors of Cutting Edge, pending investigation into the extent of their operations, but the legal and marketing connections had to be severed. Marco was taking a sabbatical of sorts, staying with the family at least until they could figure out what to do with Bruno's body. The emotional wreckage left behind learning the truth of Abe's death was something the whole family would have to resolve together.

Luce was home, dealing with her real estate business, trying to catch up, really. The plan was for me to drive up tonight. I figured I'd pick up some food from Yuan and pay Sly at the same time. Luce shouldn't have to worry about cooking tonight. She'll be tired. I smiled, her face happily in my head. I'll call her and tell her about the food. Yeah.

So everything had fallen into place. Everyone was happy. But still, there had to be something connecting Bruno's irrational murder of Abe and the sleaze going on between Hinds and Lu. Okay, if Bruno really was crazy, and as far as anyone knew, Bruno had never even visited Adfam, then maybe the timing of the break-in and that of the attempted murder were just coincidence. Maybe. But assuming there is a connection, what would precipitate Bruno killing Abe? If the connection isn't the break-in et al., what was left?

In the distance, I could hear thunder rumbling. The rain was still steady, but maybe a storm was forming. Bruno wrote that he was doing it *for the family*. What could he be referencing? More thunder, and the rain was picking up. Yeah, a storm was definitely coming. Then a flash of lightning crackled, forking out beyond the city limits. Thunder followed, and an afterimage of the lightning remained before my eyes. And there it was. Of course! How stupid was I?

***

Checking my watch, I called Luce. "Hi, it's me. How goes your day, so far?"

"Well, I'm not caught up yet, but the semiemergencies are all under control. What's up?" She sounded distracted.

"Do you have a few minutes to talk?"

"Of course. You remember we are seeing each other in a couple of hours, right?"

"This won't take long. But if you are too busy, I can get by until this evening…"

"No, no. Talk."

"I have been thinking. The investigation is over, at least officially. But there is still one nagging point that bothers me about this whole case. First, we don't know why Bruno killed Abe. Yes, he may have been operating under some sort of delusion, and the murder was a consequence of craziness. But then again, maybe he had a reason. Maybe that reason could answer my nagging question."

She said, "And what is that question?"

"How does the corruption at Adfam and the murder of Abe connect? During this whole time, we assumed that they were connected—that's what drove our investigation. Am I alone in this?"

She didn't answer at first, then she said, "I don't know, Tom. Bruno admitted to the murder. And the mess at Adfam is all resolved, or at least our part of it is. I'm not saying you are wrong, but even if there is more to it, does it really matter?"

"Maybe not, but I suspect that there is a connection, and I think I know what it is. Or let's say a plausible connection can be made, and it will drive me nuts until I know for sure one way or the other." I waited.

"Tom, you know I will help in whatever way I can. Okay? What is this connection?"

"It has to do with Bruno's reason as stated: 'I did it for the family.' I think it has to do with that, but I need more information about the Adamo family. Maybe you can help."

"Okay. I can try."

"What sort of relationship did Abe, Marco, and Bruno have? Especially when growing up, but after that, as well. Don't answer it now, I want you to give it some thought. Wait until I come over tonight. Okay?"

"All right. What time is that likely to be?"

"Is five, five thirty too soon? Oh, and I'll be bringing dinner from Yuan's, if that's suitable?" I waited. Hopefully, she hadn't started to prepare dinner already.

"Suitable? Definitely! I'm low on supplies in my cupboards, so that will be a blessing."

"Excellent! Okay, see you in a couple hours. Any requests from Yuan before I call it in?"

She sighed and answered, "Not really. How about asking Yuan to surprise me? Will that work?"

"Hah! He will love it. See ya." I hung up, called Yuan, placed the order, and leaned back.

***

Luce and I greeted each other like teenagers after being separated for summer break. Then we drank a pleasant white wine from the Finger Lakes region of upstate New York and ate Yuan's food. Luce enjoyed some sort of heavily spiced fish dish with a side of dumplings. I had my usual egg foo young. The best part of the meal was the little note that Yuan left for Lucy: "Please enjoy your surprise meal. Also, please let TB have a taste of it. I always hope that he will learn to enjoy something other than his usual eggs. Yuan." Luce gave me a forkful, and it was okay, but it clashed with my eggs. She laughed at me. Why did all my friends conspire against me? One of those eternal questions, I supposed.

After eating, we stretched out on her couch and talked about the Adamo family internal relationships. Luce's memories were particular regarding the last three years but secondhand for anything before, particularly during the childhood years. From what she remembered of casual conversations, during meals, primarily, but also references made by Tony and Gianna regarding *the kids* I learned that Marco and Bruno were very close and that Abe generally distanced himself from *the big kids* despite the fact that he was only a couple of years younger. I also learned that during those days, Tony was frequently away due to business requirements and that Gianna almost exclusively dealt with family matters. Maria, the youngest, was spoiled, according to the three boys, but doted on by both parents, especially Tony.

As she retrieved her memories, Luce fell into free association, and a lot of it was more feelings than fact, but it still gave me information that could prove useful later. For example, at one family event, Marco and Abe got into an argument over some silly matter, making Lucy feel very uneasy, frightened. Gianna told both of them to stop, and they did, but the rest of the day was uncomfortable for Lucy. Another time, Bruno and Marco were kicking a soccer ball back and forth, laughing and kidding each other, but when Abe and Lucy came up to them in the yard, Abe jumped in and tried to pass the ball to Marco. Marco and Bruno then just left the yard, ignoring Abe. Lucy recalled how upset Abe was, and when she tried to help him laugh it off, he got angry with her.

I learned what I suspected or at least enough to confirm my theory. Nothing concrete had emerged, but enough. I could take the next step.

Luce questioned me about why I wanted her vague recollections, so I explained my theory. She thought I was crazy. We went back and forth for a while, but she reluctantly accepted that there might be some truth in it. Then we discussed what to do with the theory, how to test it. We agreed to think about it, see if anything happened that might prove (or disprove) it, and go from there. And so we did.

***

A few weeks later, I was at my office desk, going over the file of a recent client, an accountant who had been, according to him, unfairly dismissed from employment because he had proven to his boss that the books were being cooked. Pretty pedestrian stuff, but he was paying me. My door was open, and I heard the phone ring in the outer office. I heard Jewels's voice, then my phone buzzed. "Yeah, Jewels."

"Ben Katz for you, TB."

"Okay, thanks." I hit the blinking button.

Ben said, "Tommy! How's life in the seedy underbelly of Concord?"

"I'm not sure, Benny. My gumshoes are stuck to the floor, and I can't get out of the office. What's up?"

"Our favorite tech company is undergoing a restructure. Thought you might be interested."

"Tell me," I said, suddenly awake.

"According to the *Journal*, it seems that Gloria Simpson, that tall blond woman with NSA credentials, has been named chief of security for Adfam Tech, and Maria Adamo, at the ripe old of age of twenty-four years, has been named VP of operations. But here's the kicker… ready?"

"You are enjoying this way too much. Go on."

"Tony Adamo himself is the newly named CEO of Adfam. What do think, Tommy?"

"Wow! That is something. Does the *Journal* say what Marco Adamo will be doing?"

"Uh-huh. Marco will be heading up the Italian-based import/export business for the family. Also, it says, he will be pursuing, and I quote, 'possible future European acquisitions.' His wife and kids are moving to Italy with him. In baseball terms, sounds like he has been sent down to the minors."

Well, my theory now had some credibility. I said, "Benny, I appreciate the update." And I did.

"You are welcome, pal. My guess is that your little investigation has had some far-reaching results. What do you think?"

"You might be right. Throw a pebble in a pond, and watch the ripples, huh?"

"I guess. Hey, not to change the subject, but my mother is waiting for a visit. Still waiting. Don't give me excuses, just give me a date."

"Ah. Hang on a second." I put Ben on hold then yelled, "Jewels, do I have anything scheduled for Thursday afternoon?"

She yelled back, "No. Go see her!"

"Benny. How about lunch day after tomorrow and the rest of the afternoon?" I waited for Ben to check with Doreen.

"You are in luck, Tommy. I'll meet you here at eleven thirty, day after tomorrow, Thursday. Right?"

"You got it. See you then."

I walked out to see what Jewels wanted for lunch. She wanted the usual, of course, and I walked downstairs. As I was halfway down, my spy phone rang. "Ernie!

What's up, man? I thought we were all through with the case, no?"

"I suppose that's true, but there are a couple of things unresolved."

"Yeah? What?"

"First, though I have a pretty-good idea, I'm curious about a couple things in your case. Not *our* case, the person leaking info at Adfam, but your case. I'm having trouble understanding the connection between Abe's murder and any kind of motive."

"You aren't buying the 'Bruno was just crazy' answer?"

"Maybe, but it seems pretty convenient."

"It will take a while to explain, and I'm on my way to get lunch. Can I call you back this afternoon?"

Yes, you can do that, but I have another idea. How about we get together for that mano a mano at the batting cage? You can fill me in then."

I chuckled to myself and said, "Ah, Ernie. I'm surprised you remember that. Once spies get what they want, the little people along the way are soon forgotten. But before you argue, yes, we can do that. When will you be ready for your humiliation?"

"Tonight? Six at the Center? I'll rent the cage, but you have to bring your own tissues for when you are crying and crying after."

"Yeah, I can do that. Six it is." We disconnected. Should be fun.

28

Ernie was as good as his word. The batting cage was as far away from other activity as possible, but it would serve the purpose. I walked up to him, and we shook hands. I said, "Good to see you, Ernie. Seems like a long time."

"Same here, TB. How are you doing?"

"Okay. The business is good though pretty mundane compared to spy work, you know." I grinned.

"Probably true. Do you miss it?" He grinned back.

I made a rude noise. "How about I give you the condensed version of Abe's murder and then we get down to it?" I pointed to the bats leaning against the wall.

He nodded. "Yeah, good idea. Let's sit over here." We walked to a bench behind the cage itself. We sat.

"Okay. In short, Bruno wasn't crazy, at least not in the sense that he was driven by some psychotic reason or impulse all his own." Ernie nodded, relaxing back against the wall. "He did murder Abe, but he did it to protect Marco."

"Protect Marco? How so?"

"This is where it gets a little murky, so bear with me. It seems that growing up, Bruno and Marco were about the same age, and Abe was the little brother always tagging along and generally getting in the way. Nothing unusual about that sort of thing, you know. But because Abe was always being ignored by the big kids, both of the parents were especially protective of Abe, giving him more attention. Again, nothing unusual. Now roll forward to the adolescent years, and Abe starts coming into his own. He has figured out that it was possible to get what he wanted from his parents, especially Tony. He was indulged. Marco and Bruno had grown up together, and their relationship was supportive and, to a great extent, exclusive. So the pattern was set. Abe generally got whatever he wanted, and Marco, or so it seemed, had to prove himself. Follow so far?"

"I think so. But there's a big leap between sibling rivalry and murder."

"Patience, spymaster," I said. He nodded, making a face. "Abe, who down deep resented being shut out of Marco's life, especially by Bruno, who was not even family, used his parents to get what he wanted but at the same time made sure that both Marco and Bruno knew it. When a child, he just told them directly, but later, as an adolescent, it was more subtle but even more keenly resented by Marco and, to a lesser extent, Bruno."

Ernie nodded, listening. He said, "I do understand the pattern. I can imagine it playing out in their respective lives long after any of them remembered why. Is that so?"

"Yes. I'm convinced of it, and here's why I think it has everything to do with the murder. When the three boys came to maturity and Tony began to parcel out family-business responsibilities to each of them, the pattern continued. First, Bruno, who was quiet and nonaggressive in most ways, was a natural for taking on the family estate. He could remain home, where he was most comfortable. And so it went. Abe took over the family's central business, real estate and property management. This was the most lucrative and secure part of the family empire. Tony trusted Abe, and Abe enjoyed the responsibility, and yet because it was a mature side of the business, it allowed him ample time to pursue his own interests. Marco was given the exploratory, diverse business group. It suited him because he could operate autonomously, and it appealed to his curious intellect. So it all seemed good."

Ernie said, "So how did it fall apart?"

"Adfam Tech. The business skyrocketed, as you know. At a point, during the ascent, Adfam profits overtook the core business, Abe's business. That's all fact. Now imagine the family business meetings with the two sons and Bruno, all reviewing their respective responsibilities. For the first time, Marco, the oldest son, reports the success of his division in hard, measurable terms. He is proud, expecting Tony's praise, at the very least. But that doesn't happen. Instead, Tony actually pulls in the reins, suspecting that the meteoric rise of Adfam would taper off. And again, this is all a matter of record, I checked. Funds were actually diverted to the real estate side and invested in some prime buildings in Boston. Granted, those buildings were a safe investment and, from Tony's perspective, a safe place to put the newfound wealth. But from Marco's point of view, Tony was once again favoring Abe, not him. And Bruno, not the sharpest knife in the drawer, sees all of this. As Marco's lifelong friend and brother, he feels the presumed slight every bit as much as Marco." I paused.

"Sounds to me like a great deal of guesswork. How do you know all of this happened?"

"I know from speaking with the family, Marco and Tony included, that the childhood relationship between the three brothers is exactly as told. I also know that Bruno committed the crime. Additionally, I know that Tony sent Marco and his family to Italy, effectively exiling him."

"Okay. I get that. But why in the world would it be necessary for Bruno to kill Abe? For a slight to Marco? There would have to be more."

"Tony suspected something was going on at Adfam, something unsavory. He hires Gloria Simpson, ex-NSA, to investigate it. Do you seriously think Abe wouldn't have known about it? Of course, he did. My guess is that Abe dredged up some hard evidence that Marco knew all about what was going on between Lu and Hinds and then confronted him with it. Marco is terrified that Abe will let Tony know, just like when they were kids. Marco shares his fear with Bruno, who then *solves* the problem by killing Abe."

"Well, that connects the dots, for sure. Still seems speculative, though a compelling theory. Any way to prove it?" Ernie gave me a look.

"Nope. But effectively, if it's all true, the punishment for Marco's complicity has already been served. He has had his part of the empire taken away, and I'm absolutely sure that Tony, through legal means, has made it impossible for Marco to ever have anything to do with running the larger family businesses ever again."

"Interesting. Well, you answered my question." He stood up, stretched, and said, "Okay, T. B. Stone. Ready to get your ass kicked?" He reached for a bat and swung it menacingly.

EPILOGUE

I'm going to break with an unspoken compact here and go from *first person* to *person to person* in my narrative, because I know that if the solution to this investigation isn't clear yet, it never will be. But having said that, the rest of the story can be told, if not the underpinning of said story.

After Benny's call, I knew that all my perseverance, in faith, thought, and action had paid off; I knew who was behind the murder of Giorgio Abraham Adamo. I can't say that it changed very much in the final, overarching scheme of things. After all, even though rainbows promise many things, tracking them to their terminus never ever yields that mythic pot of gold.

Now this is where it gets a bit dicey, so hang on. Tony intervened following the murder. It is unclear how soon he knew who was behind the murder, as we measure such things, but at the point where it all became clear, he set in motion everything you have read so far, including my beloved Lucia's stubborn persistence and my dogged investigation. And perhaps even the loving consequence of our inevitable meeting, although I can't be sure of that.

Now, considering this, one may wonder, how can Tony Adamo be responsible for all these threads of human action and interaction? I can blithely point to all human behavior being a consequence of some previous event, human or otherwise, but that gets way too messy for a guy like me—determinism, free will, trying to reconcile the two in reality or even perception… I'm just a small-time PI from Concord, New Hampshire. So what I will say is that all of us have to work that stuff out for ourselves. And I like to think that Tony would agree.

But it is abundantly clear that however unsatisfying Tony's response seems to have been, any other course of action would have been worse. Could he subject his last living son to the humiliation and cruelty of a trial in the public square? And what of the scandal and subsequent unraveling of Adamo Enterprises? The public wasn't ready for that. Maybe later, but certainly not then. So Marco and his immediate family were moved to Italy, where sun and sea, wine and pasta, and joy and tragedy dance in beauty and sadness as nowhere else on earth. Call me a romantic, but I like to imagine Marco's children growing in their Italian cradle to love one another over those ephemeral years together as brothers and sisters of the sun rather than the shadow.

As for me, I'm off to spend an afternoon with Mamma Katz and my friend Ben. Then, by grace alone, a lifetime with Lucia.